Wendy Soliman was brought up on the Isle of Wight in southern England but now divides her time between Andorra and western Florida. She lives with her husband Andre and a rescued dog of indeterminate pedigree named Jake Bentley after the hunky hero in one of her books. When not writing she enjoys reading other people's books, walking miles with her dog whilst plotting her next scene, dining out and generally making the most out of life.

Visit her website at:
http://www.wendysoliman.com/

PORTRAIT OF A DUKE

Rumours abound that the famous artist Patrick Trafford has taken Parkstone Manor, the run-down estate bordering the Duke of Winchester's country seat. When Lord Vincent Sheridan, the duke's brother, discovers the speculations to be true, his interest is piqued by Niamh Trafford, Patrick's granddaughter. But Nia, apparently impervious to his charms, is determined not to marry, fully committed to her responsibilities of running the household and protecting her beloved grandfather's reputation by keeping his diminished mental capacities secret. Meanwhile, someone is exploiting the artist's wandering mind by dealing in forged Trafford portraits. Can Vince assist Nia in tracking down the criminal — and perhaps win her heart too?

Books by Wendy Soliman
Published by Ulverscroft:

LADY HARTLEY'S INHERITANCE
DUTY'S DESTINY
THE SOCIAL OUTCAST
THE CARSTAIRS CONSPIRACY
A BITTERSWEET PROPOSAL
TO DEFY A DUKE
AT THE DUKE'S DISCRETION
WITH THE DUKE'S APPROVAL

MRS DARCY ENTERTAINS:
MISS BINGLEY'S REVENGE
COLONEL FITZWILLIAM'S DILEMMA
MISS DARCY'S PASSION

WENDY SOLIMAN

◆

PORTRAIT OF A DUKE

Complete and Unabridged

ULVERSCROFT
Leicester

First published in Great Britain in 2014

First Large Print Edition
published 2016

A catalogue record for this book is available
from the British Library.

ISBN 978–1–4448–2979–2

Published by
F. A. Thorpe (Publishing)
Anstey, Leicestershire

Set by Words & Graphics Ltd.
Anstey, Leicestershire
Printed and bound in Great Britain by
T. J. International Ltd., Padstow, Cornwall

This book is printed on acid-free paper

1

Winchester, England
Spring, 1819

'What the devil . . . '

Cursing, Vincent Sheridan struggled to control his stallion as a small dog streaked across the road in front of him, spooking the young horse. 'Steady, Forrester.'

He reined the animal to a shuddering halt in the centre of Compton's main street, watching the dog who had almost brought them to grief run triumphantly off with a string of sausages dangling from its jaws. The butcher's boy ran after it, shouting and brandishing a meat cleaver. Not unnaturally, the episode had attracted quite a crowd. Two boys Vince didn't recognise came bounding along, calling to the dog.

'Ruff, where the devil are you?'

'Come here at once.'

To Vince's astonishment, the dog looked up at them, quickly dug a hole to bury his contraband and trotted over to them, as innocent as you please. Vince could see the funny side of the incident, but the butcher's boy appeared unimpressed. Supported by a growing band of local lads, he approached the dog's owners.

'Your dog's a thief,' he said, not without just cause.

'He should be shot,' said another.

His supporters murmured their agreement.

'What sort of dog is he, anyway?' The questioner cast a scathing glance over the canine criminal. 'Don't look like no dog I've ever seen.'

'Who are you two and what're you doing 'ere?'

'They're probably from Shawford,' some-one suggested, without giving the two being subjected to Compton's version of the inquisition an opportunity to respond. 'Sent here with that miserable excuse for a dog to spy on us.'

Vince shook his head, saddened that the rivalry between the villages had deteriorated to the extent that children mistrusted their perfectly acceptable neighbours. The dog *had* helped himself to the sausages, but that was hardly a hanging offence. The butcher should have dealt with the matter himself by demanding restitution for his loss from the boys' parents. Instead he stood back, arms folded, and encouraged a mob of village urchins to act as judge and jury.

How the feud had started was a mystery, but it was generally assumed that Vince's ancestors were to blame for disobligingly situating Winchester Park precisely midway between the two villages. The Park was home to the Sheridan family, the eldest of whom was Vince's brother Zachary, the Duke of Winchester. Each village was fiercely determined to claim the Sheridan family as its own and bask in the reflected glory accorded to such a connection. It had once been an endless source of amusement to the Sheridan males, but was now in danger of spiralling out of control.

'Looks more like a rat than a dog,' another boy sniffed, to the great amusement of his friends, who clearly thought he was the wittiest of fellows.

'Take that back,' said one of the dog's owners, puny clenched fists raised in the animal's defence.

'Will not!'

A stone was hurled to emphasise the refusal, at which point Vince realised he would have to intervene. Several Compton adults had paused to observe the scene and it was evident that none of them had the smallest intention of restoring order. The dog at the heart of the dispute — or the excuse for it — was a small, wiry terrier mix with a tan, black and white coat, and ears that sat at different angles. He whimpered when the stone skimmed past his head, and ducked behind the boys' skinny legs.

'Get off with ya,' the bully who had displaced the butcher's boy as leader of the gang snarled, raising much meatier fists. 'We don't hold with no strangers around here.'

Another stone was hurled and then all seven of the Compton boys set upon the two with the dog. Sighing, Vince removed one glove, placed two fingers in his mouth and let out an ear-piercing whistle. It had the desired effect and all combatants turned in his direction. Seeing who had broken up the dispute, the Compton boys scattered. The agitating bully, Vince was pleased to note, had a bleeding calf. In spite of his peace-loving tendencies, presumably the dog had come to the defence of his outnumbered owners.

Vince dismounted and approached the two boys, curious as to their identity. They were still on the muddy ground, battered and bruised, but, as far as Vince could ascertain, without broken bones. The dog growled upon Vince's approach. When he offered up his re-gloved hand for inspection, the canine sniffed it, appeared to find nothing objection-able, and graciously permitted Vince to rub his spikey head.

'I planted that big boy a right facer,' one child proclaimed.

'No, Leo, you missed. That was me.' The second boy flexed bruised and bloodied knuckles to emphasise his point.

'Well, I kicked him, then.' The first lad examined his wounded knee, looking pleased with his battle injury. 'His leg was bleeding, Art. You must have noticed that.'

Leo and Art? Well, at least Vince now knew their names, even if they were so alike — twins, presumably — that it was impossible to tell one from the other. Both had curly chestnut hair, the same colour as his stallion's coat, mischievous green eyes, and skinned knees that implied they were no strangers to rough and tumble. Typical boys. That was all it was possible for Vince to discern about their features, other than that the one without the cut knee would have a splendid black eye to show off come the following morning.

'That's only because Ruff bit him.'

'I say, did he really?' Leo — or was it Art? — patted the dog's head. 'Good boy, Ruff. I expect Aunt Nia will find you a beef bone as a reward.'

Vince could tell that the boys were totally indifferent to the mud seeping into the seats of their trousers as they sat in the street, squabbling about their own roles in a battle they had now convinced themselves they had won unaided. Vince felt a moment's nostalgia for his own childhood: a time when similar scrapes had seemed equally important to him and his three brothers. The only difference was that, when he had been Leo and Art's age, he had been brawling at prep school rather than in village streets. Different location, different class of opponent, same principle.

He sobered when he considered what could have happened to these two if he had not put a stop to the incident.

'Well, lads,' Vince said amiably. 'That didn't go too well.'

'It wasn't our fault . . . '

'We were minding our own business.'

'We would have offered to pay for the sausages, but they didn't give us a chance.'

'They just wanted to fight with us.'

Vince held up a hand to put a stop to the endless flow of words. 'Has it happened before?'

'We only just moved to the area.'

'Well, I think you ought to get off home. That knee needs attending to.'

They clambered to their feet, but Vince could see that the injured party couldn't put much weight on one leg. Blood still flowed freely from a bad gash where he had fallen on one of the jagged stones being hurled at them. Vince produced a handkerchief, tied it around the wound, and then lifted the boy onto Forrester's back, in front of the saddle. He then mounted up himself, held a hand down to the other boy, and pulled him up behind.

The butcher watched, scowling, arms akimbo.

'Here.' Vince reached into his waistcoat pocket and flipped him a coin far in excess of the value of the sausages. 'For your loss.'

The butcher doffed his cap. 'Thank you, m'lord. I hope you'll see to it that those lads have their backsides tanned.'

'Why?' A hint of sarcasm shaped the arch of Vince's brow. 'Did *they* steal from you? Was it they who started the brawl?'

Without waiting for a response, Vince turned Forrester down Compton's main street. They made a strange spectacle, as evidenced by the astonished looks directed their way by the residents who turned out to watch them. Here was he, Lord Vincent Sheridan, brother to a duke, in all his sartorial elegance, accompanied by two mud-caked urchins on one of the finest horses in the district. Oh, and a dog, too. Art or Leo — the lesser-injured combatant — had tucked the little dog under his spare arm when Vince pulled him up behind. He shrugged, rather pleased that the boy thought to protect the cause of their problems.

'Where to, boys?' he asked.

'We live at Stoneleigh Manor . . . '

'It's on the southern edge of the village.'

Vince knew where it was, since it adjoined the boundary of the Park. It also answered the question of the boys' identity. The Manor had recently been re-let, but mystery surrounded the identity of the new tenants. All efforts to welcome them to the district had been met by closed and locked gates, which was unusual enough to foment endless speculation. Vince's family were consumed with curiosity, but his mother, the dowager duchess, would not leave her card until she was satisfied she would not be intruding upon their new neighbours' desire for privacy. Overtures from a lady of the duchess's consequence could not, after all, politely be ignored.

The fact that the new residents had not hired any servants locally — another cause for grievance amongst Compton's residents — implied that they had brought their own people with them. Whoever lived there was reclusive by nature, and rumours abounded that Patrick Trafford, the renowned Irish portrait painter, had taken the house. Lady St. John, a close neighbour and friend of Vince's family, as well as an intimate of

Trafford's granddaughter, insisted it was so, but the rumour had yet to be substantiated.

Now, purely by chance, it appeared Vince would soon be in a position to satisfy his family's collective curiosity.

'I say, this is a bang-up horse, sir,' said the injured boy in front of him.

'Absolutely first rate,' agreed his brother.

'Is he fast?'

'Can he jump?'

'Well, thank you,' Vince replied when they paused long enough for him to respond. 'I'm very glad he meets with your approval. He's still young.'

'We could help you to train him.'

'We're very good with horses.'

'We're Irish, you see, and everyone knows the Irish have horses in their blood.'

'You can't have a horse in your blood, Art. That's stupid.'

'Aunt Nia says we have a real affection.' Leo shook his head. 'No, that's not right, but it was aff-something.'

Vince was endlessly amused by their ability to carry on a conversation in tandem, even when separated by the solidity of Vince's body. The stallion the three of them were riding, and which met with the lads' approval, had been bred by Vince's brother, Amos, at the stud he ran on Zach's behalf at Winchester Park.

'An affinity?' he suggested in response to Leo's dilemma.

'That's right.' Art sniffed. 'Not sure I like the idea of affinities, though.'

'I should say not,' Leo agreed.

'Right, here we are.' Vince halted Forrester at rusted gates that were firmly locked. He could see the grounds of the manor house beyond, overgrown and neglected: a haven for small boys to get into mischief. Perhaps the occupants hadn't thought to bring any outdoor servants with them. The Compton men would be glad if there was work to be had here after all. If so, Art and Leo would be able to walk the streets in safety. Anything was possible if one possessed an optimistic nature. 'But it seems our entrance is barred.'

'You can leave us here, sir.'

'It might be best if I took you inside,' Vince replied, his curiosity getting the better of him. 'I need to speak with your mother.'

'You won't tell that we were fighting, will you?' Leo appeared a little anxious at the prospect. 'Aunt Nia will make the most frightful fuss.'

'She's a girl,' Art explained helpfully. 'She doesn't understand these things.'

Vince eyed their bloodied and dishevelled state impassively. 'I rather think she might take one look at you and work that much out for herself.'

'That's true,' Art conceded, screwing up his nose. 'What a nuisance. Aunt Nia is always fussing about our clothes.'

'And she did tell us most particularly to stay clean this morning.'

'It's not our fault Ruff got out.'

'We had to go after him. She would have been upset if he got lost.'

'She loves that dog.'

Fearful that the conversation would continue indefinitely, Vince cleared his throat to gain their attention. 'How did you get out of the grounds?' he asked.

'That way.'

Leo pointed to a small side gate almost hidden by the undergrowth. The track was just wide enough for a man on a horse, or for a narrow gig, to pass along it. The thick bed of bluebells underfoot had been flattened by hooves and wheels, thus confirming his suspicions. Art, with the dog still beneath his arm, slid down from behind and opened the gate. The dog raced ahead through a jungle of greenery created by close-packed trees with branches that meshed overhead. Art ran after him, gangly limbs flying at all angles. Vince, with his remaining passenger, followed along at a more sedate pace.

'Ruff, boys, where are you?' called a feminine voice that sounded irritated. 'It's

11

past time to come in.'

'Oh Lord,' Leo muttered. 'Now we're for it.'

As they got closer to the front of the house, the bluebells gave way to neglected gravel interspersed with muddy puddles and sprouting weeds that strangled struggling shrubs. The woman calling for the boys came into view, standing on the edge of an equally neglected terrace with cracked paving and a crumbling stone balustrade. At the boys' mention of their Irish heritage, Vince had thought the rumours about Trafford having taken this place were most likely true. He was interested in art and would be glad to have such a talented neighbour, even if he possessed an artist's taciturn and unsociable disposition.

Now that he saw the state of the place, and its relatively small size, he decided it couldn't possibly be Trafford who had taken it. He was reputed to be richer than the Prince Regent — which admittedly wasn't saying much, since the prince made an art form out of living beyond his means. But even if Trafford had decided to settle in such a quiet backwater, surely he would have taken a larger property; or, at the very least, arranged to have this one repaired before taking occupation?

As he rounded the final turn in the path, he

got his first proper view of the woman and almost lost his balance. The sight of such an individual female in this unlikely location was as welcome as it was unexpected. He had spent the entire season dodging the match-making mamas and their equally determined daughters, none of whom had engaged his interest. This creature, on the other hand, already had his complete attention, although he wasn't entirely sure what it was about her that interested him. He halted Forrester and observed her for a moment or so, wondering at his extreme reaction to a woman he knew absolutely nothing about.

The boys kept referring to their aunt, and presumably this was she, since she didn't look old enough to be their mother. She, too, had an abundance of chestnut curls, held back by a ribbon from which they appeared deter-mined to escape and cascade insubordinately over her shoulders. She wore a green-striped muslin gown with a high military collar — a style his sister Annalise had adopted more than three years previously, but probably wouldn't be seen dead in today, since it was no longer fashionable. Its wearer was irritated and the muslin swirled around her tall, lean body as she paced back and forth, giving Vince a graphic view of the rather enticing curves beneath it.

'Here we are, Aunt Nia,' Leo said, sliding over Forrester's withers and running up to her at the same time as Art. So much for Leo's incapacity, Vince thought with a wry smile. His knee was swollen, but if Leo felt any discomfort, he disguised the fact well.

'Where the devil have you been? I've been calling you this half hour.'

'Sorry, but we — '

'Excuse me, sir,' she said, noticing Vince and stiffening. 'This is private property. I must ask you to leave.'

Vince did not leave. Instead, he dismounted and approached her. At close quarters he observed that her eyes, almost too large for the delicate face that housed them, were greener than her gown. They also showed signs of considerable strain, and she seemed tired and preoccupied. Her features were attractive rather than beautiful, freckles dotted the bridge of her pert nose and her slightly jutting cheekbones were pink with annoyance — whether at him or the boys was less easily determined. She scowled at her charges, slight horizontal lines forming on her forehead as she did so.

'This gentleman brought us home,' Art said.

'We had to run after Ruff.'

'He got out, you see, and you told us most

particularly to keep him in the garden.'

'And the boys in the village, they — '

'He stole some sausages from the butcher's cart, and — '

'Ruff?' She fixed the dog with an exasperated expression. The dog responded by dropping to his belly and squirming away from her. Vince couldn't help it. He laughed aloud at the precocious mutt, causing the lady's scowl to give way to a reluctant smile. 'I shall deal with you later,' she said, wagging a finger at the canine offender.

'This gentleman paid the butcher — '

'We wanted to say we were sorry, and that you would — '

'But they didn't give us a chance — '

'Boys, boys!' She held up her hands, shaking her head. 'I beg your pardon, sir. I can see they have been scrapping again, and I thank you for returning them in one piece.' She screwed up her nose as she contemplated them. 'More or less.'

'It wasn't our fault, Aunt Nia,' Art protested.

'The pleasure was all mine,' Vince quickly interjected, before the boys' tongues ran off on another of their dual explanations that could keep them standing on this crumbling terrace for the next ten minutes. 'Vincent Sheridan at your service.' He offered her an effortless bow and the ghost of a wicked smile, because . . . well, because his mind had been taken over by highly inappropriate thoughts the moment he set eyes on her.

Her eyes widened and she clapped a hand over her mouth, which was when Vince noticed what appeared to be paint encrusted beneath her fingernails.

'Lord Vincent Sheridan?' she asked.

2

'The very same.'

Nia took a moment to recover her composure. This was a disaster! She had told the boys to remain within the grounds because they were in no fit state to entertain visitors; especially those of Lord Vincent's stature. Since he had gone to so much trouble on the boys' behalf, he would naturally expect to be invited into the house and offered refreshment, but she would die before she allowed him to see the state of their living conditions. The grounds and the shabby exterior of the building gave a bad enough impression. Oh Lord, why could not the boys have done as they were told, just this once?

Nia had heard talk of the four Sheridan brothers: their eligibility and good looks. Indeed, when suggesting this area might be just the place for Nia's family to settle quietly, her friend Frankie St. John had warned her what to expect when her path crossed with that of her elegant neighbours, as eventually it was bound to. She had not exaggerated. Lord Vincent was at least six feet tall, with thick black hair falling across the collar of his fashionably-cut coat. A coat that was now caked in mud, thanks to her rebellious nephews' propensity for finding trouble — or creating it. Much as she loved them, she was not blind to their faults.

Returning her attention to Lord Vincent, Nia decided that if he had noticed the blight upon his pristine tailoring, he didn't seem unduly concerned about it. Well, she supposed he had his own valet, ready and waiting to clean up his apparel, so why *would* it trouble him?

He observed the world through eyes that were a deep, arresting blue. They sparkled with unsettling intelligence and, if she was any judge, a modicum of cynical enjoyment. His rugged features were all planes and angles, enhanced by a chiselled jaw and straight aristocratic nose. His body appeared to be a solid wall of muscle. Well, of course it was! He was disturbingly poised, damn him, while she was a bundle of uncertainty. He exuded easy charm and yet there was an aura of danger about him, too.

'Oh . . . Niamh Trafford,' she responded belatedly, bobbing a curtsey and blushing when she realised she had been staring at him for a little too long. He was probably used to invoking such a reaction from females, and Nia so disliked being predictable. 'And these

18

are my nephews, Leonard and Arthur.'

'We're twins,' Art piped up.

'But I'm older, by ten minutes,' Leo added proudly.

'We're eight.'

'Eight and a half.'

'Are you really a lord?' Art asked, peering up at Lord Vincent suspiciously.

'Art!' Nia was horrified at his manners, or lack of them. 'How badly are you hurt this time?' she asked, crouching down to examine Leo's knee. She removed the fine lawn handkerchief binding it that was now caked with dried blood.

'It will need washing and bandaging,' Lord Vincent remarked. 'But no permanent damage has been done.'

'Only to your handkerchief,' Nia replied with a wry smile.

'That's of no consequence.'

No, Nia thought, to him it most likely was not. Why she was so determined to be out of charity with him when he had rescued the boys and taken the trouble to see them home was a mystery to her. She had hoped to avoid meeting her neighbours at all, especially the Sheridans, by keeping her grandfather's identity a secret. She could see now that had been a hopelessly naïve ambition, but still . . .

Satisfied that Leo's injury was indeed not

life-threatening, she shook her head and turned her attention to Art. She brushed the hair away from his forehead, shook her head for a second time when she observed he had one eye swollen half-shut, and tutted.

'Run off and find Hannah,' Nia told them. 'Ask her to clean you up and bandage your injuries, and put you into clean clothes. No, on second thoughts, don't worry about the clothes.' The boys looked very pleased to hear it. 'We can delay our outing until tomorrow since it's almost time for luncheon. I see no reason for you to dirty a second set of clothes in one day.'

'We don't do it on purpose,' Leo said.

'It wasn't our fault.'

'No,' Nia said with a heartfelt sigh. 'It never is.'

'Don't forget we have horses in our blood,' Art said, addressing his comment to Lord Vincent. 'We can help you with your stallion at any time.'

'You are very kind,' Lord Vincent replied gravely.

'Oh, it's no trouble.'

'Unlike the two of them,' Nia said, unable to suppress a smile as she watched them charge off into the house, pushing at one another in order to be the first to tell Hannah of their adventures.

'Do they do everything at a breakneck pace?'

'Pretty much.' Nia chanced a glance up at him. 'Were you not the same as a boy? No, I don't suppose you were,' she added, not giving him the opportunity to respond. 'Your upbringing would have been worlds apart from theirs.'

'Not in the least.' He waved a negligent hand towards the unkempt grounds. 'My brothers and I would have been in seventh heaven if we had found ourselves here at Leo and Art's age. We would have climbed trees . . . and fallen out of them, naturally. Built dens, had battles, fought one another . . . all of the things that your nephews so enjoy.' He shrugged impossibly broad shoulders and treated her to an engaging smile. 'It's simply the way of boys everywhere.'

'You are as bad as they are.'

His smile was broad and infectious. 'Very possibly.'

Their conversation stalled. Nia felt unsettled beneath the full force of his lazy scrutiny, resenting the fact that he probably found all manner of things to criticise in her looks, her manners, her appearance in general. She wanted to call the boys back on some fabricated pretence. Their chatter would have broken the razor-sharp tension that was definitely not a product of her imagination. But if Lord Vincent felt it also, it didn't appear to worry him. She glanced up at him and noticed a teasing smile playing about his lips. She thought of the many occasions upon which she had craved solitude in her busy, unpredictable and disorganised life. It had chosen a most inconvenient time to oblige her. There again, if any of the residents of Stoneleigh Manor decided to show themselves, she would be mortified.

But if that did happen, it would rid her of him in record time. Which was what she wanted, was it not?

His smile turned positively lethal as she continued to look at him. Unsure what it implied, she hastily lowered her gaze, only for it to collide with strong thighs encased in tight-fitting inexpressibles. Heat invaded her cheeks as a firestorm of alien emotions filled her senses and a tremor of awareness rocked her entire body. Perdition, things were going from bad to worse! Nia made a monumental effort to control herself. Glancing lower, she took comfort from the fact that his hessians, which she was sure must usually be polished to a glossy shine, were now caked in mud, also thanks to the part he had played in rescuing her troublesome nephews.

'Art's right, you know, it really wasn't their fault.' Lord Vincent's deep, arresting voice snapped her out of her reverie. 'Well, not entirely. Boys are simply made to behave in such a fashion. I know my mother despaired of the four of us. I am surprised we didn't manage to turn her hair grey.'

Now that the conversation had returned to safer ground, Nia risked chancing a glance at his face. 'You got up to the same sort of things?'

Lord Vincent shrugged. 'Worse, I would imagine. Boyish pursuits don't recognise social boundaries.'

'No, I suppose not.' She bent to scoop up Ruff, who had been dogging her footsteps. 'And you have a lot of explaining to do,' she told him severely. 'I asked you to remain in the grounds for a reason. It's not as though there aren't enough rabbits and squirrels here for you to chase without the need to turn thief. Those boys don't need an excuse to find mischief.'

Ruff sat in her arms, cocked his head to one side and adopted an appealingly innocent expression that made it impossible for Nia to remain angry with him.

'He's incorrigible,' Lord Vincent said, tugging one of the dog's ears, which sent him into a state of near delirium.

Nia rolled her eyes. 'On a good day.'

She returned the dog to the ground and he shot off somewhere, presumably in search of his partners in crime.

'Am I to assume you are related to Patrick Trafford?' Lord Vincent asked after a moment's silence. 'Lady St. John mentioned he might be taking this house.'

'I am his granddaughter. The boys are my brother's children. He is away on business at the present.'

'And their mother?'

'Is dead.'

'I am sorry to hear it.'

Lord Vincent smiled at her, and she heartily wished he had not done so. All the time they were making polite conversation she could play her part, but that smile of his was her undoing. She looked away, again trying not to see the dilapidated house and grounds through his eyes. She felt the need to explain, but stubbornness held her back. It really was none of his business. She was grateful to him for rescuing the twins, but she didn't owe him explanations.

'They appear to look upon you as their mother,' he remarked.

'They have, through necessity, spent more time in my care than their father's recently.'

Lord Vincent sent her a curious glance. 'You love them very much,' he suggested softly.

'How could I not?' She flashed a genuine smile. 'But they need their father. They need proper schooling — '

'Excuse me, they do not go to school?'

'Not since we arrived here. At the moment I teach them myself, but that is hardly a satisfactory arrangement.'

'Presumably you could you engage a tutor if your plans are not settled and you don't wish to send them off to school.'

Tutors cost money. 'It's one possibility, but without my brother's approbation, I cannot make long-term decisions.'

'That must be very frustrating for you.'

'Hmm.'

His mouth. It fascinated Nia, constantly making her lose the thread of their conversation. Her artistic eye was drawn to the shadows between his nose and the tantalising shape of his lush lips. She noticed that deep vertical clefts appeared on either side of his mouth whenever he laughed. She imagined those same lines would become tight with irritation if he was annoyed, and thought how challenging it would be to paint such a mouth. Almost impossible to get it exactly right. It was too expressive. A dangerous weapon he undoubtedly employed with considerable success, even if he was not conscious of doing so. She wondered how it would feel to be kissed by those full lips. Lord Vincent would know how to kiss with conviction, she suspected, just as he most likely did everything he set his mind to with skill and precision.

'I take it your grandfather decided to come to the district for peace and quiet. He undoubtedly has commissions to finish.'

'Yes, that is why we are not receiving guests,' she said emphatically, crossing her fingers behind her back.

The blast of a hunting horn from an upstairs window made her start violently and stumble. Lord Vincent's strong arm caught her before she fell. His horse whinnied and tugged at the reins which Lord Vincent had tied to one of the stouter pillars skirting the terrace. It did not crumble — which, she supposed, was something.

'What the devil is that?' Lord Vincent asked, glancing at the window in question.

Nia closed her eyes for an expressive moment, not needing to follow the direction of his gaze to know precisely what it was. *Oh, Grandpapa!*

'What-ho, Nia my dear,' her grandfather cried cheerfully, before sounding the horn again. 'Are we to have some sport today?'

Unable to avoid looking up, for fear of what her grandfather might do if she did not, at least it gave Nia an excuse not to look at Lord Vincent and be subjected to his derision.

'It's not the hunting season yet, Grand-papa,' she said softly, sighing inwardly when she noticed he was still wearing his nightcap, wisps of white hair sticking out at angles from beneath its frayed hem. He had on his favourite, stained, satin jacket, but since she couldn't see the rest of his body she was spared knowing what other garments had caught his eye that morning. 'Go back inside and I shall be there directly.'

'I say, is that another travelling artist there with you, Nia? Do bring him inside. There's always room for another beneath this roof.'

'Where is Sophia, Grandpapa?'

Tears pricked at Nia's eyes when, even from a distance, she noticed her grandfather's blank expression. 'Who?' he asked, sounding as bewildered as Leo or Art did when they had nightmares.

'I'm here,' Sophia said from behind her grandfather. 'Sorry about that, I only left him for a moment. Come along, Patrick,' she added gently. 'Let's get you settled.'

Nia was unsure if she was grateful or sorry when Sophia coaxed her grandfather inside and closed the window. She was now alone with Lord Vincent again, and she supposed he would expect an explanation for the embarrassing incident. If she did not offer one, he would draw his own conclusions, and tell the world what she had been desperately trying to keep confidential. Her beloved grandfather had lost his mind and barely knew his own name.

She chanced a sideways glance at him, still trying to decide how much or little to tell him about her circumstances. If she saw pity in his expression then he could go to the devil. She could cope with anything but that. To her intense surprise, she merely observed understanding and compassion in the set of his features.

'You cope remarkably well, all things considered,' he said softly.

Before she could respond, the sound of approaching footsteps caused her to glance up and inwardly groan. Mr. Drake; that was all she needed! His ill-fitting black coat billowed behind him, giving him the appearance of a scrawny crow, but his ever-present air of superiority fit him like a second skin.

'Miss Trafford,' he said, raising a hand in greeting. 'Your grandfather is asking for you.'

'I beg your pardon, Mr. Drake.' It was one thing to have her grandfather's lame ducks foisted upon her, but quite another to have them tell her what she should or should not be doing.

'Excuse me,' he replied. 'I did not realise you had company.'

Of course you did not. With no other choice available to her, Nia reluctantly made the introduction. 'Lord Vincent Sheridan, may I present Mr. Drake. Mr. Drake is a poet who enjoys my grandfather's patronage.'

Mr. Drake bowed, for once struck speechless, which was a blessing. Lord Vincent merely inclined his head, clearly not seeing much to be impressed by. Well, at least there was one area in which they were in complete agreement. 'I don't believe I'm familiar with your work, Drake,' he said, turning towards Nia and offering her the ghost of a wink.

He understands. Nia felt overwhelming gratitude.

'Well, I . . . er, that is, my opus has not yet seen publication, but I have every expectation of it very soon being read in all the best salons.'

'How very optimistic of you.'

'Can I escort you inside, Miss Trafford?' Mr. Drake proffered his arm in a proprietary manner that irked Nia. 'It is time for luncheon.'

'No thank you, Mr. Drake.'

Her incivility had no discernible effect and he continued to hover. At that moment the boys burst onto the terrace again, along with Miss Tilling, and Nia's humiliation was complete.

'Hannah says I shall have a scar on my knee, most likely,' Leo said triumphantly.

'And I shall have a black eye.'

Nia smiled her approval at their clean hands and faces, well aware that situation would not endure.

'Shall we walk Forrester up and down for you?'

'It doesn't do to keep fine horses standing around, you know.'

'Did you know that Forrester was bred on our stud here at Winchester Park?'

Nia stifled a smile when, wonder of wonders, Lord Vincent's comment rendered the boys round-eyed and speechless. But not for long.

'Gosh, that must be jolly,' Leo said.

'I should love to see it.'

'Then perhaps it can be arranged,' Lord Vincent replied. 'With your aunt's permission.'

'Can we, Aunt Nia?' The turned identically appealing expressions upon her.

'We shall have to see.'

Annoyed with Lord Vincent for placing the idea in their heads, she shot him a look of disapproval. It bounced harmlessly off his indolent expression. Determined not to be bullied into a situation that would create more problems than she was ready to handle, Nia introduced Miss Tilling to his lordship as an aspiring artist. That much was true, but it seemed indelicate to add that she was a hopelessly inept one, living off her grandfather's goodwill and dwindling resources.

'How lovely to have such a distinguished neighbour,' Miss Tilling trilled, making it sound as though *she* was the mistress of this house, infuriating woman! 'I hope we shall see a lot of you.'

Nia choked on her indignation. 'Boys, take everyone back inside for luncheon,' she said, saving Lord Vincent the trouble of formulating a response. 'I shall be there directly, once I have seen Lord Vincent on his way.'

Mr. Drake looked as though he wished to argue the point. Nia fixed him with a steady gaze and he turned back towards the house, taking a reluctant-seeming Miss Tilling with him. The girl was exquisitely pretty, very dainty, flirtatious by nature, and used to engaging the attention of men from all walks of life. In short, she was everything that Nia was not, and never wished to be.

Emily Tilling looked back over her shoulder and batted her lashes at Lord Vincent. If he noticed, he gave no sign, and Nia was hard-pressed to hold back a smile.

'I hope I did not speak out of turn just now,' Lord Vincent said when they were alone again. 'I ought to have sought your permission before inviting the boys to the stud.'

'Yes, you should have.'

'I can see that you already have too many responsibilities, what with your grandfather —'

'He paints at night,' she said quickly. 'Which is why he sleeps half the day.'

'I see.' Nia very much hoped that he did not. 'Leaving you to run his household?'

'My grandfather collects people in the same way that others collect stamps,' she replied, unable to keep a note of ill-usage out of her tone.

'So I just observed.'

'He means well.' She shrugged as they strolled the length of the crumbling terrace. 'He likes to encourage talent, but is sometimes too soft-hearted for his own good.'

'Do bring the boys over tomorrow morning,' he said, fixing her with an entreating look. 'I believe Lady St. John will be back, and she is bound to call with news from her visit to my sister.' He smiled. 'Make that, demands for my sister's new charity with which she is totally absorbed.'

'It would be nice to see Frankie again, but I'm not sure I can spare the time.'

'The boys will plague you night and day until you agree.' The expression in his eyes was compelling, and Nia suspected he knew it. 'I shall never know a moment's peace, thinking of you being overset by their demands.'

'Behave yourself!'

'Oh, excuse me.' He arranged his features into a convincingly innocent expression that almost, but not quite, fooled Nia into believing it was genuine. 'Did I say something to offend?'

'Do you always say whatever you like?' Nia bit her lip to prevent an inappropriate laugh from escaping. Lord Vincent's reckless mood appeared to be rubbing off on her. 'Well, I suppose someone in your position can do as he pleases and get away with it.'

'Does that mean you will agree to bring the boys?'

Nia could think of a dozen reasons why she should not, but could also not remember when her nephews last had a proper treat. Nor could she recall when they last interacted with a man whose company they enjoyed as much as Lord Vincent's. Or was that Nia trying to justify her own desire to spend more time with him? She thought of Mr. Drake, of Sophia and Miss Tilling. Her grandfather's fragile mind, and of all the responsibilities resting upon her own shoulders. When did *she* last have a treat, come to that?

'Very well, Lord Vincent,' she said, tossing her head and offering him her hand to seal the arrangement. 'We shall be happy to accept your invitation.'

3

Having secured Miss Trafford's agreement, Vince took his leave of Stoneleigh Manor and its strange assortment of residents. Upon return to the Park, he found all of his family in the drawing room, including Lady St. John, already returned from Southampton. Their beautiful young neighbour was a widow, recently settled in the district following the death of her husband, and now an intimate with the Sheridan family.

'I assume we have Annalise's enthusiasm to thank for your early return,' Vince said, smiling as he took her hand. 'She can be rather intense when she gets to grips with a new passion.'

'On the contrary, Lord Vincent.' Lady St. John treated Vince to a specious smile. 'Your sister's fresh ideas are an inspiration to those of us who have become jaded over the years. I came home because I felt I had outlived my usefulness. As well as setting up her charity, your sister is tearing Romsey House apart and completely redecorating. She didn't need me getting under her feet.'

'From what I have seen of the house,'

Vince's mother, the dowager duchess remarked, 'it certainly needs some attention. The place hasn't been touched for decades and is shockingly neglected.'

'Where have you been to get yourself so covered in mud, Vince?' Zach asked.

'Oh, sorry about that, Mother,' Vince replied. 'I should have changed before showing myself in your drawing room.'

'Stop procrastinating and tell us why you're bathed in mud,' Portia, Vince's younger sister, demanded. 'Don't tell me you fell from that new stallion of yours.'

'Sorry to disappoint you, but it was nothing quite so dramatic.'

He told his family about the incident in Compton. 'Really, Zach, this dispute is getting out of hand,' he said. 'Something needs to be done.'

Zach, who was elegantly draped against the mantelpiece, shrugged. 'So I am constantly being told. What is less clear, is what *can* be done. I rather think the villagers enjoy being at odds with one another, and I can hardly order them to befriend each other if they would prefer not to.'

'We need a cause which they feel strongly enough about to overcome their prejudices,' Lady St. John said pensively. 'They put aside their differences each year to challenge your family and friends to a cricket match, Your Grace, so it's not impossible to get them to cooperate.'

'Do you have anything specific in mind?' Zach asked her.

'It's simply a case of coming up with an idea and then convincing the villagers they thought of it themselves.'

Vince's youngest brother, Nate, laughed. 'I admire your optimism,' he said.

'Who were the urchins you rescued?' Amos asked, standing behind his wife, Crista's, chair.

'I dare say you know the answer to that question, Lady St. John,' Vince replied.

This time she did roll her rather expressive eyes. 'Leo and Art, I would imagine.'

'Precisely so. We now have Patrick Trafford and his family living on our doorstep,' Vince told his family.

'Did you see Trafford himself?' Lady St. John asked.

Vince nodded. 'I had no idea he was so . . . well, I expect you know.'

'Yes, unfortunately, I do.'

'I feel very sorry for your friend, Miss Trafford. She has a lot to contend with.'

'Do explain,' Nate urged. 'Why all the mystery?'

'Trafford has lost his wits.' Vince went on

to explain all he had seen and heard at Stoneleigh Manor. 'People take advantage of his good nature and Miss Trafford is left to deal with the consequences. I did not go inside the manor, but it was evident from what I did see that the place is in chaos.'

The duchess shook her head. 'Does Trafford still paint?'

'Apparently so.' But Vince thought about the paint he had seen beneath Miss Trafford's nails, and the manner in which she had looked at him as though preparing to commit his features to canvas — the look of an artist — and doubts crept into his mind. He wondered now if the scent of jasmine that had clung to her might actually have been linseed oil, used for mixing oil paint. There was no reason why she should not mix her grandfather's paints, it didn't mean she herself was an artist, but Vince would not discount the possibility. 'I suspect that if people knew the true state of his mind, he would quickly fall out of fashion, and therein lies Miss Trafford's difficulty.'

'His eccentricities might make him more famous,' Zach suggested. 'Artists are supposed to be temperamental and impolite. It adds to their fascination.'

'That is most unkind,' Lady St. John chided. 'But very likely true.'

'The boys are mad about horses, Amos,' Vince remarked, 'and so I've invited them and Miss Trafford over here tomorrow morning.'

Amos shrugged. 'I am sure I can find something for them to do to make them feel useful.'

'Nia has agreed to come?' Lady St. John sounded surprised. 'It's unheard of for her to leave her grandfather to take up social engagements. She's very protective of him.'

'Vince must have deployed his disgusting charm,' Nate suggested, smirking.

'Really?' The duchess looked interested.

'I have my moments,' Vince replied indolently. 'You will call in the morning, I hope,' he added to Lady St. John. 'Your friend would enjoy seeing you.'

'Don't tell me,' Nate taunted, 'you had to bribe Miss Trafford with the prospect of seeing Lady St. John. Ah-ha. Perhaps your charm is not so potent after all.'

'I can give you lessons at your convenience, little brother.'

'Excuse them, Frankie,' Portia said, grinning. 'They have yet to grow up.'

'Why ever would we want to do that?' Nate asked, perplexed.

'Yes, thank you, I shall.' Lady St. John smiled in response to Vince's invitation. 'It is a long time since Nia and I saw one another.

How did she seem?'

'Distracted and overworked. I don't suppose I helped much when I appeared uninvited.'

A speculative smile played around Lady St. John's lips. 'No, I don't suppose you did.'

'How did you meet Miss Trafford?' the duchess asked Lady St. John.

'In Brussels, at the end of the war. Trafford was fully functional then, with dozens of commissions for portraits of officers before Waterloo. I thought it was insensitive of their families to commission them. It was as though they thought their loved ones would perish and wanted to preserve their likenesses before the battle, just in case.' Lady St. John shook her head, setting her curls dancing. 'Anyway, the boys' mother and Nia's parents were all alive then, and Nia did not have so many responsibilities.'

'I did not know her parents were dead as well,' Vince remarked.

'They and her brother's wife returned to England, and sadly fell victim to the scarlet fever epidemic. The boys, their father and Nia remained in Brussels with Mr. Trafford while he finished his work. The irony is, they ought to have been in more danger, what with them being so close to the fighting, and yet it was the English contingent who perished.' Lady

St. John lifted her shoulders and sighed. 'It was all very sad.'

'Perhaps that's what made Trafford lose his senses?' Zach suggested.

'Very possibly.' Vince nodded. 'It would certainly explain why he switched from portraiture to landscape painting. Everyone who knows about it — and it is not public knowledge yet — seems to think it's a brave change of direction by a talented man who has made a fortune from his art and can afford to indulge his whims, but — '

'But he cannot paint portraits anymore because the people sitting for them would see that he's senile,' the duchess finished. 'How very sad.'

'You are right, both of you,' Lady St. John said. 'Nia Trafford confided in me that her grandfather had made the switch at her suggestion for that reason.'

'I wonder why he doesn't just retire, if he is so unwell,' Portia mused.

Vince wondered the same thing. From what he'd seen that day, he had a few ideas, but decided against voicing them. 'On a different note,' he said, 'something occurred to me on the ride back home, Zach.'

Zach's lips twitched. 'Some insightful thought you have a burning desire to share?'

'All of my thoughts are insightful.' Vince

ignored Nate's scoffing laugh and concentrated his attention on Zach. 'We are agreed that we need to find a solution to the feuding between the villages, are we not?'

Zach nodded. 'Go on.'

'It has got more intense since Amos married Crista.'

'I hope I haven't made things worse,' Crista replied, looking alarmed by the possibility.

'Not in the least. It's just that you happened to be living in Shawford when Amos found you and had the good sense to marry you.'

'Ah, I see what you mean,' Amos said. 'Since I am the first brother to marry and chose a lady Shawford claims as its own, that gives Shawford the edge in this ridiculous feud.'

'But now that Trafford is living in Compton,' Zach added, 'it could even the score.'

'Except Trafford won't show himself in public. Nia won't permit it because she never knows if he will be coherent,' Lady St. John said.

'He may not need to,' Vince said pensively. 'Just knowledge of his being there would give Compton reason to boast.'

'But people wouldn't leave him in peace, and it sounds as though peace is what the poor man needs,' the duchess pointed out.

'Quite so.' Lady St. John stood. 'Please excuse me, Your Grace.' She bobbed a curtsey for the duchess. 'Time is getting on and I have things to do.'

'Of course.'

It was Zach who answered her as he rang the bell for Faraday to show her out. Vince was aware that their mother lived in hope of Zach and Lady St. John forming an alliance. Frankie St. John was beautiful, intelligent, and gave as good as she got in her frequent bouts of verbal sparring with Zach. She showed no particular ambition to become a duchess; which, in Vince's view, was the surest way to make it happen. Vince could see his brother was attracted to her, but he had never voiced his intentions, and Vince would never ask.

*　*　*

'Can we really go, Aunt Nia?'

'Will we be able to ride any of the horses, do you suppose?'

'Forrester is a jolly fine beast.'

'I expect they have lots more like that, Leo.'

'I dare say there are things we could do to help out.'

'I shall bear you company,' Miss Tilling said with alacrity.

42

'The invitation was not extended to include you,' Nia said shortly. The events of the day had left her with a headache, and she had no patience to spare for her grandfather's lame ducks.

'I am sure that doesn't signify.'

'If you wish to be useful, you can help Hannah. There is plenty to be done in the house.'

'I think it would be better if I took the boys,' Mr. Drake said portentously. Since he made little effort to disguise the fact that the boys irritated him intensely, Nia assumed he was ... well, assuming too much responsibility for her — again. 'You know nothing of these people, my dear, and might feel overwhelmed in such august company. I, on the other hand, have had a great deal of exposure to good society. Indeed, when I read some of my verse in Lady Effingham's salon last summer, my audience was quite overcome.'

Of all the patronising, egotistical, controlling ...

'Probably with a collective case of boredom,' Sophia whispered in Nia's ear, loud enough for the entire table to hear.

'Your desire to be of service is as unexpected as it is welcome,' Nia said with asperity. 'However, I do not need anyone's help to drive the gig a few miles. When I *do* need something done, on the other hand, you all appear to be fully occupied.'

'You should accept offers of assistance when they are forthcoming,' Miss Tilling said, waving her fork rudely in the air. 'Those of us with artistic souls cannot put our creativeness to one side simply to oblige you; not when the muse is upon us.'

'Let us hope the muse strikes tomorrow, then,' Sophia muttered.

Nia patted the older lady's hand, aware she was the only person beneath this roof whom she could take to Winchester Park and not be ashamed of. Paradoxically, she could not possibly ask them to receive her.

Her grandfather sat at the head of the table, looking dazed and confused, his luncheon barely touched. Even Sophia's gentle coaxing failed to have its usual effect. Grandpapa's earlier exuberant mood had changed in the blink of an eye, and he had now retreated to a place where she could not reach him. It broke her heart to see him that way, but she could no longer deny that the episodes of distraction, unawareness — call them what you will — were becoming more frequent and prolonged. Soon, they would have to give up the pretence altogether. It filled her with fury that, in part due to his own trusting nature, her beloved grandfather could not already enjoy a luxurious retirement.

His near-catatonic state killed what little appetite Nia had, and she placed her knife and fork aside.

'Come along, Grandpapa,' she said, standing and kissing his brow. 'Why do we not sit outside in the sunshine for a little while? You would enjoy that, I'm sure.'

Her grandfather stood and shuffled from the room with her, more compliant than the boys when they were on their best behaviour. She steered him towards a stone bench on the terrace, now bathed in afternoon sunlight. The two of them sat side by side, Nia firmly grasping her grandfather's wrinkled hand. A hand that had created such beautiful works of art, but which now struggled to grasp a brush. When it did so, there was no telling what the result would be. Sometimes he produced something extraordinary — images conjured from the vast recesses of the functioning parts of his brain that took her breath away. At others, his efforts looked like something Leo or Art might have produced.

Nia stared at the wild jungle of a garden, the sweet fragrance of wild honeysuckle competing with the heady perfume of early-blooming rambling roses and rhododendrons. Ruff and the boys spilled from the dining room and tumbled onto the long grass: boys and dog tangled together in a jumble of limbs. Nia was about to warn them not to tear their clothes or reopen the cut on Leo's leg, but closed her mouth again, knowing better than to waste her breath. She watched them with a combination of anxiety and envy, trying to remember when her life had last been so carefree.

Hannah, faithful, loyal Hannah, stepped quietly onto the terrace and sat on Nia's opposite side.

'Don't let it upset you, lamb,' she said, nodding towards Nia's grandfather, now dozing upright in the sunshine. 'He's had a long, successful life, and wherever his mind takes him off to nowadays, it's a damned sight better for him than reality, that's for sure.'

'I know.' Nia sighed. 'But that doesn't help us much, does it?'

'Perhaps your brother will return with good news.'

'Perhaps,' Nia replied, with more hope than conviction in her tone.

'We need to start making changes,' Hannah said, as though Nia didn't already know that perfectly well. 'Issuing Drake and Miss Tilling with their marching orders would be a good place to start.'

'Don't you think I would, if I could? They

have nowhere else to go, and no means of supporting themselves. If they tell what they know about Grandpapa, out of spite, necessity, or for whatever reason, we really will be finished.'

'And they know it, the ungrateful wretches. That's why they continue to live off us like the parasites they are.' Hannah pursed her lips. 'Well, if they are to stay, they must start pulling their weight.'

Nia stifled a giggle. 'I find it hard to imagine Miss Tilling scrubbing floors or peeling vegetables.'

'You do all of those things. Why should not she?' Hannah scowled. 'Anyway, I'm sure I can find her other occupations that will not be beneath her dignity.'

'If you suggest it, you can be sure the muse will come upon her and she will be filled with an urgent desire to finish her dreadful paintings.'

Hannah sniffed. 'At least that will keep her from under my feet. She's deliberately taking her time because she will have no excuse to remain with us when they are done.'

Nia smiled. 'What about her grand exhibition we hear endless talk about?'

'Bah, you know as well as I do that even if she manages to make the arrangements, no one will attend it. And if they do, who in their right minds will purchase her canvases?'

'Which is why she wants her paintings added to Grandpapa's exhibition of landscapes.' Nia pulled a face. 'She is depending upon Grandpapa's patronage to make a name for herself. As his protégé, people might buy because they assume Grandpapa has recognised a budding talent.'

Hannah blew air through her lips. 'Dicked in the nob, they would be, to think that.'

Nia sighed. 'Don't be downhearted, Hannah. I know I take the most dreadful advantage of you, but I do appreciate your loyalty. You have stuck by us through thick and thin, and I don't know how I would manage without you.'

'Go on with you, lamb.' Hannah wiped her eyes with the back of her hand. 'At least we have Sophia to ease our burden.'

Nia managed a brief smile at the thought of the brazen, kind-hearted, outspoken and often deliberately provocative courtesan who had been her grandfather's mistress for Nia's entire life. She had been between protectors, Grandpapa at the height of his fame, when he first saw her in Paris. He became fixated on her, the two of them hit it off immediately, and had been together ever since. At first Sophia had been his paramour, his muse and his hostess: keeping him entertained, his

48

mind focused on his work, and the hangers-on who gravitated towards him at arm's length. When Grandpapa's mind became fragile, Nia was terrified that Sophia would up sticks and leave him. It would have broken her grandfather's heart to see her go; and Nia's too.

She should have credited Sophia with more loyalty. Instead of leaving, she adapted to their changed circumstances, knuckled down, and had remained a constant source of support to Nia throughout the travails of the past few years. She now acted as Grandpapa's nurse, companion and best friend.

Nia rested her head on the plump shoulder of the woman who had been more of a mother to her than her own ever had. Tears of exhaustion spilled down her cheeks and she made no effort to check them.

'Will you be all right if I take the boys to Winchester Park in the morning?' she asked when she regained her composure. 'They are so looking forward to going.'

Hannah fixed Nia with a probing look. 'And you are not?'

'I know what you're thinking, but you're quite wrong. I came here because . . . well, you know why. We were desperate, the rent was cheap, and this place is hidden away. I had hoped to stay hidden a little longer, though.' Nia expelled a long breath. 'I suppose I was naïve to imagine word of Grandpapa's presence here would not leak out.'

'I was watching Lord Vincent from inside. He didn't seem critical of your grandfather, and bear in mind he saw him at his worst.'

'He is a gentleman. He wouldn't allow his true feelings to show, but I can easily imagine what he must have been thinking.'

'And yet he invited you to his home. He wouldn't have done if he felt you were beneath him.'

Nia squared her shoulders. 'Who said anything about being beneath him?'

'That's the spirit.'

Nia caught sight of Hannah's satisfied expression and wagged a finger at her. 'You said that deliberately, just to provoke me.'

'Someone needs to remind you that you have nothing to apologise for.'

'I think his lordship took a shine to the boys. It would be hard not to when the devil gets into them; although, I suppose, I am biased in that regard. Anyway, they want to see the horses, were not afraid to say so, and so Lord Vincent could hardly invite them and not me.'

'Ah, I see.' Hannah smiled broadly. 'That's what it must be.'

Nia tossed her head. 'You don't see anything at all.'

The boys were scrambling up an old oak

tree, causing the branches to wobble as they played a game that appeared to involve dislodging one another. Ruff scrabbled at the trunk and barked encouragement. Nia opened her mouth to warn them of the dangers but Hannah patted her hand.

'Let them be. It's a soft landing if they do fall, and expending all that energy will wear them out. We won't have the usual tussle getting them to bed tonight.'

'They have had no lessons today,' Nia said, feeling guilty. 'Once again the morning got away from me. I really must talk to Sean about employing a full-time tutor for his sons when he returns, before they run completely wild. We can surely find the money for that?'

'Mr. Drake is always offering — '

'Not on your life.' Nia shook her head emphatically. 'I have yet to hear him utter two sensible sentences in succession. He doesn't even like children, and I have no intention of becoming beholden to him.'

'No, you're right; insufferable little man! I wasn't thinking straight for a moment there.'

'Perhaps Sean will finally agree to sell one of Grandmama's necklaces.' Nia was referring to the jewellery owned by her grandmother that had passed to Sean's wife. 'Any one of them would raise enough money to pay a tutor's salary.'

'Your brother won't hear of it. He insists the jewellery items are family heirlooms and will be passed on to the boys' wives.'

'My brother must face reality.' Nia sighed. 'We do not have any heirlooms in this family. Grandpapa bought that jewellery when he first became famous. There is no sentimental or family history attached to it.'

Hannah shook her head. 'You will have the devil's own job convincing him of that.'

'Perhaps when he's lived here for a few days, when he realised what we have been reduced to, it will finally make him see reason.'

Hannah sniffed. 'And perhaps the moon is made of cheese.'

Nia smiled. 'Are you coping all right in the house with just Annie and Beth for help? We were so very fortunate to find those girls while we were still in Brussels.' Sir Edward Fairstock, the Englishman they had worked for, had died unexpectedly. Lady Fairstock had no further need of their services, leaving them stranded and without employment. Nia was glad their plight had been brought to her notice and they could help one another. 'They are grateful to have regular work, and know better than to gossip about the family when they go into the village.'

'They are good girls, although Annie can

sometimes be lazy. And I have you, as well. You're always doing things to help that ought not to fall to your lot.'

'I wish we could employ more servants locally.' Nia expelled another of her seemingly endless supply of sighs, justifying it by reminding herself she had a great deal to sigh about. 'Goodness only knows what we are going to do about these gardens. They are already a jungle and it's still only spring.'

'We could furnish Mr. Drake with a scythe and set him to work.'

Nia choked on a laugh. 'Now, that I would very much like to see.'

Hannah hauled herself to her feet. 'For once, think about yourself. Decide what to wear for your engagement tomorrow. How about the rose-pink sprigged muslin?'

'Hannah, that's far too smart.'

'You are likely to meet a duchess.'

'Oh Lord, so I am.'

Hannah grinned, causing Nia to suspect she had somehow played into her capable hands. Again. 'Right; and you could scrub your nails to remove all that paint if you want to make a favourable impression.'

'I am not trying to make an impression.'

'No, lamb, of course you're not.' She offered Nia a gap-toothed grin. 'Come on. Let's get your grandfather inside.'

4

'Don't worry, love,' Sophia said the following morning as she insisted upon dressing Nia's hair. 'Your grandpapa's having a good day today. He won't even notice you are gone.'

'There's no rhyme or reason to his actions,' Nia replied, sighing. 'Last night, when I sat with him, he kept mistaking me for Morag. I didn't have the heart to tell him Grandmama has been dead these twenty-five years.'

'It *is* heartbreaking to see him the way he is now, but I reckon it's us as suffer, not him. Wherever he goes to inside his head, he's happy for the most part.'

'I sometimes think it's like having a third child in the house. I want to give that child back and demand the return of my lovely, vibrant grandfather.'

'He's better-behaved than those boys, that's for sure,' Sophia said, chuckling as she did something clever with the heavy sweep of Nia's hair, deploying pins that actually looked as though they might keep it in place.

'I can reason with the boys,' Nia pointed out with a sad little shake of her head. 'Well, sometimes.'

'Your grandfather can still produce inspired work; which is why we are here, of course. I took a peep in the studio and see he made good progress on his latest landscape last night. We won't need to throw this one out.'

Nia turned away from the mirror so she wouldn't have to look at her own tired eyes and drawn features. So she wouldn't have to meet Sophia's enquiring glance in the glass. She knew — or suspected. Nia's secret would be safe with Sophia, but she wasn't ready to share it yet, and Sophia had the good manners not to press her.

'Make sure you keep the studio locked while I'm away, Sophia. I don't want Mr. Drake or Miss Tilling snooping around. I don't trust either of them.'

'Don't you worry.' Sophia firmed her jaw. 'The scrounging beggars won't get past me.'

Nia grinned. 'I remember the last time Miss Tilling tried to sneak into Grandpapa's studio, before we came here, when she thought you were in London for the day. You chased after her with a riding crop, and the look of abject fear on her face was hysterical. She actually thought you would use it on her.'

Sophia chuckled. 'She was right about that. You don't get to rise to the top of my profession . . . former profession,' she amended, 'without knowing how to take care of yourself. Some gentlemen do get the strangest notions in their heads about how they can treat ladies who are not their wives.'

Nia sat up a little straighter and took an active interest in the conversation. Sophia was quite open about her past career as a courtesan, and Nia found everything she had to say on the subject highly informative.

'Do tell more,' Nia urged when Sophia's words dried up.

'We don't have the time right now. If I had had someone to advise me when I was your age . . . no, I was younger than you the first time it was necessary for me to . . . but still, all in all, I have no regrets.'

'When you talk like that, it makes me feel ashamed to complain about my lot.'

'We all make the best of things, love. In my case, I would not have met your grandfather if I hadn't been what I was, so it worked out for the best. In those days just about every single female under the age of forty was keen to get her hooks into him because he was so talented and so popular, invited everywhere. But Patrick was not of a mind to marry again. He said no one could replace your grandmother in his affections. I didn't try to. I just made him laugh, and he knew I didn't want more of him than he was prepared to give.'

She caught Sophia's eye in the mirror and smiled. 'Just look at the wonderful times we have had since then. I really do love him, you know, and I didn't think a person like me was capable of love.'

'Sophia, that's nonsense. I know life has been difficult for you, but you are the most loving, giving, fun person I have ever had the good fortune to know.' Nia flashed an impish smile. 'To say nothing of the fact that you talk to me about all sorts of interesting things that most people would deem inappropriate.'

And she did. Nia knew all about the various men who had kept Sophia in style before she happened upon her grandfather. Nia could well understand how Sophia had caught those gentlemen's attention. She had seen some of the sketches Grandpapa had made of her twenty years ago — sketches that formed part of his private collection, never available for public viewing. Sophia's vivaciousness radiated from the paper, and Grandpapa had skilfully captured her sensuality and that certain something in her expression — a delicacy and susceptibility that would appeal to any man's protective instincts.

Sophia was no longer in the first flush of youth, and her body had spread along with the passing years, but she was still vibrant, delightfully irreverent and quite shockingly outspoken. Sometimes, Nia thought she would join her grandfather and lose her wits completely, were it not for Sophia and Hannah — so different, but between them the bedrock of Nia's struggle to keep her family's collective heads above water.

'We're a right mixture,' Sophia said, echoing Nia's thoughts. 'There's me, a has-been harlot who's no better than she ought to be. Hannah, who was your father's nursemaid and as reliable as it's possible for a woman to be. And then there's you. Pretty as a picture but too blind to see it, working your fingers to the bone to try and atone for the hedonistic pleasures that have seen your family reduced almost to bankruptcy.'

Nia laughed. 'And they say opposites don't attract.'

'Why you insist upon remaining in England defeats me. Stubbornness runs in your family, and I hate to see what it's doing to you.' Sophia's voice softened. 'Why don't you take your grandfather back to that monstrosity of a house in Ireland straight away? We both know it's where he wants to finish his days, and I dare say I shall adapt to the wind and rain soon enough.'

'Oh, Sophia, don't you think I would if I could?'

'If you won't do that, can't I persuade you to auction off those sketches your grandfather did of me all those years ago?'

'No!'

'You can't afford to be sentimental.'

'It's not that. It's just the thought of your . . . well, nude . . . body being displayed to all and sundry that upsets me.'

Sophia chortled. 'Bless you, darling, but after the life I've led, I'm hardly going to be worried about that. In fact, I'd enjoy the notoriety.'

Nia smiled. 'I'm sure you would, but it's not only up to me. I shall see what Sean has to say when he returns. If he doesn't bring good news it might come to that, but I do worry that it will show Grandpapa in a desperate light.'

'How so?' Sophia tugged at a stubborn curl.

'Ouch!'

'Sorry.'

'Releasing old sketches for profit, I mean. After all, we are trying to pretend all is well with his world, and that he's turned to landscapes from a position of strength.'

'Well, the offer's there.' She put her brush aside and stood back. 'What do you think?'

Nia, distracted by their conversation, hadn't been watching Sophia's progress. She did so now, and let out a startled *oh*. Sophia had transformed Nia's hair by fashioning her rebellious locks into a neat chignon, leaving coppery-gold curls cascading about her face.

'I didn't know I could look like that,' she said with a wry smile. 'Thank you, Sophia. At least I don't have to apologise for my appearance.'

Sophia laughed. 'You never have to, especially in that gown.'

The sprigged muslin walking dress was a relic from better days, purchased for her by her grandfather when they were still in Paris. The feel of the delicate petticoats whispering around her ankles reminded Nia that she had lived all over Europe, attended a lot of sophisticated salons where she had been introduced to princes, counts and royalty of every persuasion. She was perfectly equal to meeting a duchess, and a duke, and . . . well, whoever else happened to be in attendance. Lord Vincent's opinion did not matter in the slightest. She had made this effort not to impress him, but to ensure she did not disgrace her family. She trusted to luck that the boys would be sufficiently awed by their surroundings to behave themselves.

Nia picked up her decorated straw bonnet, carefully fitted it over Sophia's handiwork and tied the ribbons beneath her chin.

'Hopefully Hannah will have scrubbed the

boys clean and made them look presentable,' she said. 'Not that I expect that situation to endure.'

'You look a picture.' Sophia hugged her. 'Your Lord Vincent will be enchanted.'

'Sophia!'

'There's nothing you can teach me about animal attraction,' Sophia replied with a throaty chuckle. 'Lord Vincent is attracted to you. I kept my distance, of course, when I realised who your handsome caller was. Can't shock him by having a courtesan brought to his notice — '

'I am not ashamed of you, Sophia. And if Lord Vincent is offended by your presence then he can go hang himself.'

'Come on now, love, time's a-wasting.' Sophia squeezed Nia's shoulders. 'Have a lovely time, and I want to hear all about it when you get back. You know how I thrive on gossip.'

'Let's go and find those boys.'

Nia groaned when she found Mr. Drake loitering in the vestibule, and Miss Tilling fussing around Hannah and the boys.

'You look quite nice,' Miss Tilling said grudgingly.

'I really think I should come with you,' Mr. Drake said. 'It isn't seemly for a young lady to accept an invitation from an unmarried gentleman without male protection.'

'What do you imagine I need protecting from, Mr. Drake?'

He shook his head and tutted. 'Really, there is bound to be something.'

'We're ready, Aunt Nia.' Leo bounded up to her, saving Nia from saying something she might regret. Or, worse, *not* regret.

'Hannah made the most dreadful fuss over us,' Art complained.

Nia shared an amused glance with Hannah over the boys' heads. She couldn't remember the last time she had seen them looking so clean, or so excited. Leo was literally hopping from foot to foot in his impatience to be gone. Nia was scarcely less impatient to escape Mr. Drake and the impossibly self-centred Miss Tilling, who made little effort to conceal her jealousy.

'Come along then, boys.'

A short time later Nia drove their gig, drawn by an accommodating if plodding cob, up the never-ending driveway to Winchester Park. Even the boys, who had not stopped chattering until that point, seemed subdued by their surroundings.

'I say!' Art bounced up and down on the seat when they took a right-angled turn and the house finally came into view. 'It's enormous.'

'Hundreds of people must live there,' Leo

said, his jaw dropping open.

'It makes our house in Ireland look tiny.'

'Do you think Lord Vincent will remember he invited us . . . '

'Or will we be asked what business we have here?'

Nia was wondering the same thing.

As she drove closer to the magnificent mansion, she observed Lord Vincent standing on the front steps, raising a hand in greeting. Her treacherous heart did a strange little flip at the sight of him, and she was glad she was still too far away for him to observe the colour that flooded her cheeks. The boys were less reserved and returned his wave with vigour.

Nia brought the gig to a halt and a footman ran up to take the horse's head. The boys leapt down before the conveyance had even stopped. Lord Vincent walked up to the gig and offered Nia his hand to help her alight.

'Good morning, Miss Trafford. I am so very glad you were able to come.'

'Good morning, Lord Vincent. There was not the slightest possibility of my not keeping the engagement,' she replied, with a signifi-cant look at the boys.

He chuckled. 'No, I don't suppose there was.'

'I say, sir, can we see the horses now?'

'We are most frightfully keen.'

'I hardly slept a wink, I was that excited.'

'Yes, I was the same.'

'Boys, boys,' Nia said sternly. 'Remember your manners, please.'

'It's perfectly all right,' Lord Vincent replied, tousling their heads by spanning one large hand across them both at once. 'Ah, and here is Amos, come to show them around. Miss Trafford, may I present my brother, Amos Sheridan.'

A gentleman as tall and elegant as Lord Vincent assessed her for a moment or two before treating her to a devastating smile. Nia dipped a curtsey, feeling a little overcome.

'Your servant, Miss Trafford,' he said, extending his hand.

In spite of their elevated position in society, it appeared this family did not stand on ceremony, although Nia would reserve judgement on that point until she had met the duke and dowager duchess. *If* she met them.

'Lord Amos,' she said. 'It is a pleasure to make your acquaintance.'

'And these are Miss Trafford's nephews, Leo and Art,' Lord Vincent said, indicating the boys with an elegant wave of one hand. 'But please don't ask me which is which because I simply couldn't tell you.'

'I am Leo, Lord Amos.'

'And I am Art.'

'We are most frightfully keen to see your horses.'

'We are Irish, you see, and so we understand all about horses.'

'Ah, that would explain it.' Nia watched the brothers exchange an amused glance as Lord Amos placed a hand on each of the boys' shoulders. 'If you will kindly excuse us, Miss Trafford.'

'With the greatest of pleasure, Lord Amos. Boys,' she added sternly, 'make sure you don't get in anyone's way, or make nuisances of yourselves.'

★　★　★

The forger mingled with the flow of patrons leaving the Drury Lane theatre and heading for the hostelries that littered Covent Garden. He bypassed the more popular establishments where brassy whores rubbed shoulders with potential customers, distracting them with their questionable charms while pickpockets went about their business. His destination was The Lamb and Flag, a slightly more respectable establishment where the whores were of a higher class, the clientele more selective, and the ale not watered down.

Removing his opera hat as he ducked beneath the lintel, the forger made his way to a table at the rear of the taproom. Its location enabled him to keep his back to the wall and afforded him a decent view of the doorway. He politely declined several offers of company from attractive lightskirts, but did order a tankard of ale from a harried barmaid. When it arrived, he supped it slowly. He was here on business and needed to keep his wits about him. He had been assured his quarry would be here this night, after the theatre. Each week, Lord Barrington selected a different whore to cater to his needs as part of his regular routine. He paid well and didn't require anything too extreme, so competition for his custom was keen. The forger knew all this because he had been watching him for a while, waiting to make his move.

The forger cursed his bad fortune. He had been convinced Trafford would remain safely out of the way in Europe for a lot longer yet, where it was easier for his connections to conceal the fact that he was losing his wits. Had he been courteous enough to do so, it would have enabled the forger to continue making a dishonest living by faking his work. But that silly granddaughter of his had persuaded him to return to British soil. What the devil had she been thinking? Oh, she was trying to hide her grandfather away in the country, but how long could the presence of such a renowned artist remain secret? More to the point, how long would it be before word of the paintings he was passing off as original Traffords reached Miss Busybody's ears?

He thumped his fist against the table, drawing curious glances from one or two patrons in spite of the noise and raucous laughter that made conversation near-impossible. He had been hoping to continue exploiting men with more money than sense for a little longer yet. Still, he reasoned, even if Miss Trafford's suspicions were aroused, what could she do about them?

Thoughts of Nia Trafford had their usual effect upon him, and he was obliged to move his hat onto his lap to disguise the evidence, just in case one of the whores noticed and jumped to the wrong conclusion. Hell and damnation, he wanted the little Trafford minx! He always had, but when he favoured her with his attentions she had looked down her pert little nose at him. No one, but no one, spurned the forger and got away with it, so what he had been forced to do to her grandfather's reputation was all her fault. Damned if he knew what it was about her that had got under her skin, but it was slowly driving him as insane as her grandfather. Perdition, if he didn't stop thinking about her, he would have to engage the expensive services of one of the whores, and that was unthinkable.

Returning his thoughts to his lucrative trade, the forger convinced himself that, even if the Traffords became suspicious, they could prove nothing. The three men to whom he had sold his *alternative* Trafford portraits hadn't looked too closely at their provenances, and would not willingly accept they had been duped. No man of consequence enjoyed admitting he had been taken for a fool. Besides, Trafford would be expected to step forward and disclaim the works personally. The moment he did that, his mental state would become apparent, and he would become a laughing stock. Miss Trafford, for all her cock-teasing ways, adored her grandfather and would never permit that to happen.

The forger chose his marks carefully, made sure they were serious collectors, and did thorough research into their resources. He also ensured they did not already have Trafford originals in their collections. His work was good, but if a connoisseur were to place his beside the real article there was an outside possibility he might become suspicious. To be on the safe side, he disguised himself when he met potential clients and, naturally, used a false name.

Now, thanks to Nia Trafford and her determination to bring her grandfather home, he was obliged to move faster than he preferred. The gentry talked to one another: boasted about new acquisitions for their collections. If too many previously unheard of Trafford portraits became available all of a sudden, then someone, somewhere, would become suspicious. Still, needs must, and the forger was capable of adapting his plans as he went. Moving fast was risky, but if anyone heard of the fakes flooding the market, he would be tipped off. A small voice inside his head sometimes told him not to be greedy and to get out while he still could, but he chose to ignore it.

Ah, he was here at last. The forger sat a little straighter as several whores made a beeline for Lord Barrington.

'Good evening, ladies,' he said politely, doffing his opera hat.

The forger watched Barrington's every move. It didn't take him long to select a woman, and they disappeared to an upstairs room. Barrington returned less than an hour later, ordered a brandy, and stood alone at the bar to drink it. The forger stepped up beside him and introduced himself as a dealer in fine arts.

'I hear you are in the market for an original Trafford, my lord.'

5

Vince stood beside Miss Trafford, grinning at the speed with which the boys had shed their shyness, chattering away to a rather bemused Amos.

'Do they fall to your responsibility all the time?' he asked, watching them go.

She lifted one shoulder. 'When their father is away on business.'

What business? He transferred his attention from the boys to the far more edifying sight of Miss Trafford herself, pleased by the transformation in her since yesterday. His approving gaze started at the brim of her bonnet and worked its way at a leisurely pace to the hem of her gown, lingering for longer than was polite on points of interest in between.

What the devil were the Traffords doing, burying themselves away in a run-down manor house in the middle of nowhere? Patrick Trafford ought to be living in the lap of luxury, with servants falling over themselves to do his bidding. The fact that he was not, and that responsibility for the entire family appeared to fall upon the slender shoulders of a girl who could not be more than two and twenty, was as disturbing as it was intriguing.

What business took her brother away so frequently, leaving her to cope alone? And what had happened to all the blunt her grandfather had accrued at the height of his fame? Who were all the parasites living beneath his roof? He sensed that Niamh Trafford was a very private person, slow to trust, reluctant to confide in strangers. Vince intended for her to look upon him as a friend in whom she could confide. Unless he read her all wrong, she had great need of one.

There was evidence of strain around her eyes, as though she had not slept well. Her cheeks coloured as he continued his lazy perusal of her person.

'You are staring at me, Lord Vincent.' The corners of her lips lifted. 'I'm sure your mama taught you that it's bad-mannered to stare.'

He chuckled. 'Mothers don't know everything.'

The capricious light left her eyes and she seemed to withdraw into herself. 'I am well aware of that.'

What the devil had he said to overset her? 'Come,' he said, offering her his arm. 'My family is anxious to make your acquaintance. We are all a little awed to have such a famous family living on our doorstep.'

She placed her hand on his sleeve and looked at him askance. 'I find it hard to imagine your family being awed by us, or anyone else for that matter. I mean, just look around you . . . this magnificent house, these beautiful grounds.'

'Which just goes to show how little you know us.' He looked down at her with a reassuring smile. 'We might have money and rank, but both were inherited so we can take no credit for that. We have never, any of us, achieved anything remarkable in our own right, and fully intend to bask in the reflected glory of having your grandfather as a neighbour.'

'Please don't do that, Lord Vincent,' she said, alarm flaring in her expressive eyes.

'If you would prefer us not to, then of course we will not.' He fixed her with a probing gaze. 'It is not my intention to make your life more difficult than it already is.'

'I had hoped to keep my grandfather's presence here a secret for a little longer. But, I suppose, now that you all know — '

The hand resting on his arm trembled and Vince impulsively covered it with one of his own. 'We shall respect your privacy, Miss Trafford, and that of your grandfather. You are right to say that word of his presence will most likely spread, but if the Sheridans make it known he is to be left in peace, no one from either of the local villages will go near him.'

She canted her head and subjected him to cool appraisal. 'You sound remarkably sure of yourself.'

'I would refer you back to all that inherited wealth and consequence. The villagers bicker all the time for the privilege of *owning* us, and would never ignore a ducal decree.'

'But I do not even know the duke.'

'You are about to meet him.'

'I see,' she said simply.

He sensed she wanted to say something else, but they were now approaching the double doors to the drawing room, which a footman opened before they actually reached them. The pulse beating at the base of her throat was the only indication of her nervousness.

As they entered the room, five heads turned in their direction. Lady St. John eased the momentary awkwardness by jumping to her feet and engulfing Miss Trafford in an affectionate embrace.

'My dear, it has been too long.' She held Miss Trafford by the shoulders and submitted her to an exacting scrutiny. 'You look very well, but have lost weight since we last met.'

'Whereas you are more beautiful than ever.'

'Nonsense.' Lady St. John waved the suggestion aside. 'I am now quite established as an aging widow.'

Zach turned a laugh into a cough, drawing the ladies' attention to him.

'Miss Trafford,' Vince said. 'May I introduce my brother, Zachary Sheridan, the Duke of Winchester?'

Zach was his usual urbane self as he stepped forward and offered Miss Trafford his hand, effortlessly raising her from her curtsey.

'Miss Trafford, it is a great pleasure.'

'Your Grace,' she replied.

'I hope you and your nephews will be regular visitors to the Park while you are living here.'

'Lord Amos might take a different view after spending time with them.'

Zach laughed. 'It will be good practice for him.'

Vince introduced everyone else in turn — his mother, his brother Nate and sister Portia, and, of course, Amos's wife, Crista. Miss Trafford appeared particularly taken with Zach's wolfhounds, Phantom and Phineas. When she offered them her gloved hand for inspection and then tickled their ears, the pampered beasts recognised a soft touch and settled themselves at her feet the moment she took a seat.

'I hear your nephews have a dog, Miss Trafford,' Zach said, 'which was how you came across my brother.'

'He did rescue the boys from a rather awkward situation,' she replied with a smile.

'I don't suppose you will remember who we all are,' Portia remarked cheerfully after a short pause in the conversation. 'There are rather a lot of us. I expect it's a bit daunting.'

'I am fairly good with names and faces, Lady Portia. My grandfather has met so many people over the years. Recently it has become my responsibility to remember who they all are and where we were introduced.'

'I admire your ability to remember who people are,' the duchess remarked. 'I myself have a terrible memory for names, but never forget a face.'

'My grandfather recalls people by the shape of their heads. If they happen to have unfortunate features, well . . . that just makes them more memorable and fills him with an urgent need to capture their likeness. Or, rather, filled,' she amended with a sad shake of her head.

Vince accepted a cup of tea from his sister's hand and, standing beside Zach, observed Miss Trafford as she conversed with his mother and the other ladies. She looked perfectly at home in their drawing room, rather as Crista had done when she first entered it as, of all things, a jeweller's assistant. It had transpired that she was a great deal more than that. She was responsible for the design and manufacture of some incredibly intricate jewellery — but, as a woman, could not claim credit for her skill.

Zach showed no inclination to embrace matrimony and had named Amos, as the brother closest to him in age, as his heir, with Vince and Nate following thereafter. That being the case, Vince had wondered about his mother's reaction to Amos's obvious infatuation with Crista. A jeweller as possible mother of the next duke? Was that feasible? Vince ought to have known better. His mother's only priority was Amos's happiness, and she put up no objections to the match.

'Do you intend to remain in Compton for long, Miss Trafford?' Crista asked.

'Our plans are fluid, Lady Amos. It depends upon a lot of things.'

'Did I hear you mention you have an older brother?' Nate asked.

'He is currently in London, transacting some business on behalf of my grandfather. We expect his return any day.'

'It must be very difficult for you,' Portia said, 'to have lost both your parents.'

'Portia, I'm not sure — '

'It's all right, Lord Vincent. My grandfather's fame ensured our loss was reported in the newspapers at the time. It is not a secret.'

'It would have been especially hard for your brother, since he lost his wife, too,' the duchess said sympathetically. 'And now your nephews rely upon you.'

'I do the very best that I can, but I have help.'

'Speaking of which, how is Sophia?' Lady St. John asked.

Miss Trafford's cheeks bloomed a becoming shade of pink. 'I don't know how I would manage without her.' She gave her head a defiant toss. 'Sophia is my . . . well, was, my grandfather's muse.'

That *was* news to Vince, but if Miss Trafford expected a shocked reaction, she was to be disappointed.

'How interesting,' the duchess said, her eyes widening. 'I should enjoy meeting her.'

'Oh, would you really?' Miss Trafford looked rather alarmed at the prospect. 'We are all rather at sixes and sevens at the moment, I'm afraid.'

Vince noticed Lady St. John pat Miss Trafford's hand. Vince had to assume Sophia was Trafford's paramour, as well as his muse, accounting for Miss Trafford's embarrassment. What a very interesting family they now had on their doorstep.

The visit lasted the prescribed half an hour, after which time Miss Trafford thanked the duchess and the rest of Vince's family for receiving her.

'I hope we shall see you again, Miss Trafford,' the duchess said, shaking her hand.

'I understand your desire to keep your grandfather's presence here confidential,' Zach said when it was Miss Trafford's turn to take her leave of him, 'and you may rest assured that he will be left in peace, at least by the villagers.'

'Thank you, Your Grace. That is very good of you.'

'Would your grandfather be equal to dining with us?' the duchess asked. 'Naturally you are included in the invitation, as is Sophia.'

'Thank you, Your Grace, but I'm really not too sure if it would be possible, or advisable. Can I consult with Sophia and send word?'

'I am sure Vince will call upon you again in the very near future,' the duchess replied, her eyes sparkling in a manner that immediately set Vince on his guard. He wanted to tell her not to interfere in his affairs, she assumed too much; but couldn't raise the subject in Miss Trafford's presence. 'Please convey your answer to him, and we will fix a date if you decide to come. I hope you will. And naturally Frankie will come, too.'

Vince shared a pained look with his brothers. His mother was meddling — and rather clumsily, too — this time in Zach's affairs.

'Shall we see if your nephews are still in one piece, Miss Trafford?' Vince asked.

'Rather more to the point; has Lord Amos survived unscathed?'

'I did not know my mother planned to invite you and your grandfather to dine,' he said as soon as they were clear of the others. 'I hope she hasn't made things awkward for you.'

'You would prefer it if we did not come?'

'On the contrary, nothing would give me greater pleasure, but — '

'But, you saw my grandfather at his worst yesterday, and are worried he will cause embarrassment.'

'Is that what you really believe?' he asked, fixing her with an earnest look.

She sighed. 'You are probably right about Grandpapa. He is nothing if not unpredictable. I doubt we shall be able to accept. Some days Grandpapa is quite his old self, perfectly equal to sitting down to table and conversing intelligently. Other days, he barely remembers my name, or his own. His moods swing so very quickly. One moment he is coherent, the next . . . well . . . '

'I understand better than you might imagine. My suggestion is that you ask Sophia what she thinks of the proposal.'

'I will certainly speak with her, but she will not come herself.'

'Why ever not?'

'Sophia has been with my grandfather since before I was born. If you must know, she was a courtesan when they met, and is the kindest, wisest, funniest person I have ever had the privilege to call a friend. She would not disgrace your mother's table, Lord Vincent, but the problem is, she will *think* she might.'

'In which case, provided your grandfather is equal to the occasion, Sophia's excuses will not be accepted. You have seen for yourself how relaxed we all are.'

They walked outside into bright spring sunshine, and her eyes immediately went to the paddock where Amos schooled his horses. She gasped when she espied her nephews sitting bareback on the same horse while Amos lunged it at a lively canter.

'Don't worry,' he said, steering her towards a bench where they could watch proceedings. 'Amos wouldn't have put them up if he didn't think they were capable.'

She bit her lip but made no reply. Vince

swished the tails of his coat aside and sat beside her.

'Tell me more about your family, and what brought you to our part of the world,' he said.

6

It was obvious that Nia's nephews were having the time of their lives. She watched them intently, pretending not to notice Lord Vincent's indulgent smile. She was not used to receiving kindness from anyone who did not expect something in return, but every member of his family had taken pains to make her feel at ease. Did they go out of their way to welcome every new neighbour, or was it her grandfather's reputation that ensured she received special treatment? Their curiosity about the straitened circumstances of a man who a few short years previously had been feted throughout Europe must be piqued. Thankfully, they were too well-mannered to ask searching questions.

'Be careful!' Nia clapped a hand over her mouth when Art waved both hands at her, grinning from ear to ear, and almost lost his balance.

'You should worry about yourself.' Lord Vincent transferred his gaze from the boys to her. 'Things cannot be easy for you.'

'I tell myself frequently that I am luckier than most because I have my grandfather. I cannot recall a time when I have not been with him. Wherever he happened to be living, Sean and I were always there too. Well, until Sean married, and then things changed. But, my point is, we have had the most wonderful times, seen such things.' She threw back her head, closed her eyes, and smiled at the memories. 'No one can take that away from me.'

'Is your brother Sean older than you?'

'By five years.' She paused. 'I am two and twenty, in case you were wondering.'

'You never thought to marry yourself?'

'Heavens, no; it is too late for that now.'

He looked at her as though trying to decide if she was serious. Presumably realising that she was, he laughed. 'Too late at two and twenty?'

'Certainly. Most young ladies consider themselves to be off the marriage mart by that age. Besides, I have to look after my grandfather. That is far more important than becoming some man's chattel. Not that men are throwing themselves at my feet precisely . . . well, not for reasons I would find acceptable to embrace matrimony.'

'They want you for your connections.' Shades of irritation and disapproval filtered across Lord Vincent's expression. 'What fools!'

'Everyone who is anyone in the artistic

community will do whatever they think necessary to get close to my grandfather.'

'Drake, and the flighty young woman I met yesterday? I don't recall her name.'

'Emily Tilling. Drake is quite the worst poet in the world.'

'My sister Annalise might give you an argument on that score. One of her suitors this past season kept writing the most dreadful verse in praise of her eyes. It drove her demented.'

Nia smiled. 'She has my sympathy.'

'Why did your grandfather agree to sponsor Drake if he is so very bad?'

'Grandpapa has a reputation for affording young people the opportunity to explore their creativity.'

'He sponsored them?'

'Yes, I suppose that's what he did, and still does. He had so much trouble getting recognition himself, until a philanthropist took him under his wing. He wanted to return the favour, and has done so many times over. A lot of people now making a living from their art owe their start to my grandfather. When he held an exhibition, he would permit his more talented students to exhibit alongside him. Naturally, that ensured their work was seen by people in a position to acquire it and they were established by that means. When his mind started to go, people took the most shameful advantage. That is the only reason I can come up with for his taking Drake under his wing. He used to be a much better judge.'

'What about Miss Tilling? Is she any good?'

'Not good enough to deserve my grandfather's patronage. But he has agreed she can be a part of his next exhibition, and I cannot do anything about that.'

'He still intends to exhibit?'

'His landscapes. He can't do portrait work anymore, for obvious reasons.' Nia dashed impatiently at an errant tear. 'I don't want his reputation to suffer because he is unwell. I mean, if he had gout, or . . . oh, I don't know, some other obvious physical impairment, he would receive universal sympathy. But because he is losing his senses, people will make jokes about all truly gifted artists being a little insane.' She shook her head. 'I couldn't bear that. He is the most giving person I know, and does not deserve to be ridiculed.'

'You love him very much,' Lord Vincent said softly.

'More than you could possibly imagine.' She turned towards him, her smile wide and uncontrived. 'If you could have known him when he was at the height of his fame; he was so vibrant. He lit up a room just by walking into it, bursting with enthusiasm about something or other. It could be simply the sight of a spring flower blooming. *Look at that, Nia,* he would say. *Only imagine nature creating something quite so beautiful.* And then he would dash off a sketch or a painting of that flower, reproducing its likeness so precisely that it would take my breath away, but he saw nothing remarkable in his talent.'

'I wish I could have known him then.'

'I think you would have enjoyed his society, and he yours.' Nia shook his head. 'Now, he barely knows what day of the week it is. It is as though our roles are reversed. He is now the child and I am the parent.'

'What of your own parents? I hope it is not too painful a subject, but you must have felt their loss terribly.'

'Of course I do not wish them dead . . . '

'But,' Lord Vincent prompted when her words stalled.

'I saw very little of them. My father managed my grandfather's affairs, and so he and Mama travelled ahead of us most of the time, making arrangements and doing . . . well, whatever they did to ease Grandpapa's path. Mama was not maternal, and my father was remote and unapproachable: as different from my grandfather as it's possible for two men to be. The caring and compassion skipped a generation, but found a home again in my brother, Sean.'

'And in you,' he said softly.

'Thank you. I like to think so.'

'I am perfectly sure of it, otherwise you would have given Drake and Miss Tilling their marching orders long since.'

'Don't think I haven't considered it.'

'Forgive me, but they do not contribute to the household expenses?'

'Not a penny. They are both near-destitute.'

'Even so, they have seen the deterioration in your grandfather. They ought to have the good manners to leave him in peace.'

'I agree, but it won't happen. There were several others I did manage to get rid of, but the two that remain are what I can only charitably describe as tenacious, single-minded and — '

'Selfish?'

'Thank you.' Nia nodded. 'That is the word I was looking for.'

'My opinion is that you should send them on their way, regardless of the fact that they have no means of support. You have given them more hospitality than they had any right to expect, and don't need the added burden of their welfare.'

'I would, but if I were to do so . . . ' She flapped her hands. 'Let's just say it might create more difficulties than it solved.'

'Ah, of course. I was being obtuse. Far

from being grateful, they might repay you by spreading rumours about your grandfather's condition.'

'I can't take the risk. I live in expectation of Sean having made arrangements for Grandpapa's exhibition to take place sooner rather than later. If it's a success, he will be able to return to Ireland and live out his days there in peace and seclusion.'

'He has property there?'

'Yes, and often speaks about wishing to return to it.'

She sensed that Lord Vincent wanted to ask why they didn't do so immediately, but the answer must have been obvious. Their living conditions, Grandpapa's need for another exhibition, highlighted the fact that they were clean out of funds.

'Miss Tilling can exhibit her ghastly paintings, and we can hide Mr. Drake away in a corner where he is least likely to be an inconvenience, and let him drone on with his poetry. After that we shall be free of them.'

'Did your grandfather pass on his artistic talent to your father?'

'No, Papa could barely lift a brush.'

'But you can.'

Nia's head jerked up. 'Why do you say that?'

'Linseed oil, Miss Trafford. The aroma is quite distinctive. And, forgive me, I observed paint beneath your nails yesterday.'

'I mix Grandfather's paints for him.'

'You don't paint yourself?'

She couldn't look at him. 'I have a little talent, but nothing compared to Grandpapa's.'

'Naturally not.'

His gaze, dark and intense, rested on her profile for so long that she began to feel uncomfortable. She experienced an urgent desire to ease the awkwardness by speaking, but words failed her. If this sophisticated, charming, contradictory and infuriatingly self-assured aristocrat thought to discompose her, then he didn't know her at all. She set her chin and stared stubbornly straight ahead, until his deep, throaty chuckle finally broke through the brittle silence.

'I have offended you in some way, Miss Trafford, for which I apologise.'

'You ask too many intrusive questions,' she replied, still refusing to look at him.

'If I have been impolite, I apologise, but it is all your fault.'

Finally, she deigned to give him her full attention. 'How am I to blame?'

'You interest me.'

She widened her eyes, genuinely surprised. 'Good heavens, why?'

He shrugged impossibly broad shoulders. 'I wish I knew.'

'There is absolutely nothing about me that is interesting, other than my family connections.' The familiar feeling of being cultivated for that reason alone washed through her. 'Is that what this is about?'

'Now it is my turn to be offended,' he replied softly.

'Yes, that was unjust. I'm sorry.'

'As to your being uninteresting, you are quite wrong about that.'

Nia shook her head. Bandying words with Lord Vincent was exhausting. He was too self-assured, his wits too astute, and she struggled to keep pace with him.

'Must you always have the last word?' she demanded crossly.

His smile was annoyingly appealing. Against her will, she found herself responding to it and could not remain angry with him.

'Always,' he said, riveting her with a gaze that made her feel light-headed.

She fell into momentary silence, watching the boys slide from the horse they had been riding and lead it back into the stables beneath Lord Amos's watchful eye.

'Amos will have them brushing the horse down now, I expect,' Lord Vincent remarked, breaking the edgy silence that had settled about them. Well, edgy for Nia, anyway. Lord Vincent still seemed perfectly relaxed. 'It might take a while. In fact, the boys are enjoying themselves so much they will probably make sure it does. I hope you are not in a hurry to be gone.'

'I am sure you have better things to do than entertain me, and I am perfectly happy to wait here alone for the boys.'

'Nonsense.'

He regarded her with absorption for so long that she reacted to his intense scrutiny somewhere deep within her core. When heat invaded her face, it occurred to Nia that he probably knew precisely what he was doing to her: insufferable man! She felt herself drowning in the depths of his intelligent eyes, helpless against the raging desire she felt for this compelling, at times confusing, and yet always elegant, aristocrat. She was unsure whether she was more relieved or disappointed when he eventually looked away first.

'There is nowhere I would prefer to be,' he said casually, as though nothing remarkable had just passed between them. From his perspective it probably had not, and that knowledge helped Nia to regain her dignity.

'Then you are easily pleased,' she said, more sharply than she had intended.

'And you must learn to accept a compliment.'

'Thank you, then,' she said primly.

His lips quirked. 'You are entirely welcome, Miss Trafford.'

'We have spoken a great deal about my family. Now it's your turn. Tell me about yours.'

'We must seem like a very dull lot in comparison to your colourful existence. Zach is now duke. Amos is his heir, and he and Crista are about to produce the first member of the next generation.'

'Her Grace must be delighted.'

'She is very glad to have two of the six of us married, that I can assure you.'

'And there is less pressure on you as a consequence.'

He smiled a devastatingly engaging smile. 'Unfortunately not.'

Nia laughed at his theatrical shudder. 'Your sister is married to Lord Romsey. I know that because Frankie mentioned it to me in her correspondence. I believe I met him once in Belgium. A very distinguished diplomat, if memory serves.'

'Quite so. He is leaving the diplomatic service, or attempting to, but the Foreign Office keeps finding reasons to delay his departure. Annalise is busy setting up a charity school for the underprivileged. She was kidnapped from a society ball in the dead of winter, you see.'

'How awful.'

'Fortunately, she managed to escape, and find her way home in the middle of a blizzard.'

'Good heavens!'

'She saw a lot of destitution that night, and it left her with a firm resolve to do something to help the disadvantaged.' Lord Vincent smiled. 'She will, too. Once she sets her mind to a project, she possesses the Sheridan determination to see it through.'

'Is that what I am to you?' she asked on a whim.

Lord Vincent elevated one brow. 'I beg your pardon?'

'You mentioned the Sheridan determination to see projects through, and I wondered if you saw me as a project.'

He fixed her with a confused expression. 'Why ever would you think that?'

She spread her hands. 'Why else would you want to know my family?'

'And yet your grandfather attracts attention everywhere he goes.'

'He did, once.'

'But now you have reason to hide him away, and think that diminishes your own value.' Lord Vincent shook his head. 'What a very low opinion you have of your own self-worth, Miss Trafford. We shall have to do something about that.'

'The way I look upon myself is no concern of yours.'

Their gazes locked, and held. 'I have decided to make it so.'

'I cannot for the life of me begin to imagine why.'

'Which only goes to prove my point.'

Keeping up with Lord Vincent's conversation was making Nia's head ache. Even so, a small part of her was glad he had taken an interest in her. It was a very long time since she had met a gentleman who made her heart beat a little faster. She was serious about remaining unmarried and seeing her grandfather comfortably through his remaining years. By having warned him that she had no marital expectations, he felt safe in her company.

That was a good thing. Definitely a good thing.

'We have drifted away from the subject of your family, Lord Vincent.'

'So we have. What more would you like to know?'

'I have always wondered what gentlemen of means do with themselves all day. I suppose it is possible for you to remain idle if you wish, but in your case, I can't imagine it. Lord Amos runs the stud, and presumably, the duke looks after his various properties. But what of you and Lord Nathaniel?'

'I take care of the family's investments. I have a head for figures, you see, and make sure all our funds are earning as much as they possibly can.'

'I see.' Nia wished her own family could have had someone as responsible as Lord Vincent to manage their finances. Perhaps then they would still have some left to manage. 'And Lord Nathaniel?'

'Annalise's husband and Zach are talking about arranging proper policing of the area between Winchester and Southampton. There is too much crime, and not enough authority figures to contain it.'

He stretched his long legs out in front of him and Nia tried very hard not to focus her gaze on his strong thighs, encased in tight-fitting buckskin. She did not manage it, but told herself that was only because her artistic eye was interested in their shape. She blushed furiously when Lord Vincent caught her gawping. She quickly looked away, but not before she noticed a teasing little smile playing about that full mouth of his. It was as though he had guessed the nature of her thoughts: thoughts that had no place inside the head of an unmarried woman. Well, it was hardly her fault if a combination of her grandfather's circle of unusual friends and living constantly in the company of a reformed courtesan had made her a little too aware. She had attended their rather wild parties since the age of fifteen. No one seemed to think it was unusual that she should be there, and felt no necessity to restrain their behaviour as a consequence.

They had been informative times.

'Nate has not long finished university,' Lord Vincent said. 'He will most likely get involved in that enterprise with Romsey.'

'I think it very unfair that the men who *did* manage to come back from France after fighting for king and country cannot find gainful employment. One can hardly blame them for turning to crime if that is the only way for them to feed their families.'

'You have inherited your grandfather's philanthropic attitude.'

'And that is a bad thing?'

'Not in the least. I tend to agree with you, but if we did not have laws to protect people and their property from harm, then there would be anarchy.'

'That is undeniable.' Nia was in control of herself again and managed a brief smile. 'Just be prepared to be unpopular.'

This time his smile was tinged with a wicked edge. 'Just so long as you do not take me in dislike, Miss Trafford.'

'Just so long as you do not give me any reason to, Lord Vincent.'

'*Touché.*'

Where were the boys? Nia didn't feel the least bit in control of this conversation, and wished she could decide why Lord Vincent had taken such an interest in her. Why her heart fluttered and warmth streaked through her body when he looked at her in a particular way. Perdition; she was the sensible, level-headed Trafford, and could not afford unrealistic flights of fancy, even if they were conducted within the privacy of her own thoughts.

'You must also deal with feuding villagers.' Nia smiled. 'Perhaps there is more to being in a position of authority than I had realised.'

Lord Vincent frowned. 'Those boys didn't pick on Leo and Art because Ruff stole a few sausages, but because they thought your nephews were spies sent from Shawford. Heaven knows what there is to spy on, but the tragedy is that the adults encourage the children to think that way.'

'Why do they feud?'

'That, Miss Trafford, is a very good question.' He sighed. 'I wish I knew the answer to it.'

They fell momentarily silent, but Nia was

aware of his deep, penetrating gaze caressing her face and making her shiver.

'Are you cold, Miss Trafford?'

'No.' She looked away from him. 'Returning to Her Grace's invitation to dine, it will be impossible for us to accept it.'

'But it is not your grandfather's unpredictability that most concerns you?'

Busy examining her folded hands, Nia's head jerked upwards. 'What do you mean?'

He briefly placed one of his own hands over hers, and as quickly removed it again. 'You are worried about exposing my mother to the company of an ex-courtesan.'

'How did you know?'

He chuckled. 'By not denying it, you have confirmed my suspicions. You like your grandfather's paramour very much, and are not prepared to put her in a situation where you think she might feel disadvantaged.'

She acknowledged his statement with a brief nod. 'I couldn't manage without Sophia. She could have left Grandpapa when he started to lose his wits; most women in her position would have done so, but Sophia is not most people. She is loyal, loving, patient and kind, and cannot help the circumstances that made her what she is.'

His smile was a warm caress. 'You cannot protect the entire world single-handed.'

'I only want to protect my grandfather and Sophia.'

'And the boys, and your brother.' He tilted his head and sent her another of his devastating smiles. 'Did I forget anyone?'

Not *anyone*, but a great deal of *anythings*. Just for a moment, Nia was tempted to unburden herself by telling him absolutely everything. The real reason for Sean's visit to London and her fear that she would be unable to cope with the aftermath. But common sense prevailed. It was enough that he was her friend, or appeared to want to be. She would not exploit that situation.

'I hope you change your mind about dining with us,' Lord Vincent said when Nia remained silent. 'Sophia will be as welcome in our drawing room as you are.'

Nia searched his face for signs of derision, but found none. 'You really mean it, don't you?'

'I never say things I don't mean.'

'Then, thank you. I promise to speak with Sophia.'

'Then you have provided me with the perfect excuse to call upon you tomorrow for your decision.'

'Don't you have funds to manage, or criminal gangs to control?'

'Are you being flippant, Miss Trafford?'

She smiled at him. 'I believe I am, Lord Vincent.'

Once again their gazes locked, and Nia was conscious of awareness stretching between them. His presence affected her on every level, bringing her body alive in previously unimagined ways. Her tangled reflections were brought to a premature end by the sound of the boys calling to them, which was just as well. They moved slightly apart, even though a respectable amount of daylight already separated their bodies, and smiled at the twins as they barrelled towards them.

'Aunt Nia, we had the very best time . . . '

'That was a stallion. Did you see us?'

'Yes, I saw you.' Laughing, Nia stood and tousled their heads. 'I hope you expressed your thanks to Lord Amos. It was very good of him to make time for you.'

'We did.'

'I think he was grateful for our help, as well.'

Nia observed the brothers share an amused glance. 'I dare say he was. But now, gentlemen, you must excuse us. I think we have outstayed our welcome.'

'Not a bit of it,' Lord Amos replied. 'The boys are always welcome, as are you.'

'Please don't tell them that, or you will never be rid of them.'

A short time later, Nia waved over her shoulder to the brothers as she drove the gig away from the Park, wondering what she had just set in motion.

7

Vince watched until the ancient gig turned the corner in the driveway and was lost from view. He returned to the house in a reflective frame of mind, and joined Zach and Amos in the former's study.

'Engaging boys,' Amos remarked. 'And with instinctive horse sense, too.'

'Thank you for taking the time with them,' Vince said.

'It was amusing.'

Zach's booted feet rested casually on the edge of his priceless desk: a family heirloom passed down through the generations. 'What is the real reason for Trafford's impoverished state, Vince? Did your Miss Trafford enlighten you?'

'I thought you might be able to tell me,' Vince replied. 'What with Lady St. John being so intimate with the family.'

Zach flexed both brows. 'I can't imagine why you suppose she would confide in me.'

'Nothing would please our mother more,' Amos replied, sharing a glance with Vince.

'Our mother assumes too much.'

Amos flashed a wicked smile. 'If you say so.'

'What did you and Miss Trafford talk about while you were cosily ensconced on that bench for so long, Vince?' Zach asked.

'Spying on me, Your Grace?'

Zach chuckled. 'Idle curiosity.'

'You never ask a question out of curiosity.'

'Well, I am curious about Trafford and his straitened circumstances. I took a liking to the chit. She has spirit and a lively wit. She didn't appear overwhelmed to meet us lot, either, which speaks volumes for her resilience. I've heard it said we can be intimidating, especially on home ground.'

'I agree,' Amos said. 'It's unusual for one so young to be so self-assured, but I suppose she has been exposed to all levels of society for many years. Artistic types tend to play by a different set of rules.'

'What I have learned is that, once Trafford received public acclaim, he set about collecting protégés and helping them with their own careers.'

'And now he's losing his wits, they're taking advantage of the situation and flocking to him in droves, I dare say.' Zach shook his head. 'Ambitious people are never slow to exploit weaknesses. No wonder Miss Trafford wants to keep her grandfather's condition private.'

'Trafford is planning an exhibition of

landscapes, presumably because he needs the blunt.'

'Shame he doesn't still do portraiture,' Amos said. 'That is what he is known for, and he's damned good at it. Or was.'

'Miss Trafford says he still paints. Sometimes the results are remarkable, sometimes dire. But he can no longer do what he excels at because the sitter would notice his condition.'

'He could do a portrait of Zach,' Amos suggested, brightening at the thought. 'One of him in all his ducal splendour is long overdue for our gallery here at the Park.'

'Now, there's a possibility,' Vince mused. 'You won't mind if he seems a little scatterbrained, will you, Zach? Obviously, the portrait wouldn't be for sale, but it could form the centrepiece of Trafford's exhibition, and it would draw people in droves. They would see he has lost none of his talent and hopefully that would persuade them to invest in one of his landscapes, especially if you suggest they will soon be in great demand.'

'Quite right,' Amos agreed. 'If Zach told his adoring public that the king was really sane, no one would doubt it.'

'You two overestimate my powers,' Zach replied indolently.

Vince and Amos continued to discuss the

possibility of Zach's likeness being captured on canvas. The subject of that discussion leaned casually back in his chair, feet still on the desk as he idly fiddled with a paperweight.

'Do I have any say in the matter?' he asked.

'No,' his brothers replied in unison.

'The travails of being a duke, Zach,' Vince said cheerfully. 'Do your duty and stop complaining.'

'Did I complain?'

'Trafford could paint you with the dogs,' Amos suggested, nodding to Phineas and Phantom, dozing in front of the fire. 'They are your shadows anyway, and you would then have a permanent record of them.'

Zach nodded, seeming less reluctant. 'Will Trafford do it though? Is he still capable?'

'I shall speak with Miss Trafford and seek her opinion,' Vince replied. 'I am sure she will see sense in the suggestion. You will not be *that* inconvenienced, Zach, and will have a valuable work of art to show for it. More valuable than most Trafford portraits because it will most likely be his last.'

'Always thinking of the family's fortune, Vince,' Zach replied drolly.

'I live to serve, big brother.'

'This might be a convenient way to even the score between the villagers,' Amos suggested thoughtfully.

Zach sat upright and his feet hit the floor. 'Trafford having connections to Compton, you mean?'

'Yes,' Vince replied. 'But Miss Trafford is trying to keep that under wraps for fear of her grandfather being inconvenienced by unwanted callers.'

'The villagers will leave them alone if I make it clear I expect them to.' Zach shrugged. 'And the rest of the world need not learn of Trafford's presence here until he has quit the area.'

'True,' Vince said, nodding.

'Will they come to dinner?' Amos asked.

'Our mother took a liking to Miss Trafford,' Zach replied. 'And I can assure you Sophia Ash will not be an embarrassment.'

'You are acquainted with her?' both brothers asked together.

'You might have said something earlier,' Vince added alone.

'Our paths crossed at the opera in Paris some years ago. We were not introduced, but someone told me who she was and pointed Trafford out.' Zach chuckled. 'She was past her prime at that point but still stood out in a crowd.'

'Lady St. John speaks highly of her,' Vince said.

Vince glanced at Zach. Whenever Lady St.

John's name was mentioned, he affected an attitude of complete indifference. A little too indifferent?

'What is it, Vince?' Zach asked. 'You seem distracted. Your head is full of the charming Miss Trafford, I suppose.'

'I *was* thinking about Miss Trafford's problems.' He shook his head, struggling to articulate his thoughts. 'That the family is short of money is not in question. I would give much to know how they ran through it all so quickly, but that's none of my business. Miss Trafford's brother is away organising her grandfather's exhibition. She mentioned several times that she was anxious for his return, and that when he did come back things would be a lot clearer. She wouldn't say what things, though.'

The luncheon gong sounded and the three brothers headed together towards the dining room.

'I imagine you plan to call on your Miss Trafford tomorrow,' Zach said, slapping Vince's shoulder. 'Perhaps you will learn something then.'

'Do I have your permission to suggest the portrait?'

'Yes, I suppose so.' Zach rolled his eyes. 'The sacrifices I make for my family.'

★ ★ ★

107

Upon return to Stoneleigh Manor, Nia had no further opportunity to dwell upon her rather extraordinary morning. In some respects that was probably just as well. Mr. Drake was wandering about the overgrown grounds, reciting his poetry aloud, clearly waiting for her return. Miss Tilling was also hovering, but she took a perverse pleasure in not answering any of their questions about Winchester Park. It was time to emphasise the fact that they were not members of her family, and never would be. The boys eased the tension by chattering away about horses. Ruff added to the chaos by tearing about in circles, almost tripping Nia over because he was so pleased to see her again.

'Anyone would think I had left you for days, not hours,' she said, scooping the little dog into her arms and scratching his ears.

Nia headed for the house to see if Hannah needed help with luncheon, but was detained by Mr. Drake's hand on her arm.

'A word, if you please, Miss Trafford.'

He was the last person she wished to speak with, but good manners prevented her from brushing him aside. Annoyingly, the boys had taken themselves off somewhere, and she found herself alone with their resident poet. 'What is it, Mr. Drake?'

'Perhaps we could sit down.'

He indicated a bench, but Nia had no intention of sitting with the tiresome man. Given the slightest encouragement, he could hold her up for hours.

'Please, Mr. Drake. Whatever you have to say, just say it.'

'Well, I hope you do not think I speak out of turn, but the fact of the matter is that you require protection.'

Nia elevated both brows, surprised and angered by what — even by Mr. Drake's standards — was an exceptionally inappropriate statement of supposed fact. 'I beg your pardon?' she asked pointedly.

'You do too much.' *Yes, and why is that?* 'People take shameful advantage of your good nature.'

Nia laughed aloud, mindless of how rude it made her seem. 'That is certainly true,' she managed to say. Surely he was not so obtuse that he failed to appreciate he was a prime offender?

'I do not like the way Lord Vincent is manipulating you.'

Enough! 'It is no business of yours, Mr. Drake, how I spend my time, or with whom.'

'But I would like it to be, if you will allow it. I have had the honour of forming part of your establishment for some time now, and I know your grandfather looks to me to take care of you.' *Oh, for goodness sake!* 'You must be aware of how much I admire you, and I would consider myself the most fortunate of men if you would consent to become my wife.'

Suddenly Nia was in urgent need of that bench, but somehow managed to remain on her feet. 'Are you proposing to me?' she spluttered.

'You are shocked, I can see that. You are too modest to assume a man of my stature would admire you, I suppose. I have a great future in front of me, and I would like you to be a part of it.'

Against all the odds, Nia felt an overwhelming desire to laugh. She bit the inside of her cheek to prevent it. She disliked Mr. Drake and his arrogant assumption that she would be flattered by his self-serving attention; but even so, he did not deserve to be laughed at.

'A great future *how*, precisely, Mr. Drake?'

'Dear lady, my poetry. Surely you have not forgotten?'

As if she could. 'Thank you, Mr. Drake. I appreciate the compliment of your proposal, but we would not suit.'

'Don't be coy, Miss Trafford. It does not become you.'

Really, the man was insufferable. 'I am not being coy, as you so charmingly put it, merely honest. I have absolutely no desire to marry you, or anyone else. Besides, even if I did, how would you support us until your opus finds a publisher?'

'Well, I rather thought that we could . . . er . . . ' He waved his arms around in a vague manner, making it evident precisely what he had thought; always supposing he had considered anything as practical as putting bread on the table.

'Yes, that is what I imagined.' Nia turned towards the house. 'We shall not speak of this again, Mr. Drake. I have refused your proposal, and there is an end to the matter.'

'You are making a grave mistake,' he said, his voice turning sour. 'You may never receive a better offer, or any offer at all.'

'Thank you for your concern, but I am perfectly willing to take my chances.'

Mr. Drake looked shocked. Pompous, irritating little man! 'I do not say this unkindly, but you are not getting any younger. I shall not accept your refusal, since I am not persuaded you have considered your situation carefully enough. We shall speak again.'

Nia didn't trust herself to respond and swept past him into the house.

Mr. Drake brooded throughout luncheon, which at least spared them from the drone of his voice, and spent the entire meal sending Nia looks of unbridled reproach. Now that she had cooled down a little, she realised she had miscalculated in refusing him so uncivilly, even if his proposal had been made for his advancement and not hers. She now had no choice but to keep him here at Stoneleigh Manor, much as she wished to be rid of him. If she evicted him, he would forget all about the months he had lived for nothing in their household, and wouldn't hesitate to spread word of her grandfather's condition, if only to assuage his wounded pride.

Luncheon finally came to an end and Mr. Drake took himself off to compose more verse; probably focusing on unrequited love. Nia changed into an old gown and was working out her frustration on a flower border, attempting to rid it of its more intrusive weeds, when Sophia found her a short time later.

'Your grandfather is resting,' she said. 'What's wrong with Drake? He looks as though he's lost a guinea and found a farthing.'

'He doesn't have a guinea of his own to lose.'

'True.'

Nia sat back on her heels and sighed. 'He asked me to marry him and can't understand why I respectfully declined.'

Sophia guffawed. 'Ridiculous little man!'

'I wouldn't mind quite so much if I thought he actually felt affection for me. As it is, he seemed to think he was making a sacrifice and that I ought to be grateful to him.'

'What shall we do about him?'

'I have absolutely no idea.' Nia stood up and followed Sophia to the bench Mr. Drake had been so anxious to share with her. 'Hopefully Sean will return with encouraging news. We really are down to our last few pounds, you know. We shall have to do something, and soon.'

'The sketches of me.' Sophia's expression brightened. 'We shall sell them at auction. It is that simple.'

'Oh, Sophia, no!'

'At least let me get them out. We can look at them together and decide which ones will fetch the best prices. We may not need to sell them all.'

'Well, all right, get them out by all means.' Nia was beginning to accept that they really didn't have any other choices. 'But I refuse to decide anything about them until Sean returns. It is not a decision I can take alone.'

'Of course not.' Sophia smiled at Nia. 'Now, tell me all about your morning. Is the house as splendid as we have been led to believe?'

'You might soon be in a position to discover that for yourself.'

'How so?'

'Grandpapa, you and I have been invited to dine.'

'Goodness, are you sure the invitation

includes me?' Nia nodded. 'Well, that is very gracious of the duchess, but obviously I cannot go.'

'If Grandpapa goes, then you come too,' Nia replied firmly. 'Frankie St. John has explained who you are and what . . . er, role you fulfil. If you imagine the duchess swooned at the knowledge, then you have it all wrong. She is very modern in her views and I think she's fascinated at the thought of meeting you.'

Sophia flashed a wicked smile. 'Not many duchesses think that way, although I have known a number of dukes who most definitely did.'

'Oh, Sophia!'

'What of Lord Vincent?'

'What of him?'

'Don't be difficult. You know precisely what it is that I wish to know. Affairs of the heart are, after all, my business, and your coy attitude does not deceive me.'

'There is no affair of any kind involved, and nor will there ever be.'

'But you like him?' Sophia covered Nia's hand with her own. 'There is a connection between you?'

Nia laughed. 'Now you're being unrealistic. I do like him, as a friend. We somehow got onto the subject of matrimony, and I told him of my firm intention never to marry, which leaves us at leisure to be friends.'

'Ah, I see.'

'Stop laughing at me. We have discussed the possibility of my marrying on enough occasions for you to know I intend to remain with Grandpapa — and you, if you don't get tired of us. Lord Vincent now knows it too, and has nothing to fear from me.'

'That must be a great relief to him.'

'Sophia, I'm warning you — '

'Sorry, darling. I just want to see you enjoy yourself for once without putting the welfare of others ahead of your own. You are too young to be so serious.'

'And these weeds will not pull themselves,' Nia replied, crouching to return to her work.

'You ought to have withheld your answer from Drake, pretended to consider his proposal, and set him to work in the meantime.' Sophia fell to her knees beside Nia and grabbed at the first weed she saw. 'This is definitely men's work.'

Nia laughed. 'I would rather weed a dozen gardens than give Mr. Drake the slightest encouragement.'

8

The rest of Nia's day passed in a blur of activity that kept her constantly occupied, leaving her physically and mentally exhausted. She wasn't prepared to admit it to Sophia for fear of encouraging her unrealistic expectations, but Lord Vincent's interest in her did appear to transcend the neighbourly. She wondered what it was that he wanted from her; why he was going to so much trouble to ingratiate himself with her and the boys. Presumably it was to do with her grandfather. As soon as people realised who she was, it was always to do with her grandfather.

She spent several hours in the studio with her grandfather after everyone else had retired, pleased that he was lucid and creative that evening. Even so, it wasn't safe to leave him unattended. She had once done so for a short period, and he had managed to set the studio alight by moving a candle too close to the turpentine. Nia found him blissfully painting away and breathing in the deadly fumes.

Sophia had responsibility for him during the daylight hours, but was two decades older than Nia and needed her repose. Besides, Nia had duties in the studio that only she could perform. She had forgotten what it was like to have a full, uninterrupted night's sleep. Only since meeting Lord Vincent did she bother to think how that must reflect upon her appearance. It vexed her that she *had* thought about it.

When she had seen her grandfather safely to his bed and was at liberty to retire herself, sleep eluded her, even though she was exhausted. The events of this most extraordinary day — her visit to Winchester Park, the dinner invitation, Mr. Drake's proposal, concerns about her brother's return and what news he might bring with him — rattled around inside her tired brain as though on a continuous loop. But, annoyingly, the image of Lord Vincent's smiling face, his intelligent eyes and handsome profile, remained at the forefront of her mind, preventing her from achieving the sleep she so badly needed.

Lord Vincent had awoken some primeval need in her that she had not previously been troubled by. When he looked at her in a particular manner that need intensified, and there didn't seem to be anything she could do to control it. It tugged at her on a level she had no command over, making her forget momentarily who she was supposed to be.

Nia was quite out of charity with herself for being so fanciful. She took out her frustrations on her pillows, thumping them into a comfortable nest and pulling the covers up to her chin. But sleep was still impossible to achieve, and the first fingers of daylight were filtering through a gap in the curtains when she finally fell into an exhausted slumber.

'We can't — '

'We promised Hannah most faithfully that we would not — '

'But she might be unwell — '

'Aunt Nia *never* sleeps late — '

Nia sat up abruptly and blinked sleep from her eyes, torn away from a compelling dream in which Lord Vincent and she were engaged in a very interesting situation. She most particularly did not wish to part with that dream; but the boys, speaking in theatrical whispers that were louder than their normal voices, had snatched it away. She would never be able to regain it, which was probably just as well. Whatever could the time be? It felt as though she had only just closed her eyes, but sunshine streaming through the partially closed curtains told her she was indeed tardy.

'Come in, boys,' she said, loud enough for her voice to reach them.

The door burst open and Leo and Art tumbled into the room, their faces troubled.

Ruff was with them and leapt onto the bed, where he set about licking Nia's face.

'We wondered where you were.'

'Hannah said to leave you be.'

'But you never sleep late, Aunt Nia.'

'Shush, it's all right.' They sat on the edge of her bed, sporting identical wide-eyed expressions of concern. Nia ignored her headache and smiled her reassurance. 'Run and tell Hannah I shall be down directly.'

'You won't tell her we woke you?'

'She said we were not to disturb you.'

'You could never disturb me, my dears. Now, off you go. Oh, and boys — ' They turned in the open doorway to look back at her. 'If you want to help, you could tether Ned in the middle of the lawn, or what was once a lawn before nature had her way with it. He can make himself useful by eating the grass. That will save me the trouble of finding someone to cut it for us.'

'Yes, we can do that.'

Off they went at breakneck speed, their footsteps and Ruff's scrabbling claws on the boarded floor sounding like a small army on the march. Nia smiled, indulged in a slow stretch and, for once, took her time with her ablutions. She was late, but the house had not fallen down due to her absence, so she might as well be a little later still.

'There you are, lamb. I have breakfast prepared for you,' Hannah said.

'Sorry to be late.' Nia yawned behind her hand. 'The chores must be piling up.'

'Everything's under control.' Hannah grinned. 'I have Miss Tilling helping with the laundry.'

She nodded to the scullery off the kitchen to prove her point. Sure enough, Miss Tilling was there with their maid, Beth. With her clothing protected by an apron, their unwelcome house guest was half-heartedly scrubbing clothing.

'Good heavens.' Nia's mouth dropped open at the sight. 'What did you have to do to make her offer her services?'

'I told her you were indisposed, and if she didn't help there would be no clean clothing.'

Nia flexed a brow. 'That was all it took?'

'Well, I might have mentioned that Lord Vincent, or perhaps even the duke, might call, and if she had nothing clean to wear, it would be no use blaming me.'

Nia spluttered with laughter. 'I didn't say either of them would call.'

'Nor did I. I merely suggested the possibility. Anyway, just leave her majesty to me and enjoy your breakfast in peace.'

'I should have put my foot down with her long since.'

'Well, I intend to continue with the way

I've started, and if she doesn't like it, there's nothing to stop her from leaving. I don't need you in here today. In fact, it would be better if you made yourself scarce. You're not as tough as me, and would probably give way to her pathetic excuses. Just sit outside and enjoy the sunshine. You look done in, and little wonder.'

'I can't do nothing. If you insist upon me going outside, I shall continue weeding the garden.'

Hannah shook her head. 'At least you will have the benefit of fresh air.'

By the time she had finished her breakfast, Nia's headache had become a dull, bearable throb, and she felt a little more optimistic about the future. She had no reason to feel that way, at least until Sean returned and she knew where they stood with their wider concerns. But her sixth sense told her that today something of significance would happen.

The weeding was hard physical work, but at the same time oddly rewarding. The boys were with Sophia and her grandfather, doing their sums. Apart from Ned, who was obligingly chomping away at the overgrown lawn, she had the garden to herself. Of Mr. Drake, thankfully, there was no sign. She worked steadily away, removing her bonnet so she could enjoy the spring sunshine on her upturned face, not caring if it brought out more of her freckles.

Her entire body jerked when she heard the sound of rusted hinges protesting as the side gate was opened. She was furious with her treacherous heart for doing a strange little flip at the prospect of their visitor being Lord Vincent. She glanced down at her old gown and grubby hands and winced. She ought to have worn gloves, but enjoyed the feel of the soft, loamy soil slipping through her fingers too much to worry about her hands. Her hair had escaped its braid and she must look the most frightful sight. Well, she thought, standing to brush the soil from her skirts, this was who she was, and it was too late to change her ways, to say nothing of her attire.

'Papa!'

Nia's heart lifted. The boys would have had a clear view of the gate from an upstairs window, whereas only now as he emerged from the tunnel of trees was Nia able to recognise her brother. Sean grinned, jumped from his horse and picked both boys up together, one beneath each arm. Ruff appeared from the trees and scrabbled at Sean's legs, tail wagging.

'We thought you would never get back.'

'We expected you days ago.'

'Did you bring us anything?'

Laughing, Sean reached into his saddlebags and threw a package to his sons. They fell to the ground and ripped it open with great enthusiasm. Sean then opened his arms to Nia and she threw herself into them.

'Sorry to have been gone so long,' he said. 'Have you managed all right?'

'Don't I always?'

'Yes, but you shouldn't have to.' Sean held her at arm's length and examined her face. 'You look tired.'

'I wish everyone would stop telling me that.' Nia summoned up a smile. 'Now, come inside and tell me how it went.'

'I say, Papa, this is top-notch.'

'Thank you, Papa.'

The boys ran off throwing a shiny new cricket ball between them, presumably looking for somewhere to set up a makeshift cricket pitch. Ruff leaped around them, caught up in the excitement.

'See to my horse for me before you disappear, boys.'

'Yes, Papa.'

'Not inside, Nia. Let's talk out here.' Sean's expression sobered as he glanced at the house. 'Walls have ears.'

'Oh dear, is the news as bad as we feared?'

Sean answered her question with one of his own. 'How is our grandfather?'

'Not much change.'

'Has he been working?'

'Yes. Not as much as we had hoped, but . . . ' Nia shrugged, seeing no necessity to elucidate.

Brother and sister seated themselves on a bench. Sean removed his hat and wiped his forehead with his sleeve.

'The painting the Smythes have, the supposed Trafford original, is definitely a forgery,' Sean said, sighing.

Nia's heart lurched. Against all the odds, she had been subconsciously hoping they had got it wrong. 'You managed to see it for yourself?'

'Yes, they live permanently in town. So I called, left my card, and said I heard they had just acquired one of my grandfather's works that I hadn't previously seen. Naturally, they were delighted to show it off.' Sean shook his head. 'It's supposed to be a portrait of an unnamed gentleman painted before Grandpapa became famous.'

'We know such works exist, of course, but they are not catalogued anywhere amongst Grandpapa's paintings.'

'That isn't one of them.' Sean was emphatic. 'I examined it closely, and it's the best forgery I've ever seen, right down to the signature. But, it is not Grandpapa's work.'

'Grandpapa's brushstrokes are long and fluid.'

'The painter of the forgery tried to emulate that style, and made a damned fine job of it. Excuse the language, Nia, but it makes me so angry that someone has taken such shameful advantage of Grandpapa. The brushstrokes on the forgery were boxy in places, and a little too lightly applied. Only someone like you or me would notice, because the forgery was that good.'

'It is as we feared, then.' Nia rested her chin on her fisted hand and sighed. 'Whoever did this knows Grandpapa is losing his wits.'

'One of his protégés?'

'I don't see who else it could be, unless one of them spoke out about Grandpapa's condition to a third party, but I think that unlikely. We got rid of them all, except Miss Tilling, before his condition became too serious. And Miss Tilling is incapable of painting that well. Mr. Drake does not paint . . . '

'What is it, Nia?' Sean asked when her words trailed off.

'It occurred to me that Mr. Drake might somehow have used Grandpapa's illness to his own advantage.' She screwed her features into a moue of distaste. 'I would not put anything past him.'

'Told someone else, you mean?' Nia

nodded. 'It's possible, but why would he?'

'Oh, no reason.' Nia wasn't ready to tell Sean about Mr. Drake's ridiculous proposal. Besides, that had only taken place yesterday. If his feelings were hurt and he was looking to spite her, he had had no time to instigate the forgery business. They now knew of three forged portraits bearing their grandfather's signature, and they would have taken months to paint. 'He has been with us constantly, so can't have seen anyone to pass the information on. And, to the best of my knowledge, he receives no correspondence. Much as I would like it to be him, I think we can safely absolve Mr. Drake from blame.'

'I never imagined Drake was involved,' Sean said, sending Nia curious sideways glances.

'What do we do now? Did you see Grandpapa's agent?'

'Yes. Belling is beside himself with anger. He has not seen the Smythe painting, but he accepts my word for it that it's also a forgery. Like me, he can't think of any way to prove it.'

'How infuriating.'

'Even if we arranged for Grandpapa to see the painting and he claimed it was a forgery, everyone would laugh at him and say he was too demented to recognise his own early works.' Sean shook his head decisively. 'I could not expose him to public ridicule.'

'No, I agree. We, however . . . you and I are not demented.'

'Which doesn't help much,' Sean pointed out. 'We could complain to the Royal Academy, but they would take no notice of us because, unlike Grandpapa, we have no standing with them. Our assertions would not be believed.'

Nia stared glumly at the cracked paving stones beneath her feet. 'I am sure they wouldn't.'

'None of the owners of the forgeries would agree to them being authenticated by an independent expert, for fear of learning they have been duped.' Sean shook his head. 'I have now asked the question in an indirect way of all of them, and they all reacted in the same way.'

'So we cannot spread the word that Trafford forgeries exist because none of the people who own them are prepared to embrace that possibility.'

Sean nodded. 'That about sums it up.'

They sat in morose silence for a moment or two.

'I shall need to think about that. Did the Smythes provide any particulars about where they purchased their painting, or how that purchase came about?' Nia asked.

'They said the seller had wanted to keep the particulars confidential. They implied they had struck a good bargain and would respect his privacy as a consequence.'

'Which is more or less what the other owners told you.' Nia felt like screaming with frustration. 'Who is doing this to us, Sean, and why? What have we ever done, other than try to help struggling artists?'

'No good deed goes unpunished.'

'I feel so angry, so impotent.' Nia clenched and unclenched her fists. 'I wish there was something we could do.'

'We'll think of something.' Sean patted her knee. 'Oversetting yourself achieves nothing.'

'Did you make arrangements for Grand-papa's exhibition?'

'Yes, it will take place in Belling's Bond Street gallery the first week after Christmas, when the *ton* will be in full swing. I will tell you all the particulars later. He's very excited about Grandpapa's change of direction, and wanted to come down and see what he has done. I put him off. I would prefer that even he didn't know how bad Grandpapa's condition is quite yet.'

'I agree. All I need to do now is to ensure Grandpapa produces enough works to make the exhibition a success. But,' Nia added as another thought occurred to her, 'the moment Mr. Belling makes it public that Grandpapa has turned his attention to landscapes, it will make his portraits that much more valuable. The forger won't be able to help doing more.'

'Yes, that's why I asked Belling to delay advertising the exhibition. When the forger does get to hear of it, perhaps he will get careless in his haste and greed.'

Nia nodded, far from convinced. 'That's about the only chance we have of catching him.'

'IIow are finances?' Sean asked. 'As if I didn't know.'

'At crisis point. We shall have to sell something.'

'Grandmama's jewels it is, then,' Sean said, echoing Nia's heartfelt sigh.

'Actually, Sophia insists we sell some of the sketches Grandpapa did of her.'

'We can't.'

'That is what I tried to tell Sophia.'

'The sketches or the jewellery.' Sean shook his head. 'Neither course of action sits well with me. It makes me feel like such a failure.'

'It's not your fault, Sean.' Nia slid her hand into his. 'If anyone is to blame it's Mama and her extravagant ways, to say nothing of Papa's failure to control her spending.'

'I can probably get a good price for the

ruby necklace in Winchester, negating the need to go to London again.'

'Whereas the sketches would need to be taken to specialists, or placed in Mr. Belling's hands.' Nia sighed. 'Very well. I never did like those rubies much, anyway.'

'Sean!'

Sophia emerged from the house in a flurry of lilac muslin and hurled herself at Nia's brother. Laughing, Sean stood and caught her in his arms. Sean's laughter faded and Nia abruptly jumped to her feet when they both caught sight of Sophia's grave expression.

'What is it?' Nia asked, alarmed. 'Has something happened to Grandpapa?'

Sophia shook her head. 'Nia, I am so very sorry. I went to get the sketches, as we agreed yesterday.' Tears rolled down her face. 'They are not there. I have turned our rooms upside down and can't find them anywhere. They must have been stolen.'

★   ★   ★

'I think they know.' Annie twisted her hands together, her brow knotted with anxiety. 'I'm that scared. Every time the mistress looks at me, I'm sure of it. Aw, what shall we do?'

'What do you mean, you *think* she knows?' The forger struggled to maintain his temper. He needed Annie as his eyes and ears inside Trafford's household. She spied for him because he pretended to be in love with her. The silly chit was three farthings short of a shilling in that she believed someone of his ilk would actually look fondly upon a maid-of-all-work. But she actually believed that an averagely-pretty face and her willingness to warm his bed were sufficient incentive for the forger to offer her a life of luxury when he had made his fortune.

'Young Mr. Trafford has returned from London. He's been in close conversation with his sister and Miss Ash ever since. I couldn't hear much of what they said. They shooed me away when I got too close, but they were very intense.' She looked genuinely frightened. 'I'm scared. What will happen to us if we get caught? I would feel that ashamed after the Traffords were kind enough to give me work. Can we not leave now?'

The forger closed his eyes, striving to remain calm. He counted to ten and reminded himself how badly he needed Annie. 'Did you get what I asked you for?'

'Yes, I think this should suffice.'

She passed him some folded pages. The forger looked over his shoulder to ensure they weren't being watched by anyone in Compton's main street, and quickly perused the documents. For once, she had got it right. This was exactly what he needed, and he gave her an approving smile. She had earned it, and he liked to be fair.

'What if they suspect me?'

'As far as they are concerned, you just dust furniture and sweep floors.' He could see she felt insulted, and chucked her under the chin. 'They undervalue you, Annie. I know just how clever you really are, but that's our secret for now.'

Her smile was wide and uncontrived. 'I'd do anything for you. You know that.'

Why else would I bother with you? The forger was not in the best of moods, following his encounter with Lord Barrington. Unlike his other marks, Barrington was not nearly so easy to win over. Oh, he had finally agreed to look at the portrait the forger had in his possession, but was only willing to pay half as much as the others had stumped up. He drove a hard bargain which, under normal circumstances, the forger would have walked away from. But circumstances were no longer normal and time was not on the forger's side, so he had no choice but to accept Barrington's terms, which infuriated him. And now Annie was going through one of her clinging phases.

'Not much longer, my love,' he said, running the tip of one gloved finger down her face. 'And then we can be together for always.'

'Aw, that's what I want more than anything.'

The forger gave her a brief, chaste kiss on the forehead. 'We have to be careful,' he said, disengaging her arms when she attempted to cling. 'It would spoil everything if we were seen together now. I really should not come anywhere near the Traffords, but can't resist seeing you.'

She beamed, easily placated. Annie wasn't much good at writing, and even if she had been, she had no reason to be sending letters to him. Besides, he wouldn't risk having anything to do with their activities committed to paper. Ergo, it was necessary for the forger to come to the district. 'And you will be expected back at Stoneleigh Manor. Don't make them suspicious by being gone too long.'

'When will I see you properly?' she asked peevishly.

'Soon, my dear,' the forger replied, tucking the papers she had given him safely inside his coat. 'I will use the normal means of communication if I need to see you urgently. If not, be here at the same time next week.'

'You know I will.'

Oh yes, the forger knew it all too well. He

turned on his heel and walked away, noticing a fine gent on an even finer horse looking at him in a peculiar manner, as though he knew him from somewhere. Self-conscious, the forger pulled his hat lower over his eyes. He would have liked to ask Annie if she knew who the gent was. He didn't like the way he was staring at him. But Annie had already disappeared, so the forger dropped his head and strode off towards The Ploughman, where he had left his horse in the livery yard. The sooner he got away from here, the safer he would feel.

9

'Sophia, are you absolutely sure you have looked everywhere?' Nia asked.

'There was only one place to look. I kept them in a folder in the bottom of the wardrobe, and they are no longer there.'

'Grandpapa might have removed them,' Sean suggested.

'If he has, I cannot find where he has put them.' Tears continued to spill down Sophia's face. 'I am so very sorry, Nia. I should have taken better care of them.'

'This is not your fault.'

'When did you last look at them?' Sean asked.

Sophia lifted her shoulders. 'Months ago. Patrick is very fond of them and, in his more lucid moments, sometimes asks to see them.'

'Not since we have lived here?' Nia asked.

'No, definitely not.'

'So, they might have disappeared before we came here,' Nia surmised. 'That makes more sense, since the only people here who could have taken them are Miss Tilling or Mr. Drake.'

'Or the servants,' Sean pointed out.

'No,' Nia and Sophia said together.

'Why would they?' Nia added. 'And as for Miss Tilling and Mr. Drake, they know better than to bite the hand that feeds them, don't they?'

'I lock the door when we are not in our rooms because I don't want anyone snooping at Patrick's latest work,' Sophia said.

Nia nodded. Her grandfather's studio adjoined the rooms he shared with Sophia and could only be reached through a single doorway in the hall.

'I want those sketches back,' Sophia wailed. 'Selling them is one thing. Having them stolen is entirely another.'

'Don't worry, Sophia.' Nia hugged her friend. 'We will find them. Somehow.'

'First forged portraits of persons unknown, and now this,' Sean muttered. 'Someone has it in for us.'

'Someone clever,' Nia added. 'If the portraits were of well-known people, the people in question would know they didn't sit for them.'

'Whereas you are very obviously the subject of the sketches, Sophia,' Sean said.

'Grandpapa has shown them to a lot of people because he is proud of you,' Nia added. 'If they were to turn up for sale while Grandpapa is still alive, we would be able to prove they were stolen.'

'Someone is investing in their future,' Sean said, scowling.

Sophia nodding, sniffing. 'Because the sketches will be worth more when Patrick passes on.'

'They will be back in our possession long before then,' Sean replied with determination.

They turned when they heard an upstairs window open and their grandfather's voice booming out.

'Sean, my boy, where the devil have you been? I haven't seen you in months.'

It was a little over a week since Sean had gone to London. Nevertheless, Nia was pleased to see her grandfather looking clear-eyed and aware. There would be no hunting horns today.

'Hello, Grandpapa. How are you?'

'Never better, never better.'

'I shall be up directly to say hello.'

'You two go up,' Nia said to Sean and Sophia. 'I shall return to my weeding. It helps me to think.'

'Don't be downhearted,' Sean said, kissing her cheek. 'We are not beaten yet.'

Nia expelled a long breath. 'I am so tired of lurching from one crisis to the next, Sean. I'm not sure how much fight I have left in me.'

'Things will get better,' Sean assured her, patting her shoulder before walking towards the house with Sophia.

How? Nia wondered glumly. The theft of the sketches — and, in spite of the reassuring words she had found for Sophia, she was sure they had been stolen — was the final blow. If she had been angry about the forgeries, it was nothing to the way she felt now. Part of her wanted to protect Grandpapa by whisking him back to Ireland, where he would be safe from tricksters and parasites. But if she did that, the forger would become even more brazen, and she absolutely refused to sit back while he made money through Patrick Trafford's reputation. There had to be another way, but she was too emotionally charged to think coherently.

She covered her tired eyes with her hands, barely conscious of the tears that seeped through her fingers as she sobbed her heart out.

★ ★ ★

'Miss Trafford?'

Vince was overwhelmed by a torrent of protective feelings when he drew closer and saw just how distressed she was. He was intruding, but it was beyond his capabilities to leave her in such a state.

She lowered her hands from her swollen, red-rimmed eyes. 'I did not hear you arrive,' she replied accusingly.

'I would leave you in solitude, but . . . ' He spread his hands. 'Tell me how I can be of service to you.' He offered her his handkerchief. She wiped her eyes and appeared fractionally more composed.

'May I?' He indicated the space beside her on the bench.

She nodded. Vince swished the tails of his coat aside and sat beside her.

'Sometimes it helps to talk to a stranger,' he said softly.

She didn't respond, and Vince said nothing to try and persuade her. As a gentleman, it would be unthinkable to pry into a lady's private affairs. He watched a kaleidoscope of emotions chasing themselves across her countenance as she slowly regained her composure. She glanced over her shoulder at the house and abruptly stood up.

'Walk with me, Lord Vincent.'

He was surprised by the request, but immediately acquiesced. She headed for the tree-lined driveway that led to the gates. They would only be visible through the thick leafy canopy from one or two upper windows. She turned onto a track that ran through what had once been an orchard. They walked in silence, but Vince was acutely conscious of her light floral fragrance mingling with the stronger aroma of linseed oil and the sweet scent of apple blossom.

'I applaud your inventive means of keeping the lawn in check,' he said, smiling as he nodded towards her cob tethered in the middle of it, industriously chomping away.

'Needs must,' she replied with a negligent shrug. 'I suppose I ought to apologise for my appearance too,' she added, indicating her old gown covered in grass stains. Vince decided not to point out that she also had dirty smudges on her face — smudges that he was fighting the urge to remove for her.

'Never apologise for honest work.'

She veered off the weed-strewn path and took a narrower one between apple trees badly in need of pruning. It was obviously a favourite haunt of hers because the path had been regularly trodden, and recently. Vince could see that the area it opened up to beyond the orchard had once formed a part of the formal gardens. It was now a pretty wilderness with shrubs fighting a losing battle with the weeds.

There was the remains of an arbour housing a crumbling stone bench and Miss Trafford headed towards it. Seated, she idly plucked at the leaves of a rambling plant and stared off into the distance. Vince sat beside her, conscious of the absolute silence; a silence broken only by the occasional call of a bird, or the rustling leaves stirred by a gentle breeze. Never had a lady appeared in more need of comforting; never had Vince felt a greater desire to provide that service. And yet he hesitated. Miss Trafford was a very proud, self-sufficient person, and might not appreciate his interference.

'This place must have been a haven of tranquillity when it was a garden,' she said absently.

'In some instances, it's better to let nature have her way.'

She looked at him then; a long, probing sideways glance. 'How strange. I have often thought the same thing. I come here whenever I can, and the peacefulness never fails to soothe me.' She managed a brittle smile. 'Unless the boys find me.'

'Ah, the boys.'

She threw aside the leaf she had just shredded to pieces. 'Why are you here, Lord Vincent?'

'I called to see if you had decided to accept my mother's invitation.'

'Ah, I had forgotten about that.' Vince struggled not to smile. Not many people forgot invitations issued by duchesses. 'I'm sorry, that was rude of me. My brother got back from London this morning, and his arrival sent everything else from my head.'

'Is that why you are upset? He didn't bring the news you wanted to hear?'

'Not precisely.' She paused, once again either lost in reflection or struggling with indecision. She then straightened her shoulders and gave him her full attention. 'He didn't only go to London to consult with Grandpapa's agent and arrange his exhibition.'

'Who is your grandfather's agent?'

'Mr. Belling. He has a gallery in Bond Street.'

'I know of him by reputation.'

'But this isn't about Belling.' She took another deep, fortifying breath and met his gaze. 'Someone is selling forged portraits, passing them off as Grandpapa's early work.'

Vince sat a little straighter. 'The devil they are!'

'We know of three so far. Sean managed to see the third one while in London and confirms it is definitely a forgery. A very good one, but a forgery for all that.'

'Then why did he not tell the purchaser he had been duped?'

'If only it were that easy.' She sighed. 'We think the forger must be one of Grandpapa's protégés, seeking to profit from his skill because he knows Grandpapa is losing his mind and is in no position to disclaim the work. To do so, he would have to show himself in public, everyone would notice how vague he has become, and no one would believe him.' She inverted her chin. 'I cannot, I will not, expose him to ridicule.'

'Quite so.' Vince flexed his jaw, thinking about the stranger acting furtively in Compton a short time ago. He had only caught a glance at the back of the woman he had been engaged in conversation with, but she had looked familiar. Vince had seen her somewhere, and recently. 'What a very peculiar way your grandfather's students have of repaying his kindness.'

She flashed a wry smile. 'Quite.'

'Do you have any idea who might be responsible?'

'I have been racking my brains. There are perhaps three men with the requisite skill who have been with us recently enough to be aware of Grandpapa's fragile state of mind.'

'If they are that talented, can they not make their own mark?'

She shrugged. 'It is not as easy as you might imagine. Good fortune, a rich sponsor, timing, opportunity, and so many other factors play a part. I can well understand these men's collective frustration at their lack of acclaim, but to take advantage of Grandpapa . . . ' Miss

Trafford shook her head. 'It is truly wicked.'

'Can your brother connect any of them directly to the sales of the forgeries?'

Again she shook her head, a sad little smile playing about her lips. 'The forger has been very clever, claiming in each case that the portrait had belonged to a relative, recently deceased, and that he needed to sell it to pay death duties. Naturally, he did not reveal his real name, but offered the paintings at far less than they would be worth if Grandpapa had actually painted them.'

Vince scowled. 'Hmm, the buyer thinks he has made a wise investment and is willing to keep the particulars private.'

'Especially since Grandpapa no longer plans to paint portraits. When that becomes public knowledge, those that do exist will increase in value.' She curled her fingers into a tight fist. 'It's infuriating, and there is absolutely nothing we can do about it.'

'There is always something that can be done if one has the desire to set matters right.'

She glared at him. 'That is very easy for you to say.'

'If you think I was making light of your difficulties, then you mistake the matter.' He took her hand, gently forced her clenched fingers apart and linked his own through them. Goodness knew what madness drove him to do it; he just didn't seem able to help himself. Miss Trafford appeared momentarily surprised, but didn't attempt to remove her hand. 'But there is more, I think. You already knew about the forgeries, so this latest one could not have come as that much of a surprise.'

She sent him a surprised look, and, with a reckless shrug and their fingers still entwined, she started to speak. 'Twenty years ago, when Grandpapa was at the height of his fame and Sophia at the height of her beauty, he did a series of sketches and paintings of her *au naturel*. They are exquisite; but, as you can tell from our living conditions, we are exceedingly pressed. Sophia keeps saying we ought to sell some of the sketches. What we could ask for them would set us up for years, but I couldn't bear to do it, and kept putting it off. Now we have no choice. It is either that or Grandmama's jewellery that is locked away for the boys' wives.'

'What about you?'

She laughed. 'What use do I have for jewels?'

Vince was filled with an urgent desire to bestow emeralds upon her. Only emeralds would so suit her Irish heritage, her colouring; everything about her screamed *emeralds*.

'If you have made the decision to sell the

sketches, will you give my family first refusal?'

'We would with pleasure, but unfortunately they've gone missing.' He could see her struggling not to burst into tears again. 'Sophia can't find them anywhere.'

No wonder she was so upset. Her failsafe for a rainy day that had turned into a torrential downpour.

'You suspect one of your current charity cases? Miss Tilling, or the poet?'

'We can't be sure if they were taken from here because Sophia is certain she has not looked at them since we moved.' She spread her hands. 'They could have gone months ago. With all the upheaval, we would not, obviously *did* not, notice.'

'Perhaps the forger has them.'

'It would make me feel better, a very little better, if we only had one devious ne'er-do-well in our ranks.'

'Forgive the bluntness of the question, Miss Trafford, but why is your family in such a dire financial situation?'

Her responding laugh was bitter. 'My grand-father has always possessed a philanthropic attitude. He's willing to lend a hand to those with talent, encouraging them to exploit their creativeness.' She sighed. 'And look where that has landed him. But that in itself would have made little impression upon his fortune.'

'Even so, I — '

'Grandpapa threw wild parties, inviting anyone and everyone from the art world. That is how Papa met my mother. She was as beautiful as she was wilful, and I'm told he was captivated from the first.'

'Go on,' Vince encouraged when she lapsed into momentary silence.

'I hate to speak ill of the dead, but there can be no denying that they went through Grandpapa's money quicker than Ned can eat that lawn for me. Mama demanded the best of everything, you see; she considered it her birthright.'

'She was from a good family?'

Miss Trafford chuckled. 'She was beautiful. Isn't that enough?'

'Evidently.'

'Extravagance was Mama's byword, and Papa never could refuse her anything. As Grandpapa's manager, he had complete control of his funds because Grandpapa trusted his only son to have his best interests at heart.' She managed a brief smile. 'Even I must acknowledge that Grandpapa is not very practical. If he has funds he spends them, and trusts those close to him to deal with investments and so forth. Unfortunately, not only did Papa badly mismanage those funds, but he also utilised them to keep up with

Mama's extravagant demands.'

'My father was an excellent man, and you have seen for yourself just how charming and caring my mother is. We were obviously very fortunate, and never wanted for parental attention.' Vince pulled a wry face. 'We still do not. But from what you tell me, it seems your parents paid little attention to you and your brother. That must have been very hard for you.'

'It would have been, if not for Grandpapa and Sophia.' This time her smile was wide and sincere. 'They have been better parents to me than my own ever were. We have had the most wonderful times, and I have never felt anything other than cherished. Sean's wife, the twins' mother, on the other hand, was cut from similar cloth to Mama. She was the daughter of one of my mother's society friends. I don't think Sean ever loved her, and he certainly regretted his decision to marry her. He was young at the time, and I think he appreciated Mama finally taking an interest in him. He was swept along by Mama's determination that they should marry, and by his future wife's flattery. But once they were actually married, her behaviour changed overnight and she became a mirror image of Mama. I hate to say this, but the twins are better off without her. She ignored them completely, and now they almost never ask after her. Sean, on the other hand, has always been an attentive father.'

'And, in you, the boys have an equally attentive aunt.'

'I try very hard to ensure that they don't go without love and affection.'

'The male members of your family have a destructive streak?' Vince had seen several similar examples amongst his aristocratic friends. Sons inherited valuable estates and promptly lost the fortunes their ancestors had built — either through mismanagement, inefficiency or, more often than not, at the gaming tables.

'Grandpapa does not. My grandmother died before I was born, but I know she was a kind, sensible woman whom he loved very much. All I can remember is Grandpapa and Sophia being together. Sophia has never pretended to be anything she is not, and because of Grandpapa's fame she has been accepted everywhere. And so she should be. Sophia is ten times the woman my own, supposedly respectable, mother ever was.' Miss Trafford jutted her chin defiantly. 'And I would give an argument to anyone who tried to say otherwise.'

Vince raised his hands in mock surrender, glad to see her eyes now glistened with loyal determination rather than tears. 'I have not met your Sophia, but I become more curious about her by the second. I hope you will introduce me.'

She fixed him with a considering look. 'I still fail to understand why you are taking such a prodigious interest in my family, Lord Vincent.'

Vince didn't know how to answer her because he scarcely understood it himself. 'Quite apart from the pleasure of *your* company, and an overwhelming desire to see you smile,' he replied with a provocative look that made her blush, 'I also have a great curiosity to see your grandfather's landscapes.'

She punched his arm. 'Ah, so you seek to exploit Grandpapa also?'

'Not a bit of it. In fact, I intend to make myself useful and discover the identity of your forger.'

'Why? How?' She shook her head. 'I do not have the pleasure of understanding you.'

'Have you become so accustomed to people wanting something from you, that you cannot accept there are still those who have no ulterior motives?'

She gave another bemused shake of her head. 'Seemingly so.'

She appeared overcome with emotion and fresh tears brimmed. One slid down her cheek and Vince reached forward to arrest its progress with his forefinger.

'Shush, don't cry,' he said softly, delicately tracing the curve of her face with the tips of his fingers. 'Everything will be all right.'

'No, it will not.' She shook her head. 'Unless you can give my grandfather his senses back, then things will never be the same again.'

'Your grandfather has lived a long and productive life, and the magnificent works of art he leaves behind will give pleasure to generations to come. Not many people are fortunate enough to possess the skill to leave such a legacy.'

'No.' Her sigh was deep and heartfelt. 'There is that, I suppose.'

'He deserves to enjoy his retirement, and if you will permit me to interfere, I shall help to ensure that he does.' He lowered his voice to a seductive purr. 'Nothing remains the same forever, Nia, much as you might wish for it to do so.'

She nodded, making no objection to his use of her name. 'Yes, I do understand, but . . . '

Her words stalled and the tears fell again in earnest. Unable to help himself, Vince leaned forward, cupped the back of her head with the splayed fingers of one hand and briefly covered her lips with his own. Her gurgle of protest lacked conviction, but before Vince could do anything to persuade her she really didn't want to protest at all, a voice calling Nia's name had them pulling apart. Then Ruff came hurling down the path, wagging his stubby tail as he jumped adroitly into Nia's lap.

'That is Sean's voice,' she told him, looking flushed and confused. 'Over here,' she called back.

10

Nia was sure Lord Vincent had been about to kiss her. Really kiss her. Not the brief, the too brief, brush of lips they had shared before Sean interrupted them. She was equally sure she would have found the experience instructive. Curiosity had awoken something that made her yearn for pleasures she had only previously experienced vicariously through informative discussions with Sophia.

Thinking rationally again, she took calm stock of the situation, mentally cataloguing all the reasons why Lord Vincent could only have been entertaining himself. He could take his pick from the finest young ladies in the top echelons of society. And yet he conceitedly assumed that anyone who happened to engage his interest was his for the taking. She was living on his doorstep and he couldn't resist the opportunity to hone his seductive skills, probably because he was bored.

Nia understood his game now, and would not be caught unawares a second time. She threw back her shoulders, straightened her gown, and treated him to her best assault glare. Unfortunately, it bounced harmlessly off his amused expression.

'I am glad to see you looking more in control of yourself,' he said, his lips curving into a glamorous smile.

Before she could formulate a pithy retort, Sean strode into the clearing.

'I say, Nia . . . '

Nia stood, tipping Ruff off her lap, and took Sean's arm. 'Sean, may I introduce you to our neighbour, Lord Vincent Sheridan. Lord Vincent, this is my brother, Sean Trafford.'

The gentlemen sized one another up as they shook hands.

'Trafford,' Lord Vincent said amiably.

'Your servant, Lord Vincent.'

Nia released a breath she had not been conscious of holding when Sean appeared to like what he saw in their neighbour and replied with affable deference. She would not allow Lord Vincent to seduce her — if that had been his intention — but he had mentioned something about helping them, and so she needed to cultivate his good opinion. Nia was no longer in a position to stand on pride and refuse any genuine offers of assistance that came from such an influential source.

As the gentlemen fell into conversation, Nia's mind wandered. She thought about the almost-kiss she had shared with Lord

Vincent, and the most extraordinary effect it had had upon her. A deeply disturbing jolt had rocked her body, and she had felt hot all over as glorious sensation threatened. *Desire,* she thought absently. She actually desired him, and chided herself for having such a ridiculous reaction to a harmless kiss. Not that anything about Lord Vincent was harmless, precisely. Beneath all that suave sophistication, there was an element of danger that, annoyingly, only added to his allure. Sophia had told her that dangerous and powerful men made wonderful protectors. Nia bit her lip to hold back a smile. Sophia was in a good position to know.

Would Lord Vincent really have overstepped the boundaries, here in the open air where anyone might have come upon them at any time? Despite being the most decisive person she knew, Nia's thoughts were currently in a hopelessly contradictory tangle. Two minutes ago, she had decided his intention was definitely seduction. Now she was convinced he was merely being gentlemanly — well, sort of — in offering to help her family. She had been upset and he had comforted her in a manner that would come naturally to a man of his ilk. Thanks to Sophia, Nia knew all about men's desires and impulses. In theory, anyway. The opportunity to gain some practical experience had slipped away, and she told herself that was just as well.

'I came looking for you to let you know Lady St. John is here,' Sean said.

'Oh, how nice. We were about to return to the house anyway. Lord Vincent has offered to discover the identity of the forger for us.'

Sean frowned. 'You told him about that?'

'You can be assured of my discretion, Trafford,' Lord Vincent said as they made their way back through the trees together. 'I was about to ask your sister to introduce us so that I could discuss the matter with you and make a few suggestions.'

Sean nodded. It was already evident to Nia that, once Lord Vincent set his mind upon a particular course, then charm, authority and determination ensured that no one stood in his way.

'My sons have been talking non-stop about their visit to your stud, Lord Vincent. It was very kind of you to take an interest in them.'

'They are fine boys.'

When they reached the house, Frankie and Sophia were seated in the drawing room, such as it was, chatting amiably as they sipped at tea from mismatched cups. Frankie stood and hugged Nia when she entered the room. If she was surprised to see Lord Vincent it didn't show in her manner, and she greeted him with easy friendliness.

Nia disengaged from Frankie's embrace and cleared her throat. 'Lord Vincent, may I present Miss Sophia Ash.'

'Miss Ash.' Lord Vincent sent her an engaging smile as he took her hand. 'It is a great pleasure to make your acquaintance.'

'And I yours, my lord.'

Sophia had not forgotten how to deploy the feminine wiles that had helped her rise to the top of her profession. Her own smile was sultry, with a wickedly enticing edge to it. Lord Vincent appeared captivated by it, since he held her hand for longer than politeness dictated. Jealousy tied Nia's insides into a vicious knot, which infuriated her. Lord Vincent was nothing to her.

Sophia finally resumed her seat, sending Nia an approving nod as she did so. God in heaven, what was going through that calculating brain of hers now? Hannah appeared with more tea. With a wink at Nia, she closed the door as she left them, presumably to discourage Mr. Drake or Miss Tilling from inflicting themselves upon them.

'Who is with Grandpapa?' Nia asked.

'He is having a good day, *chérie*,' Sophia replied. 'The most lucid he has been for weeks. The boys are up there with him and he is teaching them to play chess.'

Nia brightened. If her grandfather was clear-headed enough for chess, it was a very good sign.

'Sean has been telling me about his findings in London, Nia,' Frankie said. 'I am so very sorry it has come to this.'

'It only confirms what we already suspected.'

'Who owns this latest forgery?' Lord Vincent asked.

'Sir Angus Smythe,' Sean replied.

'Brooke Street?'

'Yes. Do you know him?'

'He is a member of my club. Who has the other two?'

Sean gave the names, but Lord Vincent shook his head. 'I'm not acquainted with either of them.'

'They are wealthy nabobs who wouldn't move in your social circles,' Sean replied.

Lord Vincent paused to sip his tea. He was elegantly draped in an old armchair that she happened to know was excruciatingly uncomfortable, but he gave every impression of being perfectly at his ease. Nia and Hannah had done their best to brighten up the shabby room by placing around it vases of flowers plucked from the wilderness that had once been a garden, and displaying the few decent remaining ornaments in their possession. Two of their grandfather's paintings, favourites of Nia's that she had so far stubbornly refused to sell, hung on the walls.

If Lord Vincent noticed the dilapidated state of his surroundings, he was far too well-mannered to comment upon them; as, of course, was Frankie.

'You said just now that you had an idea how to expose the forger,' Nia said, anxious to hear what Lord Vincent had in mind.

'Is your grandfather absolutely determined not to do more portrait work?'

'He cannot; or, rather, he could, but we as a family are not prepared to take the risk with his reputation,' Sean answered before Nia could.

'I understand that, but if he were to be commissioned to paint a portrait of someone who knew of his condition and would not speak of it — '

'A person of consequence?' Frankie caught Lord Vincent's eye and smiled.

'Precisely so,' Lord Vincent said in reply to Frankie's question. 'I have in mind a duke.'

Nia gasped. 'Your brother . . . but I do not see how . . . ' Too surprised to string an intelligible sentence together, Nia shared a glance with an equally astounded-seeming Sean and gave up trying.

'That is a remarkably generous offer,' Sean

said, recovering first. 'But I do not see how it would serve.'

'There is nothing generous about it. Zach's portrait is long overdue, but he keeps finding reasons to delay sitting for it. To have such an eminent artist accept the commission would be sufficient to rouse even Zach from his *ennui*.' Lord Vincent paused. 'Naturally, we would pay the going rate for your grandfather's services and consider ourselves fortunate to have secured them.'

'You are too generous,' Sophia said *sotto voce*, clearly as shocked as Nia felt.

'It *is* remarkably generous of you,' Nia agreed, 'but, like Sean, I fail to see how that would help to catch the forger.'

'Nothing could be simpler.' Lord Vincent placed his cup aside and leaned back in his uncomfortable chair. Nia thought she saw him wince. So he *was* human after all. 'Does your grandfather paint quickly?'

'Extremely,' Sean replied. 'Just so long as he is mentally acute, of course, but there is no rhyme or reason as to his state of mind, unfortunately.'

'If he has his wits about him the entire time, how quickly could he complete a portrait?'

Nia and Sean exchanged a look. 'Two to three weeks should be sufficient,' Nia replied.

'Then, even allowing for twice that long, we could set a date for six weeks' time for a private preview at Winchester Park of your grandfather's landscapes, with the portrait of my brother forming the centrepiece. The viewing, as I say, would be private; but word would spread, telling the world that Patrick Trafford's star is still very much in the ascendant.'

Nia was again almost lost for words. 'You would do that for us?' she managed to stutter.

'With the greatest of pleasure, Miss Trafford,' he replied, darting her a searing smile that sent heat to her cheeks, and all the rest of her. 'The event would be invitation-only, but it would be the most natural thing in the world for you to invite Smythe, Trafford, given that you recently viewed his forgery.'

'And you intend to invite Patrick's students as well, the ones we think might be responsible for the forgeries, in the hope that Sir Angus will recognise the one who sold him his painting?' Sophia's smile was radiant. 'But that is inspired!'

'*If* the forger transacted the business with Smythe in person.' Lord Vincent raised a hand in warning. 'He most likely would have done. He couldn't risk including anyone else, unless he trusted them absolutely.'

'You know,' Sean mused, rubbing his chin between his thumb and forefinger, 'it just might work. We had the devil's own job getting rid of the three people we suspect. They would jump at the chance to have anything to do with Grandpapa again, and if one of them does not, then his reluctance will reveal him as the forger.'

'Who are the individuals in question?' Lord Vincent asked.

'There is a fellow called Parish,' Sean answered. 'Damned good artist, but prone to prolonged fits of depression. When in the doldrums, it wasn't uncommon for him to abuse those who had commissioned portraits, or destroy perfectly good work because something about it offended his artistic eye.'

'Artists can be very temperamental,' Sophia pointed out.

'He left us because he became engaged to an heiress,' Sean said.

'Well then, I don't suppose he's our man,' Lord Vincent replied.

'He might well be,' Sean told him. 'The engagement was broken when the young lady's father learned of it. He had not given his permission for it and did not approve of Parish. He seemed to think he could rejoin our household at that point, but I set him straight on that matter.'

Lord Vincent nodded. 'In which case, he could be set upon revenge.'

'There is another gentleman by the name of Kenton,' Nia said, looking at her hands as she spoke his name.

'Bounder tried to take liberties with my sister,' Sean said, scowling. 'I sent him packing as soon as I heard of it.'

'The devil he did!' Lord Vincent muttered.

'Actually, he proposed to me; I declined, and he accepted my decision. The unpleasantness exists only in Sean's mind,' Nia said, blushing. 'We got along quite well, but he mistook my friendship for something more. I don't think he is responsible for the forgeries.'

'Is he capable of painting them?' Lord Vincent asked.

'All three of the men in question are,' Sean answered before she could. 'But my sister is right, I suppose. Perhaps I overreacted a little.'

Nia quirked a brow. 'A little?'

'Kenton remained in Belgium when we returned to England, and my understanding is that he's starting to make a name for himself in his own right. Unless his fortunes took a downturn, he would have no reason to turn forger.'

'All right,' Lord Vincent said. 'I will bear his name in mind. Who is the third suspect?'

'A man by the name of Weale,' Sean said. 'He returned to England with us, but left us a few months ago because he received several commissions after exhibiting his work with Grandpapa's last collection. However, there was some unpleasantness over one of them; we never did learn what. Word spread, and the rest of the commissions were withdrawn.'

'He most likely became too attached to the sitter's daughter, or wife, or some female beneath his care,' Sophia said. Nia widened her eyes. She had not realised Mr. Weale was a womaniser. 'Anyway, he tried to rejoin us when we moved here, but Sean wouldn't allow it.'

'All three of them could easily have convinced themselves they have reason to feel aggrieved,' Lord Vincent remarked in a considering tone.

'Yes, I imagine so,' Nia replied.

'Are they all in England? You mentioned Kenton remained in Brussels.'

'I believe he has now returned to these shores,' Sean replied.

'Do you have means of contacting them?'

Sean nodded. 'Oh yes, I know where they all are. Since we got wind of the forgeries, I have made it my business to find out.'

'Well then, what do you say to my suggestion? I hope, if your grandfather agrees, it would not inconvenience him to do the portrait at the Park. My brother is far too impatient to come here every day.'

Nia suspected it was more likely Lord Vincent didn't think Stoneleigh Manor a fit place for a duke to spend hours of his time and appreciated his tact.

'Yes, I'm sure he would be agreeable, provided you have a place with plenty of natural light where he could do his work,' she replied. 'I can drive him over each day and stay with him. He needs me to mix his paints, you see. Besides, he has become accustomed to either Sophia or me being with him, and he gets confused if he is alone for too long.'

'Indeed.' Lord Vincent shared a smile between them. 'Besides, we don't want Drake or Miss Tilling to interfere. I have not absolutely absolved either of them of blame for the theft of the drawings of you, Miss Ash.'

'You said you knew of a way to retrieve them,' Nia reminded him anxiously.

'We shall ensure word gets about that the preview is for collectors with bottomless pockets. The drawings are, if I understand you correctly, some of the most inspired work your grandfather has ever done.' Lord Vincent glanced at Sophia as he spoke, and sent her a rakish grin. 'Given the subject matter, I can well understand his inspiration.'

'Why, thank you, Lord Vincent,' Sophia replied with a coquettish smile.

'We must assume the thief will be amongst those invited, and I cannot imagine he would let the opportunity pass him by to attract buyers.'

Sean scowled. 'With all of us in the room? Damned impudence!'

'I think our thief would take the chance, especially if we make it known your grand-father plans to retire after this last exhibition and return to Ireland.'

'He will want to have buyers lined up, ready to bid against one another, the moment Patrick leaves the country,' Frankie said musingly. 'Our mystery forger sounds like an arrogant and rather desperate fellow who thinks he can get away with absolutely anything.'

'With good reason, to date,' Nia pointed out.

'His arrogance will prove to be his downfall,' Lord Vincent replied calmly. 'I have been meaning to ask: what servants do you have, and how long have they been with you?'

'You suspect our servants?' Sean asked, elevating one brow.

Lord Vincent smiled. 'I have a suspicious nature.'

'We have Hannah, who was Sean's

nursemaid, then mine, so has been with us forever and her loyalty is beyond question,' Nia said. 'I could not manage without her. Apart from her, we have just two maids-of-all-work, Annie and Beth.'

Lord Vincent looked surprised, as well he might. 'How long have they been with you?'

'We acquired their services in Belgium,' Sean replied. 'Sir Edward Fairstock died in an accident and his widow, Arabella Fairstock, discovered he had not left her well provided for. At least, that's what we assume must have happened, since she dismissed everyone except her personal maid, closed up the house and disappeared, leaving a string of unpaid debts behind her.'

'Annie and Beth are English, and travelled to Belgium with her and Sir Edward, making the Fairstocks responsible for their welfare,' Sophia explained. 'They had no means of getting back on their own, and were stuck in a foreign country where they did not speak the language. Fortunately we heard about their plight, were in need of discreet servants, and so counted ourselves fortunate to procure their services.'

Lord Vincent nodded. 'But they also have reason to be grateful to you, and so don't sound as though they would be a threat.'

'No, I agree,' Nia replied.

Lord Vincent stood up and smiled at her. 'Can I tell my mother she will have the pleasure of your company at dinner tomorrow so we can discuss the matter of the portrait, and this other business, at our leisure? You are, of course, included in the invitation, Trafford; as are you, Lady St. John and Miss Ash.'

'For my part, I accept with pleasure,' Frankie replied.

'As do we all,' Sean added without bothering to consult Nia. 'Thank you, Lord Vincent. We are very much obliged to you for your help.'

Lord Vincent took his leave of them. Instead of ringing the bell — which probably didn't work; and even if it did, she would not wish to inconvenience Hannah — Nia walked to the door with Lord Vincent herself.

'You need to move your horse,' he remarked, looking out at the garden. 'He has made a very efficient job of that area of grass and is probably anxious to move on to the next.'

'I shall see to it.'

'Allow me.'

Before she could protest, Lord Vincent bounded down the crumbling steps, pulled up the stake to which Ned was tethered, and moved it and him to a fresh patch of grass.

'Thank you.' Nia walked with him towards their ramshackle stable to retrieve Lord Vincent's stallion. 'You have been remarkably kind.'

'It is entirely my pleasure.'

He reached out and grasped her chin between his gloved fingers. All of Nia's recently-formed resolve to resist his charm evaporated when he lowered his head and brushed her lips with his own for the merest fraction of a second.

'Don't imagine I have forgotten what we were doing before your brother found us,' he said, a dangerous light in his eyes as he released her chin, swung up into his saddle and raised a hand in farewell. 'Until tomorrow night,' he said.

11

Vince was the first of the brothers to enter the drawing room the following evening. Of his mother and sister there was, as yet, no sign. He helped himself to whisky and stood with his back to the fire, enjoying a moment's solitude as he pondered upon the events of the previous day. He had been doing a great deal of pondering since becoming acquainted with the Traffords, and most of his mental perambulations had been centred upon one particular member of that rather unorthodox family.

Niamh Trafford both compelled and intrigued him, but he was unable to decide why. Her fierce loyalty towards her grandfather, and determination to protect him from the ugly side of human nature in his declining years, had won his admiration. Except he had been drawn to her before he knew any of that. His fixation upon her was totally baffling, especially since there was nothing remarkable about her.

Everything about her was extraordinary.

She was aware of his family's influence and standing in society; knew there were three single brothers within its ranks, and that the future of any lady marrying into it would be secured. But she appeared unintimidated by their wealth and consequence, and had no apparent interest in being admired by any of the Sheridan males. Perhaps she really did intend to remain single and devote herself to her grandfather's comfort during his declining years. Such single-minded devotion was as refreshing as it was admirable. It was also a timely lesson in humility. Vince chuckled. Perhaps he and his brothers were not so very irresistible after all.

Nia was a charismatic distraction who had come to his attention at a time when he was feeling uncharacteristically unfulfilled. His life had become too settled, too predictable, and he was in the market for a new cause to champion. Miss Trafford's appearance was opportune. It was for that — and no other reason — he planned to help her discover the identity of the forger.

Vince grinned when his mind briefly dwelt upon Sophia Ash. She must have been stunning in her younger years, and her beauty had not completely diminished. Nor had her flirtatious nature. She didn't have the hard, self-serving edge inherent to many in her profession, seemed genuinely attached to Patrick Trafford, and was a godsend to Nia.

Vince flashed a wry smile. With Miss Ash forming part of tonight's visiting party, they were assured of a memorable evening.

'What is so amusing?' Zach asked, entering the room with his dogs at his heels.

'I was thinking about Sophia Ash. Not many duchesses would agree to sit down to dinner with a semi-retired courtesan, but our mother appears rather enthusiastic about the prospect.'

'That doesn't surprise me.' Zach helped himself to whisky.

Vince moved aside to give the wolfhounds access to their favourite place directly in front of the fire. 'Let's hope Patrick Trafford is in a lucid frame of mind tonight. None of his relations will be able to relax if he is not.'

'You are thinking of Miss Trafford?'

Far too much. 'Yes. She takes on too much responsibility. She reminds me of how Crista used to be when Amos first met her.' Zach's brows disappeared beneath his hairline. 'In Miss Trafford's case, I intend to make myself useful to her family, but I don't envisage becoming leg-shackled in the near, or distant, future if that's what you are thinking.'

'The thought never crossed my mind.'

'Zach, mind your own damned business,' Vince said, irritated by his brother's superior smirk.

The rest of the family joined them at that point, but they had not been together for more than five minutes before Lady St. John was announced. She entered the room wearing a magnificent evening gown of striped satin gauze in a cornflower blue that exactly matched the colour of her eyes. Always beautiful and immaculately attired, tonight she had excelled herself, and Vince thought she had seldom looked lovelier.

'I was just remarking upon how interested I shall be to meet Mr. Trafford,' the duchess said when Lady St. John took a seat beside her. 'I feel rather intimidated at the thought of having someone so famous beneath this roof. Artistic types can be so unpredictable. What if he decides he does not like us?'

'Do not concern yourself on that score,' Lady St. John replied. 'Patrick, if he is lucid, has all the charm of the Irish. He will have you in fits of laughter with his tall stories. And if he is not on song, then Nia and Sophia between them will manage him.'

The duchess shook her head. 'His friends and relations have a lot of responsibility.'

'Yes, but I have never heard them complain.'

'I have hidden all of my sketches away,' Portia said, grimacing. 'I should be ashamed for Mr. Trafford to see them.'

Vince, aware that his younger sister possessed some artistic talent, smiled at her. 'You shouldn't have done that, Portia.'

'Your paintings aren't half bad,' Nate added grudgingly.

'Which leaves me to suppose they are not half good, either.' Portia smiled good-naturedly at what, coming from Nate, was fulsome praise. 'But thank you anyway.'

'Happy to oblige,' Nate replied.

The double doors opened and Faraday stood on the threshold. 'Mr. Trafford, Mr. Trafford, Miss Trafford and Miss Ash, Your Grace,' he said.

He stood back, and the party entered the room. Vince's gaze immediately fixed upon Nia, who was on her brother's arm. At least, he assumed it was she. He inhaled sharply, scarcely recognising the transformation that had taken place in the grubby gardener from the day before. Tonight she wore a gown of emerald green, reinforcing Vince's conviction that emeralds were the only jewels that would suit her. There was a visible underskirt beneath the gown, of a lighter shade of green, fashioned from what he thought was sarsnet.

The bustline of Nia's gown was low, giving Vince a graphic idea of the treasures concealed beneath it. Quite without his permission, his gaze lingered on her décolletage, and his breeches suddenly felt too tight. Crystal beads decorated the bodice and short sleeves of Nia's gown, but Vince's knowledge of feminine attire failed him when he attempted to name the lace flounces that trimmed her hemline. Her hair had been tamed into a fashionable waterfall of shimmering curls, held in place with a tortoiseshell clip. Her cheeks were rosy pink and those temptingly plump lips of hers were shiny and moist, crying out for the kiss he had been deprived of delivering the previous day.

She levelled a cool gaze in his direction, but looked away again almost immediately. Vince felt no inclination to follow her example and continued to look exclusively at her until Zach, still standing beside him, gave him a sharp nudge in the ribs.

'Miss Ash is playing up her role,' Zach remarked in an amused undertone.

And so she was. In figure-hugging scarlet silk, she deferred to the duchess with decorum that belied her attire. Vince wondered if, through her choice of gown, she was trying to make some sort of obscure point. People had preconceived ideas about her, and she tried not to disappoint.

'How is your grandfather this evening?' Vince asked Nia as they shook hands.

'You don't need to worry about him, my

lord. He is having another good day. He rested for a long time this afternoon, so ought to see the evening through without embarrassing anyone.'

Vince glanced at the old gentleman, and could see for himself that his eyes were bright and clear. 'That was not my purpose in asking the question. I was thinking more of your enjoyment. You will not relax unless you are sure your grandfather is comfortable being with us.'

She sighed. 'I'm sorry. That was unpardonably rude of me. You have gone out of your way to help my family and I cannot seem to find a civil tongue in my head. Please forgive me.'

'There is nothing to forgive.' Vince took two glasses of champagne from the tray Faraday proffered and handed one to her. 'Unlike mine, your life is not one of idleness and dissipation.'

She took a sip of champagne, and choked on it when his words registered with her. 'I cannot believe you said that.'

'It's what you think of me.' He sent her a taunting smile. 'Part of you is intrigued, at least in regard to the dissipation, which infuriates you because you want very much to disapprove of what you see.'

She arched a brow, hiding the lower half of

her face behind her raised glass. 'Do not suppose to know what I think, Lord Vincent.'

'Am I wrong?'

'Even if you were not, I should never admit it.'

'Anything you wish to learn about me, you have but to say the word.'

She clearly realised he was referring to their almost-kiss, and blushed. 'There is nothing you have that intrigues me.'

'You really should not have said that,' he warned.

She blinked up at him. 'I hesitate to ask why not.'

'Because I cannot resist a challenge.' He sent her an unrepentant smile. 'It's a family failing.'

She rolled her eyes. 'Why does that not surprise me?'

'What is wrong with being competitive?' he asked in a smoky, provocative tone.

'Are you flirting with me, Lord Vincent?'

'I believe I am, Miss Trafford.'

'Well, please don't. If you feel the need to flirt, I will gladly excuse you so that you can converse with Sophia. I am sure she will oblige you *and* give you a good run for your money. She knows how to play that game.'

'Then where would the fun be in that?'

She didn't answer him. Instead she glanced

towards Sophia, who was in conversation with his mother, while her grandfather's attention had been claimed by Amos. 'You can relax, Nia. Everyone is comfortable.' He paused. 'Everyone except for you. I wonder why that is.'

'You may wonder all you wish.' Her eyes sparkled as she levelled them upon his face and responded to him with lively playfulness. 'I have not the slightest intention of enlightening you.'

'Are you absolutely sure about that?'

She shook her head, setting her curls dancing around her face, but remained silent.

'What is it?' he asked. 'What are you thinking?'

'Believe me, Lord Vincent, you would prefer not to know.'

His lips quirked. 'I am not afraid of your thoughts.'

'Very well then.' She focused her entire attention upon him, the light of battle shining from her eyes. 'I was wondering if anyone has ever told you how insufferably arrogant you can seem at times.' She was clearly doing her very best to appear severe, but a tiny smile slipped past her guard, spoiling the effect.

'Quite a few jealous husbands,' he replied, grinning.

'Harrumph! I should only be surprised if

that were not the case.'

'Because you have already formed an unfavourable opinion as to my character.'

'How can that surprise you when you have just admitted that you dally with other men's wives?'

'I simply suggested that I might have invoked husbands' jealousies. I did not say their reactions were justified. It is hardly my fault if they cannot keep proper control of their wives.'

This time she did manage to look disapproving. 'I don't think I like you very much, Lord Vincent.'

He lifted one finger and placed it gently against her lips; removing it again almost immediately. 'Yes you do,' he said, in a soft, melodious tone. 'You may not want to, but you can't help yourself.'

'Definitely arrogant,' she muttered, with less conviction than previously.

'Go with your instincts, Nia,' he added in an undertone. 'I promise not to bite.'

'Go to the devil!'

He roared with laughter, attracting curious glances from others in the room. 'I very likely shall.'

Vince sobered when she appeared on the point of walking away from him. He was almost sure she was enjoying their lively exchange as much as he was. He admired the way she stood up to him and gave as good as she got. But enough was enough — for the time being. Rather than lose her, he changed the subject, moving their conversation onto safer ground.

'What is your grandfather doing?' he asked.

Nia turned her head abruptly, tension radiating through her body. Then she smiled, and he sensed it drain out of her again. 'He obviously remembers he is to paint the duke's portrait. Good, I am glad that did not slip his mind.'

'But if you only just told him, and he is having a lucid day — '

'Means nothing. Grandpapa has perfect recall about things that happened before I was born. You will discover that for yourself later, since I dare say he will insist upon telling the most outrageously exaggerated stories.' She shook her head, a tiny smile playing about her lips. 'There is no help for that, I'm afraid.'

'I, on the other hand, am not in the least afraid. I look forward to hearing what he has to say for himself. It might teach me more about you.'

'But, you see, even on good days, if you ask Grandpapa what was said to him half an hour ago, he would be hard-pressed to answer you.' She sighed. 'I am told that is not uncommon for people with Grandpapa's affliction. Short-term memory is the first thing to go.'

'It must be very hard for you.'

'To answer your original question, Grandpapa is observing the duke's profile from all angles, committing his features to memory. Amazingly, he will not forget them. The mysteries of the human brain never fail to astonish me. However, I am willing to wager that at some point during this evening, Grandpapa will call for paper and dash off a sketch of His Grace without again looking at him, and it will bear a remarkable likeness.'

'Really?'

'Oh yes, I cannot recall a time when Grandpapa has not done random sketches. We have had to persuade him not to sign them, because he always gives them away, and the recipients sell them for a lot of money simply because — '

'Because they bear his signature.' Vince sighed. 'Does absolutely everyone take advantage of his good nature?'

She spread her hands. 'Sometimes it seems that way.'

Faraday appeared in the open doorway and announced dinner.

'May I have the pleasure?' Vince proffered his arm but Nia seemed reluctant to accept him as an escort. 'My mother and your grandfather are going in together,' he pointed out. 'Your brother is escorting my sister, Amos is escorting his wife, and my brother Nate is taking care of Sophia.' Vince bit back a smile. Nate was the youngest of the four boys, still earning his spurs in many respects — respects that Sophia would have recognised. 'And Zach is escorting Lady St. John. So, I am afraid you're stuck with me.'

'How tiresome.'

But she was smiling when she finally placed her hand on his sleeve.

12

Nia felt a little dizzy as she walked into the sumptuous dining room on Lord Vincent's arm. Her light-headedness had nothing to do with the effects of the champagne and everything to do with the intoxicating presence of the elegant predator escorting her into dinner. A hungry, powerful male, stalking his prey and then toying with his catch before moving in for . . . for what precisely?

Why he chose to amuse himself with someone as unfashionable as her truly baffled Nia. Perhaps being at home in Winchester restricted his hunting ground. She happened to be there, available, and had told him she had no expectations of matrimony. Did he imagine she was cut from the same cloth as Sophia, and had made that admission to indicate her availability? She felt hot and cold all over when that possibility occurred to her. But now that she *had* thought of it, she was unable to imagine why he would not have misinterpreted her candour. The living arrangements in their household were rather unorthodox, *and* she and Sophia were staunch friends.

Now that she understood what drove him, Nia was unsure whether to be flattered or insulted. She felt heat invade her face, and a tingle of anticipation trickle down her spine. Was she actually considering playing him at his own game?

Dare she?

How matters developed between them was up to her; because, obviously, she was in complete control of the situation and of her impulses. She absolutely was!

'What is so amusing?' he asked as he held her chair for her.

Damnation, she had not realised he was watching her quite so closely. To even contemplate pitting her wits against such a master of seduction was extreme folly. She must be sickening for something. Nia thought it exceedingly unfair that close proximity to Lord Vincent rendered her incapable of rational thought, whilst he appeared to be in complete control of himself; insufferable man! She glanced around, frantically looking for something, anything, to explain her smile.

'I was wondering if Lord Nathaniel knows quite what he has let himself in for,' she said, watching Sophia working her magic on the youngest Sheridan male. She felt the dark weight of Lord Vincent's gaze burning into her profile, and inwardly groaned. By drawing attention to Sophia's overt flirting, she had probably just reinforced Lord Vincent's impression of her.

'Ah, I see.' His sculpted lips curved upwards as he waited for her to arrange her skirts to her satisfaction before taking the chair beside her.

She hadn't deceived him for one moment, but he was not the only person in the room who did not back away from a challenge. If he continued to stalk her she would remain still, allow herself to be captured, and then turn the tables on him by declining his advances.

Yes, that was what he would do.

A frisson of awareness warmed her body. He would be a dangerous person to play mind games — or any other type of game — with. Perversely, she also felt perfectly safe with him. To a degree. Endeavouring to untangle her thoughts, she conceded that her rebellious side didn't want to feel safe. In the spirit of private honesty, she was also willing to concede that her proposed course of action was not entirely selfless. Lord Vincent, all lithe muscle and graceful coordination, with his not-entirely-civilised male aura and cynical view of the world, had turned her meticulously-planned existence on its head. Her curiosity was piqued; always a dangerous sign. She really would like to have a little practical knowledge of the subjects she had discussed with Sophia.

A smile flirted with his lips as, saying nothing, he toyed with a fork and watched her fight with her conscience. She searched her mind for some innocuous comment that he couldn't misinterpret. Before she hit upon one, a loud guffaw of laughter caused heads to turn towards one end of the table. Nia's heart lurched. Grandpapa was seated beside the duchess, and it was his laughter that had disrupted conversation. God forbid that he had launched into a risque story and given offence. But, amazingly, the duchess was laughing right along with him. Not polite, contained laugher, but the genuine variety that left her eyes moist and her entire body quaking. Lord Vincent cocked his head at Nia, his eyes brimming with infectious good humour.

'I wonder what that's all about,' he mused.

'I did warn you.' Nia tried to look disapproving. 'Grandpapa is incorrigible, I'm afraid. I refuse to ask him what he just said because I would much prefer not to know.'

'If it was inappropriate, my mother doesn't seem to have taken exception to it.'

'No.' Nia smiled as she watched the sophisticated lady in animated conversation with her grandfather. 'Not many people take offence at Grandpapa's outrageous comments. I used to think they made allowances for his artistic eccentricity. But really, perhaps it's simply because he is such a charming raconteur.'

'Which, I hope, means you will stop fretting and enjoy yourself.'

'Certainly I shall.' She concentrated on her soup for a moment before speaking again. 'In which part of this vast house are you thinking of having Grandpapa work on the duke's portrait?'

'Ah, I ought to have thought to show you before we came to table, when it was still full light.'

'It is Grandpapa who needs to see it.'

His disconcertingly intelligent gaze rested on her profile for so long that she felt uncomfortable. 'Is it?' he asked softly.

He knows! Panic surged through Nia as she stubbornly refused to accept that possibility. 'Naturally, I shall view the space with him,' she said, articulating the first words that filtered through her addled brain. 'Sometimes, even when he is doing as well as he is today, Grandpapa overlooks fundamental requirements.'

'That would never do,' he replied, in a mildly hectoring tone.

'Perish the thought,' she said, transferring

her attention to Lord Amos, seated on her opposite side, when he addressed a question to her.

Slowly, Nia began to relax as she observed the casual affection and lack of formality that prevailed between the Sheridan siblings. It must be wonderful to grow up within the confines of such a tight-knit family, Nia thought, feeling a moment's envy for what she had never known. But then again, she had her grandfather. Always her grandfather had been there; the one constant in her life to gently guide, protect and nurture her. She caught his eye as he glanced down the table, looking to make sure she was all right, just as he had done for as long as she could remember. He probably wasn't aware he still did so.

'It is easy to see why you hold him in such affection,' Lord Vincent said softly. 'He is a remarkable gentleman.'

'Thank you. There I must agree with you.'

The meal came to an end and all the gentlemen stood as the ladies made to withdraw.

'Perhaps a servant could show me where you plan for the portrait to be painted, so Grandpapa and I can see if it will serve,' she said to Lord Vincent. 'There is still some daylight remaining. Hopefully enough for us to be able to judge.'

'Your grandfather will not take port?'

'I would prefer it if he did not. It doesn't agree with him.'

'Then none of us shall.'

'Oh no, I couldn't possibly ask you to — '

'Come along, Zach,' he said briskly. 'Miss Trafford and her grandfather want to see the atrium while it is still light.'

'Perhaps we should all take a look,' the duchess said. 'I should be interested to hear your thoughts on the setting myself, Mr. Trafford.'

'And so you shall, dear lady. So you shall.' Grandpapa offered the duchess his arm. 'When did you last have your own portrait painted? Your features, those eyes, would inspire the most exacting of artists.'

Nia chanced a glance at Lord Vincent to gauge his reaction to his mother being addressed as *dear lady*. He appeared amused, the duchess didn't take offence, and no one else seemed to notice.

Lord Vincent led the way from the dining room, making Nia feel self-conscious because everyone else, trailing behind them, couldn't fail to notice her hand resting on his arm. She would have liked to remove it, but that would imply there was something improper about a perfectly proper situation. She was far too acutely aware of Lord Vincent's close proximity, of his disturbingly poised stance and her extreme physical reaction to it. Dear God, if she planned to get the better of him, this was a sorry start indeed. She squared her shoulders and tried to divert herself by looking at her palatial surroundings as Lord Vincent led her through what felt like an endless expanse of richly furnished anterooms and corridors.

Finally, they came to a circular open space with a high domed glass ceiling in what must be the centre of the house. The last of the fading daylight poured through that glass, the subsiding rays of the setting sun filling the space with light and shadow. A small gasp slipped past Nia's lips. This place was not only an oasis of calm; absolutely ideal.

'Perfect!' she breathed, taking a closer look around.

'I say,' Grandpapa remarked. 'This has possibilities, wouldn't you say, Nia?'

'Yes, sir.'

Nia stood with her grandfather in the centre of a space that sported tall potted palms and several miniature orange trees, their fresh citrus aroma filling her senses. There were marble busts, vases of flowers spilling from several surfaces, and a few items of excellent-quality furniture dotted around the edges.

'Where would you want me to pose?' the duke asked.

'That depends upon whether you require a

formal portrait or something more relaxed,' Grandpapa replied.

'What do you think?' The duke furrowed his brow and turned towards his mother. 'Previous generations are depicted formally but, if these two are to be included . . . ' He indicated his wolfhounds with a negligent wave. 'Besides, all that sitting around for hours dressed up to the nines would try my patience.'

'We must all make sacrifices, big brother,' Lord Amos said, grinning.

The duke shot him a reproving look. 'Easy for you to say.'

'I think you should decide for yourself,' the duchess said.

'In that case,' Nia said, unable to remain silent, 'I would suggest a less formal setting. This atrium is not the place for formality.'

The duke wiped non-existent perspiration from his brow. 'What a relief!'

'Grandpapa, shall we ask the duke to sit on the end of that daybed, which I am sure will not be too inconvenient for him? It is low, and so his dogs would be able to sit or lie at his feet.'

Her grandfather stood stock still for a moment, rubbing his chin as he examined the atrium from all angles. Nia knew his creative imagination would be in full flow. He would be picturing the duke in this setting, trying to decide how best to depict him for posterity.

Nia was delighted to see the fervent light of creativity glowing in Grandpapa's increasingly vacant eyes. He muttered something beneath his breath, then grabbed one end of the daybed and moved its position. A footman rushed forward to help him, but Grandpapa waved him aside. Nia knew he would be thinking about the morning light pouring through the eastern side of the dome and how it would reflect upon his sitter. She sat on the end of the bed at his request. They conferred in abbreviated whispers, and finally settled upon exactly the right angle for the daybed, the orange trees in the background.

'That will serve perfectly, Nia my dear,' Grandpapa said.

'I believe it will.' Nia turned towards the duke. 'If you don't mind my saying so, Your Grace, I think casual clothing, as though Grandpapa had caught you in the middle of the day when you were not expecting visitors, will give the portrait the desired informal ambience. I noticed as we passed through your gallery just now that it will be a break with tradition, though.' Nia stifled a giggle. 'Shall you mind shocking future generations?'

'Zach excels at shocking people,' Lord Nathaniel remarked.

'I shall be happy to oblige you, Miss Trafford,' the duke replied, sending his brother a withering look.

'Splendid!' Grandpapa clapped his hands together. 'Perfectly splendid. We shall get to work tomorrow, if that suits you, Your Grace.'

'I am entirely at your disposal, Trafford; and in your debt, I ought to add.'

'How so, Your Grace?' Sean asked.

'We live with continual squabbles going on between the two local villages, whose inhabitants compete for our attention,' the duke replied. 'Since Crista joined the family's ranks, Shawford has been impossibly smug because they claim her as one of theirs.'

'Sorry, Zach,' Crista said, smiling. 'If I had known . . . '

The duke waved her apology aside. 'Once this portrait is completed, I shall show it off at our mother's next birthday party, to which all villagers are invited, and brag about you being a Compton man, Trafford.' The duke's smile was devastating, the man himself arguably the handsomest of all the brothers, and yet Nia could appreciate his charm without being affected by it. The same could not be said about her interaction with Lord Vincent.

'I am sure my grandfather is pleased to be of service,' Nia said for him because she could tell by his vague expression that he had retreated to an unreachable place somewhere in the recesses of his mind.

'If you have seen enough, Mr. Trafford, shall we return to the drawing room for coffee?' the duchess suggested.

Grandpapa snapped out of his reverie. 'Lead the way, my dear.'

My dear?

Nia wandered to the window, allowing the rest of the party to leave the room ahead of her. She needed a moment to recover her composure and untangle her muddled reflections. Lord Vincent appeared determined to remain close beside her, and she found his constant company as exhausting as it was exhilarating. She heard the rest of the party's shoes echoing on the tiled floor as they left the atrium, but sensed one member of it had not gone with them.

She turned to find him leaning one broad shoulder against the door jamb, watching her through unsettlingly intelligent eyes. She wanted to tell him to stop smothering her, perhaps because that prospect was becoming hourly more enticing, but she could hardly order him to leave a room in his own family's house. Besides, she would probably never find her way back to the drawing room on her own.

Nia looked away again and stared at the now almost dark garden, feeling breathless, disadvantaged. It was already apparent that she would have to abandon her plan to teach Lord Vincent a lesson. The moment she was alone with him, she completely lost all sense of who she was. He disconcerted her in a manner that was beyond her control, her understanding, and all common sense. The stultifying stillness embraced her as she became acutely aware of the strong gravitational pull she felt towards him. Thoughts of all the females whom he had probably charmed in a similar fashion helped to restore her senses, and she refused to become his latest conquest . . . well, not *that* easily.

Nia tossed her head, redirecting her thoughts to her grandfather and his enthusiasm for the portrait, so closely followed by his first vague moment of the evening. A fat tear slid down her cheek. She simply couldn't bear it if the portrait work proved to be beyond him.

A finger that was not her own stopped the tear in its tracks. Nia had not heard Lord Vincent move, and froze when she became conscious of his taut body standing far too close behind her.

'What is it?' he asked softly.

She should plaster a smile on her face and

say it was nothing more than momentary weakness. That was how she always responded when she became upset about her grandfather's condition. But she sensed Lord Vincent would know it wasn't true.

'What if he can't do it?' she asked plaintively.

'You must think that he can, or you would not have put him in this position.'

'But that's just it.' Anguished, she turned to face him. 'Perhaps I think he can still do it because I so desperately want it to be true. I want to turn the clock back and make things the way they once were.' She sighed. 'But wishes don't make fishes.'

His lips quirked. 'What a charming phrase.'

'It is one of Grandpapa's.'

'Which makes it even more delightful.'

Lord in heaven, he had slipped an arm lightly around her waist. Panic welled, only to rapidly subside again. It was the most natural gesture in the world if one wished to comfort a friend, which presumably was his intention. But she and Lord Vincent were most emphatically not friends; nor were they ever likely to be. There was a strong compulsion between them that precluded mere friendship. That compulsion overrode her desire to put him in his place. She no longer wanted to attempt it.

She simply wanted him.

'You saw him just now, Lord Vincent.' This time Nia made no effort to hold her tears in check. 'One minute he was being creative, the next . . . well, we had lost him altogether.'

'You mentioned that mornings are his best time. He has been here at the Park these several hours on top form, with just one tiny slip.'

Nia expelled a heavy sigh, far from convinced.

'My mother already adores him.'

Nia managed a brittle smile. 'Most ladies do. He has a certain way with them.'

'And if he does lose his inspiration with the painting, you will be here to guide him.'

Her mouth fell inelegantly open. 'What do you mean?'

'Precisely what I say.' He fixed her with a probing gaze. 'Your father may not have inherited Trafford's talent, but I suspect you did.'

'Why would you imagine that?' She fiddled with a leaf on an orange tree, not trusting herself to meet his gaze. He placed a finger beneath her chin and gently turned it until she was compelled to do so.

'I observed paint beneath your nails on that first day we met, which suggested you do more than mix them for your grandfather.

Then I considered what you told me about always being with him when he gets up in the night to paint his landscapes, even though you claim he is at his most creative in the mornings. *Why would he do that?* I asked myself. The only answer I could come up with was that he didn't — or, rather, you didn't — want other people intruding, just in case he made a mull of it. And then, of course, there is the way you look at people when you make their acquaintance. It was one of the first things I noticed about you.' His eyes gleamed with a dangerous light that caused liquid heat to spiral through her veins. 'You seemed fascinated with my mouth.'

'My eye is drawn to shapes, and your mouth, your lips in particular, happen to be most unusually shaped.'

The lips in question quirked. 'Ah, that would explain it.' He didn't believe her, but was too gentlemanly to say so.

'You see a lot.' She sighed. 'All right, since you have guessed, you might as well know that Grandpapa *is* more creative in the morning, but he does good work in the small hours too. Some nights his landscapes are perfect, and he barely knows I am there. You will see for yourself soon enough that when he immerses himself in his work, that is the way it is for him. Unless . . . '

'Unless his work goes wrong, which is when you step in.'

'Yes.' She closed her eyes for an expressive moment and nodded. 'I am nowhere near as talented as Grandpapa, but he recognised the artist in me when I was still quite young and encouraged me. Sean, too, to a lesser degree. That is partly why we spent so much more time with him rather than with our parents, although what I told you about them is quite true and we both much preferred to be with Grandpapa.'

'I can understand why. He is charming.'

'Yes, he's certainly that.' She threw her head back and sighed. 'His landscapes, for the most part, are his own work, and they are brilliant. But he sometimes gets frustrated because he remembers they aren't what he wants to be doing. That is when I step in. If I cannot reassure him with gentle words, then I try to rescue the painting and make it fit for exhibiting. Oh, don't make the mistake of assuming that I'm no better than the forger we are attempting to apprehend — '

'The idea didn't cross my mind.'

'If I have helped with any of the works that finish up in the exhibition, my name will be added to my grandfather's. Obviously, that will greatly lessen the work's value — '

'That I seriously doubt.'

'Thank you, but you have not seen them so cannot possibly judge.'

'Oh, believe me, I know.' He sent her a searing smile. 'I am almost never wrong about such things.'

'Or modest, either.'

He flexed a brow. 'I have something to be modest about?'

She punched his arm. 'Be serious.'

'I was being perfectly serious.'

'Anyway, now you know.'

'And I will respect your confidence. Thank you for telling me.'

She nodded but said nothing.

'And now, I suppose you are concerned about your grandfather painting Zach's portrait because if he loses his way, you will not be able to help him.'

'Precisely.'

'I don't mean to make light of your concerns, but what is to prevent you? Zach won't mind, and none of us will tell.'

'You give me too much credit, Lord Vincent.'

'Vince,' he corrected her softly.

She swallowed. 'Very well, but only when we are alone, and I don't anticipate that situation arising too often.'

His soft chuckle had a decidedly wicked edge. 'You underestimate my determination.'

She knew better than to ask him what he meant by that. All the time they were discussing her grandfather, she could ignore the fact that his large body swamped hers, mere inches separating them, fragmenting her senses and constantly causing her to lose the thread of their conversation. She could ignore the arm around her waist and the long fingers gently stroking her spinal column. If she didn't look at his mouth, she could even pretend she wasn't desperately hoping he would kiss her.

'I can paint a reasonable landscape, but my skills as a portrait artist don't begin to mirror Grandpapa's. That is my difficulty.'

'Have you attempted portraits?' She nodded. 'I should like to see the results.'

'Then prepare yourself to be disappointed.'

'Nothing you ever do will disappoint me, sweet Nia.'

He lowered his head, anticipation washing through her in unstoppable waves when his lips firmed against hers and he tickled the corners of her mouth seductively with the tip of his tongue. So sensuous, so reassuring. There was something important about an earlier resolve that she ought to remember. What was it? Something about keeping her distance, allowing him to imagine she would submit to him and then retreating before actually doing so.

Or not. Which had she decided upon? When his arms closed possessively around her, she could no longer recall, and gave up trying. Instead, her arms slid around his neck, quite without her permission, and she stood on her toes as she inexpertly kissed him back. Her body was on fire with need by the time his tongue, velvety and sensuous, cut a path through her mouth and she was able to savour the taste of him as he deepened the kiss. Ye gods, a small part of her brain screamed at her that this was madness; it was probably the very situation she had been seeking to avoid.

Yes, she was absolutely sure now that that had been her intention.

The feminine side of her ignored the voice of reason and revelled in this new, enticing and very educational experience. Her body pulsated and convulsed as desire swamped rationality. Sophia had not exaggerated. Being kissed by a gentleman she admired truly was paradise. But where would it lead? She probably ought to be concerned about that.

Far sooner than she was ready to be released, Vince broke the kiss, providing her with the answer to her unasked question. It would not lead anywhere, and not because she had called a halt to proceedings, but because he had. How mortifying!

'Better?' he asked, softly tracing the curve

of her face with his fingertips.

'We should not have done that,' she replied, turning away from him, breathing deeply as she struggled to regain her composure.

'I hesitate to disagree, but you might as well know that I have wanted to since first meeting you. However, if you would prefer that it didn't happen again, then it will not.' His smile was almost contrite, and contrition didn't suit him. 'But I hope you don't feel that way.'

'Thank you for that reassurance,' she said primly, staring at a point over his shoulder.

'You are entirely welcome.' He clasped her hand and placed it on his sleeve. 'Now come, the others will wonder what has become of us.'

13

'Mr. Trafford is charming,' the duchess said as soon as their new neighbours had taken their leave. 'Perhaps a little eccentric, but one expects such behaviour from artistic types. I am sure that he will make a wonderful job of your portrait, Zach.'

'It is a long time since I have seen you so agreeably engaged, Mother,' Zach replied with a smile. 'I am willing to wager that life with such a man on our doorstep will never be dull.'

'Patrick is known for his charm,' Lady St. John remarked, gathering her reticule in anticipation of her carriage arriving at the door. 'The last time our paths crossed in Belgium, it was a very different story. He kept complaining about being too warm at a smart gathering and repeatedly tried to remove his clothing. Poor Nia was beside herself.'

'She does seem inordinately fond of her grandfather,' Portia remarked.

'And we entertained a courtesan here at the Park,' Amos said, grinning. 'Poor Faraday. I'm unsure if his dignity will ever recover.'

'She is just as much of a lady as anyone

else!' Nate declared hotly, causing his other brothers to share a smirk. 'I'll have you know she is well-educated, well-read, and a lot more fun than half the dull misses I had foisted upon me last season.'

Faraday materialised to announce the arrival of Lady St. John's carriage.

'Thank you, Your Grace, for inviting me,' Lady St. John said, turning towards the duchess. 'I am so very pleased that you enjoyed Patrick's company. I knew that if he was in good form you would not be able to resist his charm. No one ever does.'

'I hope you will call often and observe the progress of the portrait,' the duchess replied. Vince suppressed a smile. His mother was becoming less and less subtle in her attempts to draw Lady St. John and Zach together.

'Patrick will not allow me, or anyone else, to look over his shoulder,' Lady St. John warned. 'Artists are very particular about their privacy.'

'Then come and talk to the subject,' Portia suggested. 'You can be as rude to Zach as you wish, and he won't be able to retaliate since I don't suppose he will be permitted to move.'

Amos shared a grin with his brothers. 'An opportunity we should all take advantage of.'

'I wouldn't be so sure about my inability to retaliate,' Zach warned.

Lady St. John's lips twitched. 'Tempting though that offer might be, Portia, unfortunately I cannot think of any reason to insult His Grace.'

Zach fixed Lady St. John with a scorching look that caused her cheeks to turn pink.

'You seek to provoke me, Your Grace?' Lady St. John tilted her chin and met his gaze without flinching. 'And yet I took your side. That hardly seems fair.'

Zach chuckled and muttered something in an aside to Lady St. John that Vince couldn't hear, but he did notice his mother observing the exchange with considerable interest.

'What does Mr. Sean Trafford do with himself all day, Frankie?' Portia asked.

Ah, Vince thought, so that's the way the wind blows.

'He manages his grandfather's affairs and has two small sons to occupy his time,' Lady St. John replied. 'I shall tell you more on my next visit, if you are interested.'

'Evidently she is,' Zach said, eyeing Portia somewhat severely.

'The question arose out of idle curiosity.' Portia blushed fiercely when the rest of her brothers joined Zach and concentrated suspicious glares upon her. 'I am starting to understand why Annalise complained so vociferously about the four of you watching her every move.'

'Become accustomed to it,' Zach warned. 'There are fortune hunters everywhere.'

'And none of them will like me for myself because I am not as beautiful as Annalise.'

'That is not what I meant.' Zach remained implacably calm in the face of their sister's rare fit of pique. 'Don't test me, Portia. You know I only have your best interests at heart.'

'I'm sorry.' Portia glanced down at her folded hands and sighed. 'But credit me with a little intelligence. I am not the dim wit you appear to take me for.'

'I must not leave my horses standing around,' Lady St. John said, 'so will bid you all *au revoir*.'

Vince was again surprised when Zach chose to escort their guest to the door himself, and was absent from the drawing room for some considerable time. When he returned to it, their mother, sister and Crista had all retired.

'Do you think Trafford really is still capable of portrait work?' Zach asked Vince as he helped himself to brandy.

Vince shrugged. 'Does an artist need to have his wits about him to exploit his talent?'

'Being half-mad is acceptable in artistic types,' Amos said flippantly. 'Some might say it enhances their brilliance.'

'Oh well,' Zach said, shrugging. 'If it

doesn't work, it won't be the end of the world.'

The conversation between the brothers became more general after that but Vince took little part in it. He was deep in thought about the deep impression Nia had made on him, his gentlemanly instincts waging an increasingly desperate battle with his baser side. It was a battle he would probably lose, especially when Nia looked at him with such burning and unguarded curiosity reflected in her eyes. She might live beneath the same roof as a courtesan, but there the similarity between their backgrounds ended. Vince had been looking forward to her visits to the Park with her grandfather. Now he accepted that if he found himself alone with her, he might not be able to control himself. Ye gods, the chit had a lot to answer for!

'You're quiet, Vince,' Nate said, swirling brandy around in his glass. 'Can't imagine what occupies that vacant brain of yours.'

Vince chastised his irrepressible brother with sardonic look. 'You are perfectly capable of talking enough for all four of us.'

Amos laughed. 'Can't deny that one, Nate.'

Nate laughed too. 'I'm an astute student of human nature and have much to say about my observations, but that doesn't make me a rattletrap.'

'We noticed you observing Miss Ash a little too assiduously,' Zach said.

'I say, what a woman! No offence to Trafford, but she's wasted on him.'

'Nate, she's old enough to be your mother,' Vince reminded him.

'Hardly that.' Nate's smile was irrepressible. 'Besides, older women have the advantage of experience on their side.'

'Leave her alone,' Zach said mildly. 'We are trying to help Trafford, not create more problems for him.'

'Which is why I don't like Portia making moon eyes at Sean Trafford,' Amos added, scowling.

'Portia compares herself to Annalise and finds herself wanting,' Vince said. 'We all know she didn't enjoy her first season, even though she received her share of attention.'

'But no offers, in spite of her substantial dowry,' Nate added.

'And now she has found a charismatic man here in the country who showed what she thinks is a genuine interest in her.' Zach frowned. 'But Trafford will return to Ireland with his grandfather and sons. I don't see Portia taking on another woman's children and his demented father. I want better for her than that.'

'I want to protect our sister's interests every bit as much as the rest of you,' Vince said pensively. 'But I think we're reading too much into one evening during which she enjoyed a gentleman's society because he had the good manners to make himself agreeable to her. Portia deserves to have some fun.'

'Then I shall not spare the matter another moment's concern,' Zach replied drolly.

'Do you really think the forger will show himself when the portrait is unveiled?' Amos asked after a short pause.

'Someone arrogant enough to forge paintings by a living artist is unlikely to resist viewing that artist's latest efforts,' Nate said in a speculative tone. 'He will assume he is above suspicion and will be interested in Trafford's landscapes, probably in the expectation that they will be easier to forge than portraits.'

'I agree with you for once,' Vince said, rotating his neck to dislodge the tension that had settled in his shoulders. 'I think I might go up to town for a few days.'

'And pass up the opportunity to enjoy Miss Trafford's society while she is here at the Park?' Nate's eyebrows shot up. 'I believe our brother thinks he might be in danger, Zach.'

That was precisely what Vince did think, but his only response was a withering glare in Nate's direction. The plain fact of the matter was that if he spent too much time with Nia, he would not be able to help encouraging her expectations; if expectations she had. Seducing a lady of Nia's class would be unthinkable, but it was all he seemed able to think about.

'Why the sudden desire to go to town?' Zach asked. 'There will be no one there worth knowing at this time of year.'

'I have a mind to set the cat amongst the pigeons,' Vince replied with a rakish grin.

'In what respect?' Zach and Amos asked together.

'I shall make myself known to Trafford's agent, Belling, and a few other leading figures in the art world. Let them know that Trafford is painting your portrait, Zach, and see what interest that produces.'

'Thinking word will get back to the forger?' Nate suggested.

'Precisely so. I shall also mention the theft of the sketches of Sophia Ash.'

'Sophia Ash in her prime, *au naturel*.' Nate sighed and dramatically clutched at his heart. 'I would pay good money to see those. You have to get them back, Vince, you absolutely have to.'

'It was just a few months ago when our baby brother was sighing over Martha at the Crown and Anchor.'

'Martha is an angel of mercy,' Nate

answered, chuckling. 'I believe she showed the three of you a range of celestial pleasures before she got round to me. The time has come to move on.'

Vince laughed. 'I shall endeavour to oblige with regard to Sophia's sketches, but I don't suppose they are being touted on the open market.'

'There is a black market for such merchandise, presumably,' Amos remarked.

'I am hoping Belling will be able to cast some light on that angle. And while I'm at it, I shall also see if I can engineer a meeting with Smythe at Whites.'

Amos looked momentarily confused. 'Smythe being the person who purchased one of the forgeries?'

'Yes. He probably knows more about the forger's identity than he realises. Not that I shall indicate any interest in that particular subject. I shall simply tell him about Trafford's activities here; he is bound to mention that he owns a Trafford original, and I will steer the conversation in the direction I wish for it to take.'

'And invite him to the unveiling of my portrait,' Zach surmised.

'Naturally.'

'Don't worry about Miss Trafford while you are gone,' Nate said as the brothers finished their drinks and headed for the stairs together. 'I shall take the very best care of her.'

Vince dealt Nate a chilling glare that set all his brothers chuckling.

★　★　★

'We have to stop!' Annie clutched the forger's lapels. 'They know something is wrong. I can sense it.'

The forger disentangled her grubby fingers from his exquisite tailoring. 'Calm yourself and tell me why you have summoned me here.'

'Mr. Trafford is going to paint the Duke of Winchester's portrait. Everyone in the house is talking about it.'

Damnation, that was all he needed. 'Then you were right to call on me.'

'This will make a difference to you, won't it?'

'I had not anticipated he would do more portraits, it's true.' He moved away from her. 'Just give me a moment to think.'

'I hear tell they are going to hold a private viewing at the duke's home in six weeks' time, along with Mr. Trafford's landscapes. Lots of people of consequence will be invited.'

'Is that a fact?'

The forger scratched his neck as he contemplated this disturbing development. If the new owners of the portraits he had passed off as Trafford originals happened to be there, it could be disastrous. Panic momentarily overcame rational thought. Forcing himself to calm down, the forger decided that, even if his customers did happen to be there, they would not have their paintings with them. Paintings changed hands all the time, through dealers and private transactions. If they mentioned their new acquisitions, no one would think anything about it. Trafford, in his prime, had produced hundreds of portraits. He couldn't possibly remember them all, especially in his current deluded state.

No, he would be safe enough. But the deal with Lord Barrington might have to be the last one. If Trafford was intimate with influential dukes, it was too dangerous to continue. It was unfortunate, but greed had seen better men than the forger scuppered, and he was too wily to fall into that trap.

14

Nia tried not to resent the fact that there were more problems than usual calling for her attention at Stoneleigh Manor the following morning. Short of sleep, all she really wanted to do was set off for the Park so her grandfather could make a start on the duke's portrait. Sophia had sent word to say he was bright-eyed and lucid that morning, but Nia knew that situation could change at any moment.

'Annie, where are the boys? Have they had their breakfast yet?'

'I'm not sure, miss.'

Nia strove for patience. Annie could be strong-willed, and sometimes seemed to forget she was there to serve them; not the other way around. 'Well, find them please, as quickly as you can.'

'I need a word, Miss Trafford.' Mr. Drake strode into the kitchen, a room into which, to her particular knowledge, he had never before ventured.

'Not now, Mr. Drake.'

'I'm sorry, but it cannot wait.'

'What is so important?' Nia impatiently pushed the hair back from her face, the ribbon holding it back having already come undone.

Mr. Drake glanced around the kitchen, looking as though he wanted to ask Hannah and Beth to leave their domain. Nia almost wished he would attempt it: she could do with a diversion. But his common sense, such as it was, prevailed. He turned away from them and spoke to Nia in a lowered voice.

'About our recent discussion,' he said. 'Have you had an opportunity to give it more consideration?'

Nia planted her clenched fists on her hips and looked at him askance. '*That* is what is so urgent? I have already said all I have to say on the matter, and think it best forgotten.'

'Forgotten?' He offered her a superior smirk. 'Dining with our aristocratic neighbours has turned your head.'

'I would thank you to remember to whom you are speaking,' Nia replied stiffly, holding on to her temper . . . somehow.

'I mean no offence, but hate to see you being ill-used. The Sheridans are above our station, you know.'

Nia sent him a chilling look. '*Our* station, Mr. Drake?'

'I cannot allow you to get carried away with unrealistic expectations.' The man was deluded, but before Nia could tell him so, he spoke again. 'Do you think it wise to risk having your grandfather paint the duke's portrait? You know very well it will be a disaster.'

Pondering upon Lord Vincent's marked attentions of the night before had kept her awake for far too long. She was tired, on edge, and Mr. Drake had chosen an unfortunate time to become proprietorial.

'Mind your own business!'

Nia glanced through the window and was relieved to see Annie returning with the boys. Her nephews, no respecters of private conversations, would put an end to Mr. Drake's nonsense. A tiny part of her wondered why he was suddenly so anxious to become engaged to her. He hadn't shown her any particular attention before they had come to Winchester.

'You *are* my business, my dear. It is simply that you are not yet ready to acknowledge how dependent upon one another we have become over the months.' Nia shook her head, astonished that Drake actually seemed to believe what he said. 'You and I are made for one another, and my only desire is to protect and care for you.'

'And I have already told you that I don't require your protection.' He opened his mouth as though to protest, but she sliced her hand through the air to silence him. Enough was enough! If he was not prepared to take a polite *no* for an answer, then she would speak plainly. 'As far as I am concerned, you are with us under sufferance, Mr. Drake, and if you continue to make a nuisance of yourself then I shall ask you to leave.'

He sent her a superior smile and slowly shook his head. 'You cannot possibly be serious.'

'My advice is not to put my resolve to the test.' She brushed past him. 'Now, you really must excuse me.'

She had the satisfaction of seeing his mouth hang open as she finally shocked him into silence. Then, with an angry hiss, he turned on his heel and left the kitchen. She had no time to dwell upon the incident before the boys barrelled into the room. They were covered from head to foot in wet mud and were closely followed by Ruff, who was just as muddy.

'What the devil — '

'We decided to help you, Aunt Nia, by pulling the weeds from the pond — '

'You did say yesterday that it needed to be cleaned up — '

'And it's difficult for the tadpoles — '

'They have no space to swim about.'

'But I fell in,' Art said, looking woebegone.

Nia expelled a deep sigh. 'So I see.'

'Ruff tried to rescue him and I had to rescue them both,' Leo explained.

'Take all three of them out to the pump,

Annie, and get them clean,' Nia said, shaking her head. 'I shall fetch them some clean clothes, although why I bother . . .'

Miss Tilling popped her head around the door. 'Is there to be any breakfast this morning?' she demanded to know.

'If you care to make it yourself,' Nia snapped.

Miss Tilling sniffed. 'I merely asked a civil question. Really, Miss Trafford, I cannot account for your sour moods recently.'

'Don't feel obliged to remain with us if you find them disagreeable.'

'Mr. Trafford needs me. I cannot let him down.'

Nia shared an exasperated glance with Hannah, and didn't bother to make any response.

'Sorry, Nia,' Sean said, bounding into the kitchen. 'I overslept. Oh Lord,' he added, espying his mud-caked sons through the window and wincing.

'They were trying to help, apparently,' Nia said, dredging up a smile from somewhere.

'They always mean well.' Sean grinned also. 'I'll fetch them some clean clothes.'

'Thank you.'

Finally, boys and dog were clean, and Sean had plans to keep them occupied all day: first with lessons, and then with work in the grounds that hopefully would not include another ducking in the pond. Sophia appeared with her grandfather's painting supplies, and they were ready to leave for the Park a mere hour later than planned.

Nia had hoped that their evening at the Park would leave her grandfather disinclined to take to his studio and continue his nocturnal painting when they arrived home. No such luck: he had headed straight for it the moment they got back. Desperately tired, her mind addled after hours of bandying words with Lord Vincent, Nia had almost taken Sophia up on her offer to bear him company in her stead. Almost. Sophia already did too much, and Nia would not exploit her good nature for selfish reasons.

The price for sticking to her guns was a feeling of total exhaustion. She needed her wits about her if she was to play Lord Vincent at the game he appeared determined to engage her in: a game to which he had not had the courtesy to explain the rules. But this morning her mind felt dull, her body lethargic. She had dark circles beneath her eyes and was almost too tired to drive Ned. Lord Vincent had not only agitated her passions, but also unbalanced her well-organised world with his charming manners, wicked smile and persuasively convincing words.

To say nothing of his lips, and that confounded kiss.

Even when her grandfather had quit his painting and she had been free to retire, sleep eluded her because she couldn't stop thinking about that kiss and the most extraordinary effect it had had upon her. Well, now that she was awake — after a fashion — she was perfectly capable of dismissing it from her mind as easily as she planned to dismiss Lord Vincent himself from her conscious thoughts. She would put all her energies into ensuring her grandfather felt comfortable, had everything he required to hand, and then she would fade into the background; read a book, close her eyes for a few minutes — no one would notice — take a walk in the grounds . . . no, not that. Lord Vincent might track her down if she ventured outside alone.

If his lordship chose to watch Grandpapa at work, there was nothing she could do to prevent him. But that did not mean she had to speak with him. Quite what she was so afraid of, Nia could not have said. He had woken something inside her, some deep yearning she had not previously been acquainted with, and the strength of her feelings frightened her. For once, she wanted to forget her responsibilities, the duty she owed to her grandfather and the rest of her family, and explore those yearnings.

But she did not, could not, take that risk.

Their arrival at the Park brought her mental perambulations to a halt and she was forced to pay attention. What the Sheridan groom who stepped forward to take Ned's head thought of their means of transportation, she did not care to speculate. She accepted the hand of another groom, who helped her to alight and collected up Grandpapa's supplies beneath Nia's watchful eye.

The Sheridans' rather intimidating butler showed them into the atrium. Coffee was offered, and the butler told them the duke would be with them in a moment, then left them alone. Grandpapa set up his easel, and Nia moved the end of the daybed several times according to his direction. Thank the Lord that he appeared to be functioning at full capacity — at least for now.

Excitement at this commission pushed aside some of her tiredness. It had been some months since Grandpapa last painted a portrait, and she could tell he was full of enthusiasm to indulge his first love. Whenever he displayed such fervour, the results were usually outstanding. Although she had warned the duke not to expect too much, she desperately wanted the portrait to be a success; for her grandfather's sake as much as anything else. His condition was worsening, and she was unsure if his talent would survive the loss of his wits. Was it instinctive or did it require a rational brain to produce his masterpieces? No one seemed to know, but Nia nervously accepted she would soon discover the answer for herself.

'There we are, Nia,' Grandpapa said, sipping at his coffee as he cast a critical eye over the arrangements they had made in the atrium. 'That ought to do splendidly.'

As soon as the duke arrived and was seated to Grandpapa's satisfaction, he would dash off several charcoal sketches before outlining the portrait proper with a soft pencil. He would refer to his sketches for direction as frequently as he looked at the duke in person, always trusting the first impressions he had captured on paper.

'Good morning.' The duke joined them, his dogs at his heels, and smiled as he offered Grandpapa his hand. 'I hope I have not kept you waiting. Always, something seems to occur that requires my attention at the most inconvenient times. Good morning to you, Miss Trafford.'

'Good morning, Your Grace,' Nia replied for them both.

'Will I do?' he asked.

The duke was wearing tight-fitting inexpressibles, shiny hessians and a loose shirt; no neckcloth, waistcoat or coat. His hair was tousled, as though he had just dismounted from his horse and entered the house after a lengthy period out of doors, bringing fresh air and explosive energy with him. If Grandpapa could capture that natural elegance on canvas, if he could somehow depict the ease, grace and charm with which the duke had assumed the position he had been born to occupy, then the project would be a resounding success. It was a challenge that would have any artist worth his salt salivating with anticipation, mainly because the duke was such an unusual and interesting person.

With the eye of an artist and the heart of a woman, Nia could appreciate His Grace's masculine beauty without being unduly affected by it. All that taut flesh over hard, rippling muscle didn't make her heart flutter. He was very attractive, with natural presence and disconcerting poise. He would be a perfect match for her friend Frankie, Nia thought. Frankie didn't have an obsequious bone in her body, and proved it by constantly taking issue with His Grace if he happened to say something she disagreed with.

Nia had supposed Lord Vincent would be here to greet them, since the portrait had been his idea, and wondered where he was hiding himself. Not that she wanted to see him. After participating so enthusiastically in that kiss, she wasn't ready to face him, and probably never would be. At the same time, she was anxious to get this initial meeting over with so they could put the matter behind them and meet in future without embarrassment. Not that *he* would be embarrassed. He probably made a habit of kissing willing females when he had nothing better to do with his time. He was certainly very proficient at it.

Perdition, was it her or was it too warm in here?

All things considered, she thought it rather bad-mannered of Lord Vincent not to pay his respects, even if she had . . . well, lost his respect.

'Vince delayed his departure in the hope of seeing you this morning, Miss Trafford,' the duke remarked.

She willed herself not to blush; but was conscious of doing so anyway. 'His departure?' she asked with as much composure as she could muster.

'He has gone up to town for a few days.'

'Oh, I see.'

'He has decided to do some sleuthing of his own, to see what he can discover about the person we referred to yesterday.'

Nia flashed a warning glare at the duke. Her grandfather did not know about the forgeries. Fortunately, he was busy arranging his pencils and charcoals, and wasn't paying attention to Nia's conversation with the duke.

'Right, Trafford,' the duke said. 'Where would you like me and the hounds?'

'If you would be so kind as to sit on the end of the daybed, Your Grace. Do you suppose the dogs would oblige by sitting at your feet?'

'Most likely.'

The duke gave them a hand signal and they did precisely that. Nia made a mental note to ask him how he achieved such instant obedience. It was not as though dogs understood ducal authority, surely? If there was a trick, perhaps she could use it on Ruff. Such an optimistic possibility made her smile.

'Would it inconvenience you to lean your forearms on your thighs, Your Grace, and try to look as casual as possible?'

'There,' he replied, doing as Grandpapa had asked. 'Will that do?'

'Admirably, would you not say, Nia?'

'I think it might work very well,' Nia replied, quietly moving to take a seat behind her grandfather, making sure to keep out of his light and not allow her shadow to fall over his easel.

*   *   *

Vince reached London as darkness fell, and headed directly for Sheridan House. Pausing only to change out of his travelling clothes and eat a hasty supper, he ventured out again, bound for White's. But his thoughts remained in Winchester. Having decided it would be safer to put distance between himself and his growing interest in Nia Trafford, he found reasons to linger in expectation of her arrival until the last possible moment. But no matter how frequently he looked down the drive from the privacy of his chamber, there was no sign of Ned plodding along it, hauling Nia's rickety gig. He had to leave eventually, or he would not have made the journey to London in one day.

Now that he had arrived, he was unsure quite what he expected to achieve. White's was sparsely attended at this time of year. Even so, he saw several people known to him, and acknowledged their greetings without being drawn into their company. Settled beside the fire, a drink on the table beside him, he was content to peruse the newspapers and bide his time, fairly confident that Smythe would put in an appearance before the night was out.

He did so an hour later, and accepted Vince's invitation to join him.

'What brings you up to town at this time of year, Sheridan?' Smythe enquired.

'A few bits of family business, and the need

for a change of scenery.'

Smythe chuckled. 'Some country chit got you in her sights?'

You have no idea. 'Not precisely.'

'It's a good time to be in London for a man in your position. Not too crowded, and no match-making mamas on the prowl.'

Vince smiled. 'There is that.' He paused to take a sip of burgundy. 'Have you never thought of taking a country estate, Smythe?'

'Heavens, no. I'm a city man through and through. The country bores me rigid. Besides, I enjoy the arts. Plenty of galleries and dealers in town to keep me abreast of anything interesting that comes on the market. It helps to be on hand and snap them up, you know.'

'Ah yes, I had forgotten about your precious collection.' Vince stretched and pretended boredom. 'Any new acquisitions recently?'

Smythe hesitated, opened his mouth as though about to speak, and then closed it again, concentrating upon his wine instead. Vince waited him out in silence.

'I picked up a Trafford portrait the other day, as a matter of fact,' Smythe replied with casual modesty. 'One of his early, lesser-known works.'

'Really.' Vince flexed his brows. 'Of whom is the portrait?'

'Some young girl. She isn't named, but

there's no question it's a Trafford, albeit not done with the flair he demonstrated in his later works.'

'Zach is interested in Traffords. He hadn't heard of one coming on the market.'

Symthe chuckled. 'Now you will appreciate the need to be here, in the hub of things.'

'Did you hear of this gem through an agent?'

'Actually, I was approached by someone I didn't know.' Smythe shrugged. 'It happens, once you become a recognised collector. Nine times out of ten, the advances are bogus.'

'But not this time? The portrait had provenance?'

'Well, no, not precisely.' Smythe seemed reluctant to make the admission. 'But I'm no greenhorn. I know an original Trafford when I see one.'

'Which makes me wonder why it was not offered for auction.'

'You're too suspicious, Sheridan. The vendor had his reasons.'

'I dare say.' Vince shrugged. 'Who was the chap who sold it to you? Do you have his direction? He might have access to others.'

'Name of Griffiths. He's from Paris, which is where I'm bound next week for a lengthy stay. There are several auctions coming up, and I'm keen to see the works before deciding if I want to bid for any of them.'

'Ah, that's a shame.'

Smythe looked surprised. 'Didn't know you took such a keen interest in my activities.'

'Actually, in confidence, it's a coincidence that you mentioned Trafford.' Vince leaned forward and lowered his voice. 'He's now in this country, living on our doorstep.'

'The devil he is!' Smythe sat bolt upright. 'I'd heard rumours about him being . . . er, a trifle distracted, shall we say?'

'Exaggerated.' Vince stretched his legs out in front of him and crossed his ankles. 'He's a little frail, so his granddaughter doesn't want it made public that he's back on these shores. He will never be left alone if that happens.'

'Is he working?' Smythe asked expectantly.

'As well as ever. He's accepted a commission to paint Zach's portrait.'

'Well, I'll be damned.'

'Most likely,' Vince replied, chuckling.

'I heard he'd moved on to landscapes, which I thought would add to the value of my portrait. Damned if Griffiths didn't deceive me about that.'

Vince flashed a wry smile. 'Glad to hear you rejoice in Trafford's recovery.'

'I didn't mean it that way. But you just wait until I catch up with Griffiths in Paris.' Smythe drained his glass and signalled to the servant for a refill. 'Still, it serves me right. I ought to have known better than to buy from someone I'm not acquainted with. I always swore I wouldn't be tempted.'

'We shall be having a small gathering to show off Zach's portrait and some of Trafford's landscapes. If you are interested, I'd be happy to send you an invitation.'

'If I'm interested?' Smythe's eyes flared with anticipation. 'I'd walk over hot coals to meet the great man. When is it likely to be?'

'As soon as the portrait is finished. Trafford works fast, I understand. It could be a matter of weeks.' *If he keeps his wits about him.*

Smythe groaned. 'I shall be in Paris.'

'You might want to delay your departure if you have a mind to get over your dislike of the country and meet Trafford.'

'I would if I could; never doubt it. But my wife has made a whole series of engagements which she will never permit me to renege upon.' Smythe flashed a hopeful smile. 'Sure I can't persuade you to give me a private introduction to Trafford?'

Vince shook his head. 'Sorry, not possible.'

'Damnation!'

'What did Griffiths look like?' Vince asked after a short pause.

'Why?' Smythe blinked, his affable expression clouding with suspicion. 'What does his appearance matter to you? He had every right to sell me that portrait. I made damned sure of that.'

'Idle curiosity, nothing more.'

'Nothing remarkable about him. Average in every way. Had a Welsh accent, so he did.'

With a name like Griffiths, Vince supposed that was to be expected. He was about to ask further questions when, to his intense frustration, other members joined them and the opportunity was lost.

Tired from his long day's ride, Vince declined to participate in the game of cards that Smythe joined. Instead, he returned to Sheridan House early, and retired. Smythe was the key to his plan to uncover the identity of the forger, or his agent, but if he was to be in Paris at the time Zach's portrait was unveiled, he would be of no help whatsoever. What he had managed to learn about the man Smythe had dealt with was next to useless. 'Griffiths' was almost certainly an alias, and the Welsh accent false. His lack of progress was disheartening.

Smythe had promised to keep Trafford's presence in Winchester a secret. He had probably promised to keep the particulars of his new portrait secret too, but had not been able to resist boasting about it. If Winchester was inundated with art collectors keen to make Trafford's acquaintance, Vince would be to blame for revealing his whereabouts to Smythe.

Still determined to find the forger, Vince wondered if the showing of Zach's portrait could be delayed until Smythe's return from Paris, but quickly dismissed the notion. Nia was anxious for her grandfather to return to the peace and familiarity of his old country just as soon as the portrait was completed and the exhibition of his landscapes arranged. It was his understanding that they would take themselves off to Ireland and return in the winter only to attend the exhibition. Vince could see the sense in that arrangement, but most emphatically did not wish for Nia to go.

He fell asleep, resolving to think of another way to uncover the identity of the forger, and recover the drawings of Sophia Ash before whoever stole them could profit from his crime.

15

'I am delighted with Grandpapa's progress.' Nia spoke in an undertone so as not to disturb the artist or his subject. 'It has been a week since he started the portrait, and the commission appears to have given him a new lease of life. I have never seen him so inspired.'

'I am delighted,' Frankie replied. 'Have there been any eccentric moments?'

The friends were seated in an alcove adjacent to the atrium. Nia had a clear view of her grandfather, in case he should have need of her, but they were far enough away not to be a distraction.

'Barely a one.' She widened her smile. 'It is almost as though someone has turned back the clock. I can't explain it, precisely. His last attempt at portraiture was disastrous. I can only surmise that something about being here at the Park inspires his creativity.'

'Well, it is hardly a hovel,' Frankie said, glancing around at its opulent splendour.

'Grandpapa has been inside many splendid buildings, so I don't think that explains it.'

'Perhaps it is the duke himself?'

Nia giggled. 'Well, he is not exactly hard on the eye.'

'But will he be pleased with the results? Your grandfather doesn't flatter his subjects, preferring to paint what he sees. The duke has never struck me as being the vain type, but who knows how he sees himself?' Frankie's tone was pensive. 'I would deny saying it if you repeat these words to anyone, but no one can accuse Zach Sheridan of being disagreeable to look at.'

'Which can't be easy for him. I feel almost sorry for him.'

'Good heavens.' Frankie elevated both brows. 'Why?'

'He is a duke. A young, single, and wealthy duke. The ladies hope to attract his attention with a view to matrimony. The gentlemen require his patronage, his good opinion, or simply want to be a part of his set.' Nia's soft heart momentarily filled with empathy for the duke's situation. 'It must be hard for him to separate the genuine people from the opportunists. Add his pleasing appearance, and it complicates everything.'

'I doubt whether the duke would welcome your sympathy. He seems to cope well enough.'

'Yes, but I *can* sympathise, because I know how it was for Grandpapa.' She thought of

Mr. Drake and Miss Tilling, of the forger, and pursed her lips. 'How it still is for him. Their situations are not so dissimilar now. But it would have been a very different story for Grandpapa when he was struggling to make a name for himself in the art world. No one wanted to know him then.'

'Such is the price of fame, my dear.'

Nia expelled an elongated sigh. 'Ignore me, Frankie. Watching Grandpapa work gives me too much time to think, and puts me in a philosophical mood.' She turned away from the duke and gave Frankie her full attention. 'I know you are curious to see the result of Grandpapa's efforts, and I can promise you, the wait will be worthwhile. I worried that he might not be able to capture the duke's mystique.' Nia grinned. 'I should not have doubted Grandpapa.'

'I am so very glad.'

'I am on tenterhooks the whole time since I have no idea how long his creativity will last, or if it will be overtaken by the angry, destructive mood.' She paused. 'It would be a travesty if frustration caused him to damage his portrait of the duke. In my view, it is the best thing he has ever done.' Nia shrugged. 'Who would have thought it?'

'I would. I am aware of Patrick's genius. Just because his mind wanders, it does not mean his talent wanders with it. I've heard it said that people who, excuse me Nia, hover on the edge of sanity, are better able to focus their talent because they have nothing else cluttering their minds.'

'I now have reason to believe it.'

Frankie covered Nia's hand with one of her own. 'You have not had an easy time of it recently, but this commission and the sale of the landscapes will see you set for life.'

Nia nodded decisively. 'And with Sean managing Grandpapa's finances, I believe we shall finally remain that way.'

'Did I see Sean in the grounds here when I drove up?'

'Very likely. To their absolute delight, the twins were invited by Lord Amos to spend the morning with the horses, and Sean is here with them.' Nia grinned. 'Sean was almost as keen as his sons to accept the invitation.'

Frankie nodded. 'I can easily believe it. Male fascination with horseflesh transcends generations.'

'Apparently so.' Nia rolled her eyes. 'Anyway, I am very much obliged to Lord Amos since the twins have been badgering me, wanting to know when they could visit again.'

'I wonder how the duke makes his dogs sit so still,' Frankie remarked after a short pause.

Nia followed the direction of her gaze.

They were seated in a place that gave them an uninterrupted view of the duke's profile, but he could not look at them without turning his head. Since he was posing, moving was discouraged.

'It might be more germane to wonder how the duke can remain still for so long. I have observed many subjects sit for Grandpapa but seldom one as obliging as His Grace. I am surprised that a man so used to being active, to giving rather than obeying orders, has the patience.'

'I think there is little the duke cannot do, if he puts his mind to it,' Frankie replied in a speculative tone, her gaze still fastened upon his features.

'Oh yes, quite so.' Nia made a valiant effort to keep her lips straight, but failed dismally.

'I know what you are thinking, but I am an aging widow, Nia. Even if I had designs upon the duke, which I most emphatically do not, I am not duchess material.'

'Good heavens!' Nia arched her brow. 'What a strange thing to say. I should have thought, with your background, you would make an ideal duchess. The dowager certainly appears to approve of you.'

'She and I are firm friends, but if she thought I had designs upon her precious son, she would chase me away with a stick.'

'Nonsense!'

'Talking of the Sheridan males, what news of Lord Vincent?'

Nia was furious when she felt herself blush. 'Why ask me?'

Frankie flashed a knowing smile. 'Who better to consult?'

'You are far better acquainted with him than me. I have met him precisely four times.'

'He went to considerable trouble to have your grandfather paint the duke's portrait.'

'That was kind of him, but you shouldn't read anything into his desire to be helpful. Once he made the arrangements, he lost no time in taking himself off to town to indulge himself in whatever debauchery it is that young men of fortune and consequence indulge themselves in.'

'The duchess told me his intention is to discover the identity of the forger.'

Or to avoid my society. 'He could hardly admit his true purpose to his mama.'

'Nia! He is trying to do you a service.'

'Then I am very much obliged to him,' Nia replied so stiffly that Frankie burst out laughing, causing the duke's head to jerk in her direction.

'Now see what you have done,' Frankie scolded. 'The duke moved, probably at a vital moment, and I shall be blamed for it.'

'And so you should be.' Nia shook a finger at her friend. 'Now, what were we talking about? And I do not mean Lord Vincent. I have nothing more to say about that individual.'

'You really are determined to bury yourself away in Ireland when this is all over?'

'Absolutely.' Nia shook her head. 'Grandpapa seems rejuvenated over this project with the duke, but I am not foolish enough to believe his recovery is absolute — '

'You would discourage him from pursuing his art for fear of his being ridiculed?'

'You know me better than that. I shall encourage him to paint as much as possible; but in private. It would be better that way.'

'Your devotion to your grandfather is humbling, Nia, but what of your own aspirations? You deserve a life of your own. Do you not desire a husband's love, children?'

'I have no need of a husband, and I imbue the twins with all my motherly affections.'

'It is hardly the same thing.'

'Pots and kettles spring to mind, Lady St. John.'

'Our situations are not at all the same.'

'Excuse me if I disagree with you.'

'One good thing has come out of this commission,' Frankie said, in what was clearly a deliberate change of subject. 'You look much fresher. I assume this project is exhausting Patrick and he no longer feels the need to paint his landscapes in the middle of the night.'

'No, thankfully he has abandoned that habit; for now, at least.'

'Well, I am very glad for your sake because it means you have been getting uninterrupted sleep. Has he completed enough landscapes for his exhibition?'

'More than sufficient.'

Their conversation came to an end when Grandpapa excused the duke, who strolled across to join Nia and Frankie. Nia left them alone and went up to her grandfather, looking over his shoulder at the quite remarkable portrait rapidly taking shape.

'It is a masterpiece, Grandpapa,' she said, hugging him.

'I have not got the angle of that dog's ears quite right.'

To Nia, it looked as though the dog was alive and might actually get up and walk off the canvas. But if her grandfather had decided his ears were not right, he would not leave the Park today until he was satisfied that they were. Aware that that difficulty would keep him happily occupied for at least another hour, Nia decided to check on Sean and the boys.

'I shall be back directly, Grandpapa,' she said.

He grandfather waved absently, totally absorbed in what he was doing, and probably didn't even hear what she said. Frankie and the duke had fallen into animated conversation, leaving Nia at leisure to slip out a side door into bright sunshine and fresh, clean country air.

★　★　★

After a week in London, Vince was no nearer to learning the identity of the forger, or the whereabouts of the stolen sketches, than he had been when he left the Park. Smythe could not positively identify the cove who had sold him the forgery, and became increasingly defensive on the successive occasions when Vince questioned him on the matter. Neither of the other men who had bought supposed Traffords from the forger were known to Vince. That would not have prevented him seeking them out, but both of them lived in the north of England.

Belling, in his elegant gallery in Bond Street, couldn't add anything to what he had already told Sean Trafford. He was delighted when Vince told him that Trafford was painting Zach's portrait, but horrified to hear about the theft of the sketches of Sophia.

'I have had the privilege of seeing them,' he told Vince. 'Trafford vowed never to sell them, and now this.' He shook his head; solemn, shocked. 'How could this have happened?'

Vince had no answer to provide.

'Whoever has them will not offer them to me to resell. No respectable dealer will touch them, and so they will have to be sold on the black market. Fortunately, I have eyes and ears in all areas of the art world, and news of such valuable works becoming available is bound to leak out sooner or later.'

Vince left London, accepting that not only had his investigations been a massive waste of time, but had also not provided the diversion he was hoping for to diminish his interest in Nia Trafford. Distancing himself from her had not cooled his ardour, and he wanted her every bit as much as he had before he left Winchester.

More so.

He had spent his time in London seeking every available distraction, but she still occupied the majority of his thoughts. While he applauded her dedication to her grandfather, burying herself in the wilds of Ireland for his sake seemed extreme. It was none of his business, of course. He had no right to interfere in her affairs, no means of preventing her from sacrificing her youth in order to do what she thought was right. But that did not mean he was obliged to be happy about it.

His growing obsession with Nia was as perplexing as it was inconvenient. Lady Marshall had somehow discovered he was in London and invited him to a family dinner. Vince knew why, and accepted against his better judgement. He had on one occasion danced twice with Miss Marshall the previous season, creating much speculation about his intentions. He *had* been briefly tempted by Cecelia Marshall. She was delicately beautiful, biddable, brought up to know what to expect from matrimony — perfect wife material for a man in need of a partner who would give him as little trouble as possible. But after half an hour in Miss Marshall's undemanding company, Vince was already missing Nia Trafford's lively, irreverent attitude.

He did not intend to marry her, and even if his thoughts did turn in that direction, he doubted whether she would accept him. Her determination to dedicate herself to her grandfather's service was no ruse. It seemed he had developed a fixation upon one of the few females in England who had no desire to marry into the influential Sheridan clan. The irony of the situation was not lost on Vince.

In spite of it, his desire to be of service to her had not diminished one iota.

All these thoughts percolated through his head as he turned Forrester from the Winchester Road directly onto the Park's driveway. He had broken his journey halfway the previous day, thus ensuring his arrival home late in the morning. Vince took a turn in the path that skirted the stud and observed Leo and Art in the paddock, lunging a young stallion under their father and Amos's watchful gazes. He waved, but did not stop, anxious for clean attire before he went in search of Nia, which his return gave him a legitimate excuse to do. Zach would have told her his purpose in visiting town and she would naturally be anxious to know what progress he had made.

He was obliged to amend his plans when he noticed Nia walking briskly away from the house in the direction of the stud. She appeared preoccupied and only noticed him when she was almost upon him.

'Lord Vincent.' She blinked up at him, as though about to ask him why he was there.

Vince dismounted. 'Nia.' He smiled at her, noticing that she look fresher, more rested, than he was accustomed to seeing her. 'How are you?'

'Perfectly well, thank you. I was about to

check on the boys.'

'Your brother and mine have them under control. They are behaving themselves impeccably.'

She smiled. 'That, I find hard to believe.'

'Horses are involved,' Vince reminded her.

'Of course.' A small smile graced her lips. 'They are not bad boys; just mischievous and apt to egg one another on.'

'They are a credit to you.'

'Hardly that. Besides, they are not mine.'

He turned in the direction of the mews. 'How is the portrait progressing?'

With an almost imperceptible shrug, she fell into step with him. 'Exceedingly well,' she replied with enthusiasm. 'I shouldn't be surprised if Grandpapa decided the duke doesn't need to sit anymore. He will finish the painting in his studio.'

'Can he do that?'

'Most assuredly. Besides, I shall be relieved if he decides the time has come to retreat to Stoneleigh Manor.'

Vince flexed a brow. 'You have had enough of us already?'

She smiled. 'Forgive my anxiety, but I have no way of knowing how long Grandpapa's creative mood will last for. It could change in the blink of an eye. I can control him better when he is in familiar surroundings, and

Sophia is there to help keep him calm. He gets so frustrated sometimes, but can't make any of us understand why.'

'Selfishly, I don't wish for you to go.'

'What a strange thing to say. You ran away to London the moment Grandpapa and I came here to start work.'

'Is that what you thought? That I ran away?'

She tossed her head. 'I barely gave your absence a moment's consideration.'

He sent her a teasing smile, and said nothing.

She flipped her hair over her shoulder. 'Really, you are impossible!'

Vince did his very best to contain his smile, ridiculously pleased that she had resented his absence. 'Very likely.'

'What possible difference can it make to you if we stay or go?'

He couldn't answer her truthfully; mainly because he wasn't sure what the truth actually was. Instead, he countered with a question of his own. 'Would you like to know what discoveries I made in London?'

'Regarding the forger?' Hope flared in her eyes.

They had reached the mews. Vince handed Forrester over to the groom and turned her towards his mother's pretty rose garden a short distance away.

'Tell me, does the name 'Griffiths' mean anything to you?'

She canted her head as she considered the question. 'That is the name of the person who sold the forgery?'

'It is the name he gave Smythe, but I doubt if it's his real one.'

'I don't recall meeting anyone of that name.' Nia wrinkled her brow. 'There is something niggling in the back of my mind. Griffiths is a Welsh name. I've heard someone speaking with a Welsh accent recently, but I can't think where, or whom.'

Vince led them onto a gravel walkway between budding roses filling the air with their musky perfume. He broke off a partially opened bud and handed it to her with a flourishing bow.

'Thank you.' She raised the flower to her nose and inhaled its scent.

'I assume none of the three protégés of your grandfather's whom we suspect have any Welsh connections.'

She shrugged. 'Not as far as I recall.'

'And Drake?'

She had been concentrating her attention on the rose bushes, but at the mention of Drake's name her head jerked up and a look of alarm flitted across her expression. 'What of him?'

Vince propelled her towards a bower and

the bench in its centre. The entwined branches in full leaf above their heads provided them with shelter and privacy.

'If I am to be of service to you, you must tell me of anything out of the ordinary that occurs with any of your grandfather's causes.'

'Mr. Drake is not an artist. He is incapable of forging anything.'

'But he is acquainted with a lot of people who are. If he feels he has a grievance, it's entirely possible that he would work with someone else to exact revenge.'

'I suppose he does have reason to feel aggrieved,' she agreed after a prolonged pause. 'But that situation has only recently arisen, so he has had no time to formulate complicated forgery strategies. Besides, he doesn't possess the wits to pull such a scheme off.'

'Tell me,' he said softly.

'Mr. Drake has little talent and an inflated opinion of his own self-worth. Grandpapa is generous with his patronage, but when he was in his right mind, even he would not have given Mr. Drake house room.'

'Because he has been taken into the Trafford household, it has convinced him that he really does have talent?'

'I am sure that is exactly how he thinks. Insufferable man!'

Vince fixed her with a probing gaze. 'Are

you going to tell me what he has done to put you in such a taking?'

'It cannot possibly have any bearing on the forgeries.'

'Allow me to be the judge of that.'

She straightened her shoulders and scowled off into the distance. 'Shortly after your first visit to Stoneleigh Manor, he proposed marriage.'

Vince burst out laughing.

'I am glad you find that revelation so diverting.' She tossed her head. 'Not everyone thinks me unattractive, you know.'

'Oh, I know. Believe me, I know.' Vince made a mighty effort to control himself. 'For once I cannot fault the man's taste. I was laughing at his pretentions. He must think very well of himself to imagine he has anything to offer that would tempt you.'

'Worse than that,' Nia replied gloomily. 'He thinks too well of himself to believe my refusal is genuine. He was very angry at first.' A mischievous smile broke through her reserve. 'I hurt his pride because I'm afraid I didn't mince my words. He repeated his proposal just the other day, imagining I would have had a change of heart.'

Vince harrumphed.

'I think he realises that we're getting close to the time when as a family we will retreat to

Ireland, where he most certainly will not be invited to join us. He has no means of support that I am aware of, and is probably worried about no longer having free board and lodging.'

'Very likely.' Vince made a mental note to keep a close eye on Drake.

'But, as I say, Mr. Drake is not a forger, and I think it very unlikely that he is working with someone who is. He seldom leaves Stoneleigh Manor, so how could he collude with his accomplice?'

'Hmm; let's put Drake aside for one moment, and consider the three possible forgers who once enjoyed your Grandfather's patronage. One of them also paid you inappropriate attentions, I collect.'

'Yes.' She pulled a disgruntled face. 'Some people will stop at nothing to benefit from Grandpapa's patronage. I know a lot of marriages are arranged for reasons that have nothing to do with mutual love and respect, but I could never be persuaded into such a union. You probably think that makes Mr. Kenton the prime suspect, but honestly, we parted on the best of terms. He is a handsome man and, unlike Drake, didn't seem particularly disturbed when I refused him.'

'Or didn't allow his damaged pride to show?'

Nia shrugged. 'He proposed to benefit from Grandpapa's reputation. When that failed, he accepted my decision and went his own way.'

'Because your brother asked him to leave?'

'Because it would have been embarrassing if he stayed. It was time for him to move on, and the last I heard, he was still in Brussels, doing quite well for himself.'

'All these men wishing to marry you, Miss Trafford.' Vince smiled at her. 'Do you leave a trail of broken hearts in your wake wherever you go?

'Don't be ridiculous,' she replied with asperity. 'Neither Kenton nor Drake are in love with me. It disgusts me, the way men will go to any lengths to secure their own comforts, even pretending affection when they feel none. That is one of the things I most decidedly will not miss when we return to Ireland and live in quiet seclusion.'

She sounded as though she was trying to convince herself. He ran his arm along the back of the bench and idly twisted one of her escaped curls around his index finger.

'You deserve much better than that,' he said softly.

Still twirling the rosebud he had given her between her fingers, she looked up at him, eyes wide and wary. Their gazes clashed and held, rendering further words unnecessary.

She looked so lost and vulnerable at that moment, and more tempting than she had any right to be. Vince abandoned his attempts to rationalise his attraction towards her, along with his efforts to overcome it. Something that felt so intrinsically right couldn't possibly be wrong. He placed his forefinger beneath her chin, tilted it backwards and slowly lowered his head. He slanted his mouth over hers, covering her lips firmly and possessively with his own, his actions driven by the fundamental instinct to protect and reassure.

Nia moaned, and he thought at first she was about to twist her lips away from his. He was about to release her when her lips suddenly firmed beneath his as she twined her arms around his neck. Euphoria swept through Vince as he took control of the situation. His arms closed around her back as he coerced her lips apart and plundered her mouth with seductive strokes of his tongue. The small part of his brain still capable of rational thought told him this was probably not the most sensible course of action he had ever taken. It would complicate everything — and, in spite of Nia's intention never to marry, create expectations he had no plans to fulfil. Nia was not the type of lady a gentleman dallied with and did not then offer to marry.

But the carnal sensations streaming through his body made him blind to the voice of reason. He gave up trying to decide what was so special about Nia, and instead invested all his skill and expertise into kissing the lady whom he was unable to stop thinking about. Elemental sparks flared as he drew seductively on her lower lip, teasing her, awakening her sensual nature because he simply couldn't resist the challenge. A small gasp slipped past their fused lips as he pulled her into a tighter embrace.

Dear God, this was madness! If he did not put a stop to this now, immediately, he might actually lose control. He somehow found the strength to release her just as they heard someone calling her name. She looked dazed, confused; exactly as though she had just been comprehensively kissed. No matter how urgently her presence was required in the house, she needed a moment to compose herself. If she encountered any members of his family, or her own, in her current state of bewilderment, no one would doubt how she had been occupying her time.

'My grandfather must have need of me,' she said, looking everywhere except at him. But when she tried to stand, her knees buckled and she fell back onto the seat again.

'Give yourself a second or two,' he said.

She ignored his advice and got up again. This time her legs supported her weight. Without waiting for him, she ran towards the door to the conservatory. Vince let her go, wondering how he could have handled the situation so ineptly; wondering why he had given vent to his baser instincts and frightened her off.

He walked slowly in her wake, conceding that everything he did in Nia's company defied rationality.

16

'There's a right to-do in the house,' Annie said breathlessly.

'Tell me about it.'

The forger fended off her efforts to plaster her body against his. They were in a quiet alleyway behind The Ploughman in Compton, where they were unlikely to be seen or disturbed. Even so, Annie was responsible for making purchases daily from the market stalls for the residents of Stoneleigh Manor. Everyone knew who she was, and it was only a matter of time before they also discovered the identity of the mystery tenant who employed her. Speculation was already rife. Such was the nature of villagers everywhere.

'The master has produced an amazing portrait of the duke, by all accounts. I haven't seen it yet, but he had it brought back to the manor yesterday so he can finish it in his own studio.'

The forger nodded, showing no emotion, even though he was boiling with rage. Of all the damnable luck! Initially he had panicked when he heard Trafford had accepted the commission, but had subsequently convinced himself that he no longer had the wits to pull it off. It seemed he had miscalculated, but the forger owed his success, to say nothing of his rapidly increasing nest egg, to his ability to adjust his plans according to circumstances. If he could not outwit an old man with an addled brain, and an arrogant slip of a girl, then he deserved to fail.

And the forger never failed.

His mind whirled as Annie prattled on, tugging on his lapels as she stood on her toes and endeavoured to kiss him.

'We have a difficulty,' Annie said. 'I heard Miss Trafford and Miss Ash talking this morning. Lord Vincent has been to London, asking questions of Smythe about the painting you sold to him.'

'What did he learn?'

The forger seethed. Damn Sheridan for involving himself in something that was nothing to do with him! Not that there was anything for him to discover. The forger had covered his tracks well. Part of him could understand Sheridan's desire to win favour with Miss Trafford. She wasn't a raving beauty, but there was an indefinable something about her that caught a man's fancy. Sheridan clearly saw it too.

'He knows the name you used and that you spoke with a Welsh accent, but apart from that, I'm not precisely sure. Hannah distracted me, and I can't make it obvious that I am eavesdropping. But I did hear Miss Trafford say that there would be an unveiling of the portrait at Winchester Park, along with Mr. Trafford's landscapes, for a select audience. You and some of Mr. Trafford's other protégés are to be invited, but so is Smythe.'

The forger jerked upright, dislodging Annie's hands from his lapels. 'Perdition!' he muttered.

'Lord Vincent is bound to ask him if he recognises the man who sold him his painting, and he very likely will, in spite of the fact that you disguised yourself in your dealings with him.' Annie's round face was pinched with worry. 'We can't let that happen. We shall have to leave these shores now. We have enough to live on, surely?'

The forger certainly had enough, but he had no intention of sharing it with Annie. He had no interest in her other than for her usefulness to him as his inside source in Trafford's household. The forger prided himself on his guile, aware that the Traffords thought they were fortunate to have secured the services of two such obliging maids as Annie and her friend Beth. They now knew about the forgeries, but suspicion would not fall upon their maids.

The forger had left the Trafford household in Belgium just as Annie and Beth found themselves out of work. He managed to have word of their plight leaked to Nia Trafford, assuring himself of Annie's abiding loyalty before he did so. She had not let him down; and, for once, she was right. The sensible thing to do would be to withdraw, but the forger lived for the excitement he got from outwitting his supposed betters.

He would not be withdrawing.

'Have the duke and his family seen the portrait yet?'

'No, it's not finished, and Mr. Trafford forbids anyone except Miss Trafford to see his work until he is completely satisfied with it.'

Indeed, the forger did know, and that fact could work to his advantage. No one, probably not even Nia Trafford, could be sure her grandfather would complete this commission without becoming frustrated and damaging the canvas. Unbeknownst to Trafford, he was about to do the same thing again. Or, at least, that was what would be assumed. Nia never left her grandfather alone when he was working, so a distraction would be necessary.

'I need you to provide me with a small service,' the forger said, flashing his most engaging smile.

★   ★   ★

Nia was considerably relieved when her grandfather decided the portrait would be completed
in the privacy of his studio at Stoneleigh
Manor. Their daily visits to the Park would no
longer be necessary, which suited Nia perfectly. The less contact she had with Lord
Vincent, the happier she would be.

Sophia kept asking her if something was
wrong. There was a feeling of great optimism
at Stoneleigh Manor because, although Sophia
was the only person other than Nia to have seen
the portrait so far, it was generally known
that Grandpapa had produced something
remarkable. And yet Nia was preoccupied
and uncharacteristically short-tempered. The
headache that her irascible mood had engen-
dered worsened when she glanced out of the
window and saw the twins dancing around
Lord Vincent and Forrester. She groaned. What
the devil was he doing here?

Sophia joined her at the window, noticed
Lord Vincent, and sent Nia a quizzical look. 'I
wonder what brings Lord Vincent calling,' she
said, with a mischievous grin.

'I'm sure I have no idea, nor do I have the
time to deal with him. I shall stay here with
Grandpapa. You go and see what he wants.'

'If you like, but I very much doubt if it is

me he has come to see.'

'Please, Sophia.'

Sophia's playfulness gave way to an expression of concern. 'What is it, Nia? Has he done something to offend you?'

'No, I'm just tired, that's all.'

Part of Nia wanted to run to Lord Vincent, throw herself into his arms, and let him assume all her responsibilities. The constant struggle of day-to-day living, of protecting her grandfather's reputation and keeping the household running on a shoestring, took its toll. In her current vulnerable state, she could not trust herself to go anywhere near the man whose face haunted her dreams. His commanding authority and annoyingly compelling charm robbed her of common sense and made her forget who she was supposed to be.

Sophia placed a reassuring hand on Nia's shoulder, and then took herself off to confront Lord Vincent.

The incident left Nia short-tempered with everyone in the house; especially Mr. Drake, whom she tripped over everywhere she turned.

'Luncheon is almost ready,' Hannah said, finding Nia on the terrace industriously weeding a flower border. 'Have you seen the twins?'

'Not recently,' Nia replied. 'I thought they were upstairs with Sean taking lessons.'

'No, lamb, Sean went into Compton a while back. You were busy avoiding Lord Vincent, so you would not have noticed.'

'I was *not* avoiding him!'

Hannah chuckled. 'I expect the boys are in the woods somewhere with that dog.'

Nia sighed. 'I hope they're not trying to clear the pond of weeds again.'

Nia plunged into the overgrown orchard, which was the quickest route to the pond, trying not to think about the occasion when she had sat there with Lord Vincent. She called alternately to the boys and then the dog. One or the other would answer her, sooner or later. When that didn't happen she returned to the house, supposing them to have entered it from a difference direction. She was not unduly worried. The boys were always disappearing, finding ever more ingenious ways to avoid their lessons.

Everyone was congregated in the dining room, awaiting Nia's return, including Sean.

'Are they not here?' Nia asked anxiously.

'Odd,' Sean replied. 'Their stomachs usually guide them back to the house at mealtimes.'

'We should start without them,' Mr. Drake said. 'The food will get cold.'

Nia sent him a scathing look as niggling worries wormed their way into her brain.

'Anything might have happened to them. You may stay here and eat if you wish to, Mr. Drake. The rest of us will conduct a methodical search.'

'Naturally, I will help to search,' Mr. Drake replied. 'Please don't imagine . . . '

Nia ignored him and exchanged a glance with Sean. She could see her brother was becoming as worried as she was.

'Sophia, take something up to Grandpapa for his luncheon and remain with him. I don't want him worried about this business. I dare say the boys *will* appear at any moment.' Nia wished rather than believed it would be so. She had a bad feeling about the entire episode.

'I will take his luncheon up,' Sophia replied. 'But he is very much on form today. I am sure it will be safe to leave him alone for a while, at least until we have found the boys.'

'Very well, if you're absolutely sure. The more of us there are to search, the quicker they will be found.'

Hannah hovered in the doorway with Annie and Beth while Sean efficiently allocated each person with a specific area of the grounds to search. She noticed that he took responsibility for the pond himself, presumably thinking that one or both of them had come to grief in it. Nia didn't think so.

She had already looked for them there — but, admittedly, had not thought to search in the murky water itself. She shuddered, riddled with guilt for not having been more thorough, and at the same time adjuring herself to remain calm. If they *had* tumbled into the pond, then Ruff would have come back alone, and would have led them straight back to his masters.

That thought only added to Nia's worries as she commenced a careful search of the outer reaches of the wooded area, constantly calling the boys' names. The only explanation she could come up with was that the boys had disobeyed Sean's adamant instructions and left the grounds. After all, they had done it once before, when Lord Vincent had come upon them. She knew from Sophia's account of Lord Vincent's earlier visit that the boys had been badgering him about the stud at the Park, desperate to pay it another visit.

But that was more than three miles away. Surely they would not have . . .

Satisfied that neither boys nor dog were in her area of woodland, Nia returned to the house, now really anxious. She prayed someone else had had better luck, unsure as to whether she would hug the boys when they were finally found, or strangle them for giving her such a fright. They really were the limit, and had aged her ten years. A good school was a priority, she decided. Boredom and lack of structure in their lives were causing them to run increasingly wild. Another reason for her to feel guilty.

The ground floor was deserted. Nia was obviously the first searcher to return, which at least meant the others had not given up hope. She was about to go and check on her grandfather when Sean returned, his expression grim. He was clutching the jars and nets the boys must have taken to the pond with them. She had not noticed them during her earlier, cursory search of the area.

'Dear God!' Nia covered her face with her hands and fell into a chair.

'They have definitely not fallen into the pond. I checked very carefully.'

'Thank goodness for that, at least.'

'Perhaps Ruff went off after rabbits or something, and they chased after him. It wouldn't be the first time.'

Nia shook her head. 'If they were still in the grounds, they would have heard us calling for them. The land is not that extensive.'

'Do you think they might have taken it into their heads to go to Winchester Park?'

'That thought had occurred to me,' Nia replied. 'But it's a long distance to cover on foot.'

Sean managed a mirthless smile. 'Not

when you are eight years old, with energy to burn and an obsession for horses. Besides, I think there is a short cut through the woods.'

'And if there is, they would have found it.'

'Precisely.'

'Will you ride over there and check?'

'Yes, I think I should. You stay here and see if anyone finds them, Nia. I am still optimistic that they will, but I think it better if I don't wait to find out. I would rather have a wasted journey than waste precious time.' Sean shook his head, his face taut with concern. 'If they have had an accident, fallen somewhere, time could be of the essence.'

'Calm yourself,' Nia replied, hugging her brother. 'What are the chances of both boys *and* the dog having an accident? One of them at least ought to be able to raise the alarm.'

Nia groaned when she saw the look on Sean's face, and realised she had only made matters worse. 'Don't despair, my dear,' she said hastily. 'I'm sure there is a rational explanation. I dare say they have wandered too far and lost track of time; nothing more sinister than that.'

Sean gave her a look that told her he didn't believe a word of it. 'Yes, I expect that's all it is,' he said, touching her shoulder.

Nia bit her lip to stop herself from crying. 'Go through Compton first. They might have taken it upon themselves to have another confrontation with the local boys.'

Sean's smile didn't reach his eyes. 'This time I will definitely make good on my numerous threats and thrash them for their disobedience.'

Nia managed a brief smile. 'Of course you will.'

She waved Sean away, took a moment to compose herself, and then slipped up the stairs to check on her grandfather.

'Grandpapa, I am so sorry to have left you alone,' Nia said brightly as she entered his studio. 'Is there anything you . . . Oh, my goodness!'

He was in his chair looking disorientated, blinking vacantly, and a bruise was forming on the side of his head.

'What happened, Grandpapa?' She crouched beside him and took his hand. 'Did you have a fall?'

He opened his mouth to speak, but no words came out. A movement in the periphery of her vision caused Nia to glance up. She hadn't realised someone else was in his studio, which was adjacent to his sitting room. Annie stared at Nia through widened eyes as she stood over Grandpapa's portrait of the duke with a dagger raised above her shoulder, on the point of plunging it into the canvas.

The forger approached Stoneleigh Manor's grounds from the edge of the woodland that skirted the Winchester Road, and made his way through a track in the woods. Annie's directions had been spot on. Hiding the curricle in which he planned to make his getaway was more difficult. He eventually found a place on the other side of the track that didn't form a part of the Manor's grounds. It was further away than he would have liked, but that couldn't be helped. The important factor was that, although the area where he planned to take the boys would be searched eventually, no one would think to do so until he was long gone.

Annie had assured him the boys would make their way to the pond the moment they were released from their lessons, and that was where the forger had concealed himself. He was infuriated when he heard voices coming from the terrace and realised one of them belonged to Lord Vincent. What business did he have here? He crept closer, concealed himself behind a stout tree, and watched, cursing the interfering cove for taking such an avid interest in Miss Trafford's affairs.

The boys were jumping all over him, begging to be allowed to visit the stud at Winchester Park. The forger seethed. If that request was granted, then the forger's plans would have to be put back a day. With every day that passed, Trafford progressed with the duke's portrait, making its destruction that much harder to orchestrate. Even so, he had no option other than to wait and hope. Passivity did not sit well with the forger, but eventually Sheridan took his leave, and the boys dragged themselves into the house with obvious reluctance, presumably for their lessons.

An hour later they came bounding down the path towards the pond, nets and jars in their hands. That damned dog of theirs was dancing around their feet, barking with excitement. The forger had forgotten about the beast, but wouldn't permit it to interfere with his plans. He pulled his hat low and a muffler high enough to cover his nose and mouth, leaving only his eyes visible. The boys knew him, but wouldn't be able to recognise him if they managed to get a look at him before he incapacitated them. He waited until both boys were leaning over the pond, flat on their bellies, bickering about the best way to catch tadpoles.

'You get the net ready, Art. I've got the jar.'

'No, I'll do the net. I'm better at it.'

'All right then, but hurry. You're frightening them.'

'You can't frighten tadpoles . . . '

No, the forger thought, smirking, but small boys were altogether a different matter.

He would never get a better opportunity. The boys were totally focused on the tadpoles and the dog had disappeared into the trees. He crept forward and pounced, placing a hand on the back of each of their necks and holding their heads beneath the water before they could react to his presence. This was the delicate part. He didn't wish to kill them; merely to render them unconscious so he could gag and blindfold them and get them away from Stoneleigh Manor.

The ultimate diversion.

He was obliged to let them up sooner than he had planned when something sharp sent a shooting pain through his backside. Damnation, the blasted dog had returned and bitten his buttock! The boys spluttered as their heads broke the surface of the rank water, weed and pond debris adhering to their hair and clothing. Before they could recover or catch a glimpse of him, the forger knocked their heads together with enough force to render them insensible. Then, kicking at the dog until he connected with its ribs and made it yelp, forcing it to crawl away from him, he blindfolded and gagged the twins.

Then he threw one boy over each shoulder and traipsed back to his hiding place.

17

Vince resisted the urge to call at Stoneleigh Manor again. He had no legitimate reason to do so, other than an overwhelming desire to see Nia. But, by failing to receive him in person that morning, she had made it perfectly clear that her feelings did not mirror his own. He had stretched out his visit to the point of rudeness, hoping she would appear.

She did not.

Facts needed to be faced. Nia was deliberately avoiding him.

Vince struggled to understand why she felt the need to distance herself from him. Surely she understood his only desire was to be of service to her? Well, that was not precisely true. From Vince's perspective, Nia Trafford's name and 'desire' were words better not used in the same sentence. His behaviour had probably been inappropriate and he had frightened her off.

No *probably* about it, he decided, grimacing. Whenever they were together, her strong sense of duty warred with unconventional appetites she had been unaware she possessed — until Vince taught her otherwise, probably causing instinct to overcome her strong sense of duty. That was a situation which would make her conflicted, giving her a legitimate reason to avoid him.

Was it her own reactions she mistrusted if she found herself alone with him again, or did she imagine he could not be relied upon to behave himself? She had good reason to think that way, Vince conceded, but Nia was entirely to blame for his misconduct. He seemed to forget the rules whenever he was in her company and was overtaken by a capricious need to explore her sensuality. That her mere presence could make him lose sight of his gentlemanly instincts, that came as naturally to him as breathing, was as troubling as it was inexplicable.

But matters got worse. When he was not in Nia's company, he spent an increasing amount of time thinking about her, desperate to help her family out of a situation that was fraught with more dangers than they could possibly realise. The forger would not be easily deterred. He had found a lucrative means by which to line his own pockets, and nothing would stand in the way of his ambitions. Nia and her family were in a vulnerable position — a position that was already being assaulted from two sides simultaneously, if the forger and the theft of the sketches were not connected, which he thought they most likely were not. Vince fully intended to protect the Traffords, regardless of the fact that they had not asked for his intervention.

He saddled Forrester himself, and set off from the Park at a brisk canter, with no particular destination in mind. He needed to clear his head and somehow rationalise his behaviour. After a flat-out gallop across the common, he slowed Forrester as he got closer to home again, wondering how the devil he was supposed to put right his friendship with Nia when she was purposely avoiding him.

Vince shook his head as realisation dawned. He wanted Nia because she didn't appear to have any particular interest in him. Nia's apparent disinterest was as refreshing as it was challenging. That's what all this was, Vince decided. A delightful challenge coupled with an overwhelming urge to be of service to a lady in distress.

Returning to the Park after an exhilarating ride, Vince handed Forrester over to a groom and wandered towards the stud. One subject he was absolutely clear upon: he did not want Nia to go off and live in Ireland. The thought of not seeing her again caused him acute physical pain, but was he prepared to compound his bad behaviour by putting his own interests ahead of hers? Besides, under what possible circumstances could he ask her not to go?

There was one obvious answer to that question: an answer he was not yet ready to consider. Or was he? One of the most decisive people he knew, for once, Vince did not know his own mind. Nia Trafford had a lot to answer for.

'Are you lost?'

Vince looked up at the sound of Amos's voice, and grinned sheepishly. He had been wandering about with no clear sense of purpose, giving Amos good reason to sound amused.

'Just taking the air.'

'Which is why you and Forrester came thundering in here like you were being chased by the hounds from hell.'

'How are the youngsters coming along?' Vince asked, referring to the yearlings Amos had started lunging.

Amos clapped Vince's shoulder. 'Come and see for yourself.'

The brothers spent a pleasant half-hour looking at the yearlings and discussing their progress. They were interrupted by the sound of hooves pounding up the gravel driveway.

'Hello,' Amos said, looking up. 'Someone is in an even greater hurry than you were.'

Vince scowled, an unsettling premonition gripping him when the horseman got closer and proved to be Nia's brother. 'What the devil?' he muttered.

Trafford jumped from his horse's back before he had even brought it to a halt. 'Lord Vincent, Lord Amos, are my sons here?' he asked breathlessly.

Vince and Amos shared a bewildered glance.

'No,' Vince said, anxiety taking a tighter grip. 'I assume they have gone missing again, or you would not be asking the question.' Trafford nodded. 'Have you checked Compton?'

'I rode through the village before coming here. No one has seen them.'

'What happened?' Vince asked.

'We did an hour's lessons this morning, then they went off tadpoling. When they didn't appear for luncheon, we instigated a search.' Trafford shook his head. 'When I left Stoneleigh Manor, they had not been found, although people are still scouring the grounds and that situation might have changed.' He swallowed several times. 'I found their tadpoling equipment abandoned beside the pond, but no sign of them.'

'And you hoped they might be here,' Amos suggested.

'I heard them begging to come back to the

stud when you called, Lord Vincent. Nia and I thought they might have found a way to sneak through the trees.'

'There is a track that leads through the woods to this estate,' Vince said pensively. 'But I doubt whether the boys know of its existence.'

'We made use of it as boys ourselves when we wanted to leave the place undetected,' Amos added. 'It is a short cut into Compton. But I doubt anyone has set foot on it for years now. It's probably totally overgrown, but I will get someone to check anyway.'

'If it's there, my boys will have found it,' Trafford replied adamantly. 'They excel at mischief.'

'I'll come and help you to search,' Vince said without hesitation.

'I will arrange for that track to be looked at, and tell Zach what has happened,' Amos added, striding towards the house. 'I'll get him to arrange for a party of his men to help scour the woods.'

'Thank you,' Trafford said tersely. 'I am very much obliged to you.'

Vince ran to reclaim Forrester, his mind occupied with just how distraught Nia would be.

* * *

'Annie, what the devil do you think you are doing?'

Annie started violently at the sound of her voice, and the dagger fell from her hand, clattering harmlessly onto the wooden boards of the studio floor. Her eyes were round with a combination of vindictiveness and fear. Nia realised then that she had never entirely trusted Annie — according to Hannah, she was slow and lazy — but she had never once doubted her loyalty.

'I . . . I just got back from searching and came up to check on Mr. Trafford. He . . . he had this dagger. I took it from him.'

Nia didn't believe a word of it. Her grandfather *had* damaged some of his works with a dagger in the past, but that only happened when the balance of his mind was disturbed. That had most decidedly not been the case for the course of this project, and she didn't believe such a change could have taken place during the short time Grandpapa had been left alone.

'Nia . . . I don't feel — '

'What is it, Grandpapa?'

Nia looked away from Annie and concentrated her entire attention upon her grandfather. He was clutching his head, and now that she looked more closely, Nia could see the imprint of a hand on his cheek. She glowered accusingly at Annie, anger surging through her in unstoppable waves.

'You struck him,' she spat. 'You did this to him. Why, for the love of God?'

Her grandfather groaned again, dazed and disorientated. Nia returned her attention to him and clutched his hand. Annie took advantage of Nia's distraction and fled from the room, sobbing. Nia was unsure what their maid would do, and didn't feel comfortable letting her go. But she was powerless to stop her. If it was a choice between comforting her grandfather and detaining Annie, who was obviously responsible in some way for harming her family, there was no question where her priorities lay. Without money or a means of transportation Annie would not get far, and Nia would deal with her later.

She helped her grandfather to sit up and fetched him some water to sip.

'Whatever's wrong with Annie? She just went running off as though . . . ' Sophia's words stalled as she burst through the door and saw the state of Nia's grandfather. 'Oh my goodness, Patrick!'

Sophia crouched beside Nia, her eyes filling with tears when she observed her grandfather's confused state.

'What happened?' she asked.

'I caught Annie trying to damage the portrait, although she pretended she had taken a dagger from Grandpapa to stop him from doing so. I don't believe her.'

'Annie?' Sophia looked as perplexed as Nia felt. 'Why? Did she harm Patrick?'

'She must have.'

Sophia looked furious. 'Just wait until I get my hands on the little hussy.'

'Where is she now?'

'She took off through the trees.'

'In which direction?' Annie must know something about the boys' disappearance. Now that Sophia was here, she could leave her grandfather and go after her.

'That way.' Sophia pointed to the track that would take her to through the orchard.

'Stay with Grandpapa.'

'Don't go alone,' Sophia urged. 'She sounds unbalanced. It could be dangerous.'

'I must go. There is no one else.'

The ladies clutched hands. 'Take Sean.'

'He has gone to the Park.'

'Mr. Drake?'

Nia made a scoffing sound as she bent to pick up the dagger Annie had dropped and slipped it into her pocket. 'He's still out searching, and would be next to useless in a crisis anyway. I have to go on ahead. Any delay, and . . . ' Nia gulped. 'The boys. I can't risk waiting. Send Sean after me as soon as he gets back.'

Sophia clutched her arm. 'Take care. I couldn't bear it if you were harmed.'

'I must go. There's not a moment to lose.' Nia struggled to contain her erratic breathing, her turbulent emotions and overactive imagination as increasingly desperate explanations for the boys' disappearance cascaded through her mind. 'I couldn't live with myself if something happens to the twins because I didn't act in time to prevent it.'

The two women briefly hugged. 'Godspeed.'

Nia flew down the stairs and out of the main door, plunging headlong onto the track through the trees that Sophia had indicated. It led directly past the pond where the boys had been innocently tadpoling a short time ago. She had never walked beyond this point, and had no clear idea where the path actually led.

They had been foolish not to consider that Annie — or, God help them, Beth too, for all Nia knew — might be involved with the forger. They had thought themselves fortunate when Annie and Beth's services unexpectedly became available when they were in urgent need of domestic help. In hindsight, perhaps it had been a little too convenient. Lady Arabella's careless abandonment of them had seemed iniquitous, and their distress would have persuaded Nia to engage them even if she had not needed them. It was obvious to her now that the forger must have somehow directed them towards the Trafford household because he needed a spy within it. Nia had not been aware of the forgeries at the time, so could be forgiven for not making the connection.

She ploughed on along the path, branches snapping at her face, brambles tearing at her clothing and hands. It had not rained for some time and the path was dry, making it impossible to judge if it had been recently used, unless she examined the crushed apple blossom littering it more closely. Nia couldn't waste the time and continued resolutely on, wondering where it would bring her out. She tried not to think how frightened the boys must be, no longer deluding herself. Some-one connected to Annie and the forger had taken them.

Why?

A flash of something immediately in front of her — some movement — caused her to slow her pace and conceal herself behind a tree. Ye gods, it was Annie, sitting on the ground, holding something in her hands — a letter, perhaps? She was reading it, speaking the words in a whisper as she struggled to decipher them, and simultaneously sobbing her heart out. A combination of anger and curiosity robbed Nia of all caution. She approached Annie and stood above her, arms akimbo.

'You have some explaining to do,' she said severely.

★ ★ ★

When Vince and Trafford arrived back at Stoneleigh Manor, optimistic hopes that the boys might have been found up to their necks in mischief were immediately dashed. Before they could decide what to do next, Sophia came downstairs to tell them the most astonishing story.

'I knew nothing about this,' Beth sobbed when news of Annie's involvement emerged. 'I knew she had a sweetheart, but she never told me his name. She said it was a secret, but that very soon he would be rich and they would be going away together. I never knew she meant Mr. Trafford any harm. If I had, I would have said; honest I would.'

Vince looked to Sophia and Hannah, wondering if Beth was to be believed. Sophia merely shrugged. Hannah looked severe.

'That was who I saw in Compton the other day,' Vince said. 'It was Annie, concealed in a passageway with a man, acting furtively. I stopped to observe them, and saw her give him some papers. It has been bothering me. I

282

knew there was something not quite right about the encounter. I also knew I had seen the girl somewhere before, but didn't make the connection to your servant, Trafford.'

'She must have been meeting with the forger,' Sean replied. 'He has been here on our doorstep all this time, and we were blissfully unaware.'

'I doubt if he is based here,' Vince said. 'You must know him, and would be bound to run into him in such a small village.'

'Damn it, Annie must have stolen the sketches!' Sean thumped the table with his clenched fist. 'That's what she would have been giving him.'

'There is no time for this now.' There was an urgent edge to Vince's voice. 'We must concentrate on finding your sons.'

Vince seethed as he thought of the manner in which the forger had actually cultivated a member of Trafford's household to do his spying for him. And now Nia had gone charging off, alone, to try and rescue her nephews, putting their welfare ahead of the danger. Vince didn't doubt now that the forger had taken the twins as a distraction so Annie could damage the portrait. Determination coursed through him. If anything happened to the boys or Nia, Vince would discover the identity of the forger and track him down if it was the last thing he ever did.

Only now that Nia had impulsively put herself in danger did Vince realise the answer to his earlier conundrum. His actions with her were so out of character because he was in love with her. The realisation was as startling as it was obvious. All of his brothers had sought to avoid emotional entanglements; but when Amos met Crista, he claimed to know almost immediately that true, abiding love was to be embraced and celebrated, not feared. Vince had not believed him at the time.

Now he understood completely.

'The track Annie took comes out onto a spur that leads to the Winchester Road,' Vince told Trafford. 'It's the opposite end to the one that my brothers and I used when we were boys.'

'So if someone has taken my two, they will most likely finish up somewhere on the outer reaches of the Winchester Park estate.'

'Very likely. Go back to the Park, Trafford, and tell my brothers what we have discovered. The forger is probably still in the district. He will want to be sure that Annie ruined the duke's portrait before he . . . '

'Before he what?' Trafford asked tersely.

Vince shook his head, unable to lie to Nia's brother. 'I honestly can't hazard a guess because I don't know the man's character or what he is capable of. We must act at once. You ensure their escape route is cut off at that end, I shall do the same thing here.'

'Cannot someone else go to the Park? I ought to stay here and lend you support.'

Vince flexed his jaw before setting it in a rigid line of determination. 'Go!' he said.

Trafford went.

★ ★ ★

'What do you have there?' Nia asked Annie is a castigating tone.

Annie looked up, her eyes red and swollen from crying, her face a blotchy picture of misery.

'He lied to me,' she said bleakly, the earlier belligerence Nia had perceived in her stance replaced by raw misery. 'He told me he loved me, that we would be together for always, if only I would help him to . . . '

Fresh tears rendered the rest of Annie's words unintelligible.

'Who did, Annie? Who have you been helping?'

She held up the letter she had been reading. 'It must have fallen from his coat pocket when he . . . he took the boys. I wasn't supposed to see this.'

Anger radiated through Nia. Her precious nephews were in danger, and all Annie could think about was her broken heart. But she needed Annie's co-operation to find them, and in order to obtain her assistance she first needed to understand who had motivated her. She took the letter from the girl's shaking fingers and quickly perused it, drawing in a sharp breath when she saw to whom it was addressed. And who had written it.

'Kenton!'

The man whose proposal she had rejected. She shook her head, thinking that it made no sense. She was absolutely convinced that his feelings for her were entirely imaginary and that he bore her no ill-will for rejecting him. Nia returned her attention to the letter, anxious to see if it lent any clues. When she realised it had been written by Lady Fairstock, Annie's former employer, the pieces fell into place. The forgeries, and Annie being placed in their household, were aspects of a carefully orchestrated plan, presumably put into place because Nia had not accepted Kenton. If she had done so, of course, it would have been so much easier for him to exploit Grandpapa's reputation.

Swiping away tears of anger, Nia's brain was slow to realise she was reading a love letter, full of plans for Lady Fairstock's future with Kenton. Nia quietly seethed. The lady in question wielded considerable influence in society's circles, and could help to secure Kenton's reputation. Was Kenton exploiting her in the same fashion as he had exploited Annie's trusting nature? In the same manner he had tried to exploit Nia?

'He was just using me.' Annie sniffed. 'They both were. It's as clear as day, and I was fool enough to believe every word he said to me.'

A thousand questions rattling around inside Nia's head, but explanations would have to wait. The boys were her most immediate concern.

'Kenton took the boys so you would have the house to yourself and could damage the duke's portrait?'

Annie nodded, hugging her torso, looking pathetic and miserable. Nia felt no sympathy for her, wondering instead how far Kenton would be prepared to go to protect his illegal activities.

'Where has he taken them, Annie? What does he plan to do with the boys?'

'He won't hurt them. I wouldn't have countenanced that.' Nia suppressed the urge to question this sudden fit of conscience. The time for recriminations would be after the boys had been rescued. 'He just wanted to hide them until . . . until I could . . . ' She sniffed again, wiping her nose on the back of her hand. 'He blindfolded them so they wouldn't be able to recognise him, but . . . ' More sniffing. 'I saw this at first, not the letter.' Nia's heart lurched when Annie held up a knotted handkerchief. 'I think one of them must have managed to shake it off, and somehow found that letter in his pocket.'

'And dropped it for us to find.' Nia nodded, well able to imagine her nephews doing just such a thing. They might be terrified half out of their wits, but still had the presence of mind to try and leave clues for their rescuers to follow. 'Where are they, Annie? You can make amends by helping me to get them back.'

Annie stopped crying and set her chin pugnaciously. 'I was to meet him on the other side of this track, on the edge of Sheridan land. There is an old barn, and I was to go there and let him know the portrait had been destroyed. I wanted us to go off together at once, before I could be held to account for what I had done. I knew it would only be a matter of time before suspicion fell upon me, and I thought he cared enough to take me to safety.' She glowered at the branches above her head. 'Anyway, he said we had to wait a little longer. He had one more commission to complete first, so I agreed. And all the time he was just stringing me along. I have been a blind fool. Can you ever forgive me, ma'am?'

'You are not the first to be taken in by a smooth-talking rogue.' Nia offered Annie her hand and pulled her to her feet, feeling little compassion for her. The brutal manner in which she had treated her grandfather could not go unpunished, nor could the fact that she had aided in the abduction of eight-year-old boys. But her misdeeds would have to be addressed at a more convenient juncture. 'Come, let's go and confront him.'

'Let me go alone. If he sees you, there is no telling what he might do to the boys.'

Nia thought quickly. 'I will stay just behind you. If one of the boys has dislodged his blindfold and seen Kenton, then Kenton can't allow them to live.' Nia's heart quailed. 'Is he capable of killing innocent children to save his own hide?'

'If you had asked me that question yesterday, I would have denied it absolutely.' Annie's expression hardened. 'Now . . . I don't know what to think.'

'It's too risky for you to confront him. You have outlived your usefulness and he might try to do away with you, especially if he realises you know his true intentions. I shall stay here and keep watch. You run back to the house and fetch help. My brother should be back from the Park by now.'

Annie opened her mouth to protest; but before any sound could emerge, other than a surprised gasp, her knees buckled and she crumpled slowly to the ground. Kenton stood behind her, holding the pistol with which he had just struck Annie on the head. He waved it now in Nia's direction.

'Miss Trafford,' he said politely, sweeping an elegant bow. 'How pleasant to see you again.'

18

'What have you done with my nephews?'

'They are asking for you. Please come this way, and you will soon be reunited.'

'Why did you strike Annie?' Nia demanded hotly.

He answered her question with one of his own. 'How do you think I knew of your arrival? I was looking out for Annie, and heard your voices before I even saw you.' He shook his head. 'It's impossible to buy loyalty in this day and age.'

Nia refrained from comment.

Still holding the pistol in a disconcertingly steady hand and keeping it trained upon Nia, Kenton used his free hand to drag Annie to her feet and pull her along. Annie, who had regained her senses, stumbled awkwardly, a string of unladylike curses spilling from her lips as she fought Kenton like a wildcat.

'You deceived me!' she spat at him.

Kenton sent a contemptuous glance her way as he ushered the two of them into a dilapidated barn. 'After you, ladies,' he said with the utmost politeness.

Nia walked through the door with her head

held high, fraught with worry for the twins' welfare, anxious to see them for herself. Leo and Art were sitting back-to-back on the cold floor, their small torsos bound together with a length of rope; their mouths gagged, faces filthy, clothing torn and dishevelled.

'If you have harmed them, it will be the worse for you,' Nia said in a glacial tone as she crouched beside them, tousling their hair while she checked them for signs of injury. 'Are you all right, boys?' she asked.

They nodded in unison, eyes bulging with a combination of fright and, presumably, indignation.

'They wouldn't stop talking. I had no choice but to gag them.'

'Oh, so it's *their* fault for objecting to being abducted.' Nia sent Kenton a scorching look and the boys a reassuring smile. 'We shall soon have you home again,' she told them.

'I hesitate to disagree with you, Miss Trafford, but that is no longer possible.'

'You have created a diversion, Annie has destroyed Grandpapa's finest work, and you are free to do whatever it is you planned to do.' Nia tossed her head as she told the lie, striving for an aloof demeanour that would disguise her fear. Kenton was deranged: the manic light in his eye gave him away. But surely even he must realise he couldn't kill them all and hope to get away with it. 'You can take yourself off. By the time we get back to the house, you will be long gone.'

'If these tiresome brats had not dislodged their blindfolds, that is what I would have done.' Kenton shrugged. 'As it is . . . well, you only have yourselves to blame.'

'I recall now that one of your most irritating traits is a propensity to blame others for your own shortcomings,' Nia replied disdainfully. 'Did you really imagine I would fall for your quite disgusting self-centred charm and agree to marry you?'

'It would have been convenient if you had. I confess, I didn't expect you to decline. In fact, I thought you would be delighted to receive my proposal; a mousy little thing like you.' He screwed up his nose as he rudely ran his glance down the length of her body. 'Although, in the interests of fairness, those expressive eyes of yours prevent you from being absolutely plain, and your body hints at certain delights that might cause a man to overlook other defects of nature.'

'How very reassuring.'

'Your refusal to see reason required me to rethink my plans.'

'You thought that if we were married, there would be nothing to stop you from passing off your own inferior paintings as Grand-papa's work?'

'Inferior?' He arched a brow. 'Hardly that. The ones that I have sold so far have fooled many so-called experts.'

'Many, but not all. I am sorry to have put you in the position of having to deceive them by declining your proposal.' Nia imbued her words with a wealth of sarcasm. He was unbalanced and it was probably unwise to antagonise him but Nia was too angry to play the shrinking violet. 'How fortunate that Sir Edward happened to pass away when he did, leaving a very vulnerable widow at your mercy.'

He smirked. 'Quite so.'

From his manner, it was evident that Nia was missing something. She was filled with horror when the truth dawned. 'Just a moment,' she said slowly, her eyes flaring with anxiety. 'Sir Edward didn't die in an accident, did he?'

'How very clever of you.' Kenton smirked, keen to boast about his achievements. 'Arabella was more than happy to warm my bed, but if I needed her to introduce me to good society, she had to be more than a willing mistress. So . . .' He spread his hands and smiled. 'Needs must. Sir Edward is no great loss. In fact, Arabella is heartily glad to see the back of him.'

'You used me,' Annie said sullenly.

'Oh, come now, Annie.' He chucked her under the chin, keeping a rock-solid grip on his pistol as he did so. 'You are a sweet, obliging girl, but did you really imagine society would accept me with a parlourmaid as my paramour?'

Annie screamed and launched herself at Kenton, attempting to gouge his eyes. He clearly anticipated the attack and struck her face hard before she got close enough to inflict any damage. She crumpled to the ground and didn't move.

'How gentlemanly of you,' Nia said, sending Kenton a withering glare as she crouched beside the fallen girl to ensure she was still breathing.

Annie slowly regained her senses and Nia helped her into a sitting position, leaning against the wall. The boys were watching their every move; eyes agog. Damnation, where was Sean? Why had he not come to look for her? She had to believe he was on his way and if she kept Kenton talking, presumably he would hear their voices and not simply barge in, making matters worse. There was no other way she could think of to save them. The boys were bound together, Annie was insensible and it probably wouldn't be long before

Kenton tied her and Nia up, also.

Or worse.

'My grandfather showed you the utmost encouragement and generosity.' Nia sent him a scathing look. 'This is a sorry way to repay his kindness.'

'That was his mistake.' Kenton abandoned his polite tone and now sounded distinctly Welsh. Of course, that was why the name Griffiths and a Welsh accent had struck a chord when Lord Vincent mentioned those characteristics in connection with the forger. In happier times, when Kenton had been a member of their household, they had involved themselves in play-acting once or twice to pass away wet evenings. Kenton had excelled as a Welsh ne'er-do-well and mentioned Welsh relatives on his mother's side with the name Griffiths.

'Do you never take responsibility for your own actions?'

'At your grandfather's age, life ought to have taught him that no good deed goes unpunished.' Kenton flashed an evil grin. 'He has had more than his fair share of fame and acclaim. It's time to move aside and give younger talent its opportunity to shine, especially now that he has become so . . . hmm, shall we be charitable and call it muddled? I offered to become his one and only apprentice, and to take over from him eventually, but he would not hear of it.'

'And then I made matters worse by declining your proposal. How vexatious for you.' She noticed him wince as he turned away from her and Nia had the satisfaction of noticing a rip in the back of his breeches, the fabric covered with blood. Ruff's work, she imagined, hoping it hurt like the devil. She wondered what had become of the boys' dog, hoping he'd had the good sense to run back to Stoneleigh Manor and guide the rescuers in the right direction.

'I will confess that your refusal surprised me, Miss Trafford. I didn't realise you were quite such a frigid chit.'

'Is that what you imagine?' She thought of Lord Vincent and sent her antagonist a sultry smile that clearly surprised him. 'Perhaps you should take a closer look at yourself and apportion blame where it belongs.'

'You tell 'im,' Annie muttered.

'Charming as this discussion is, I must bring it to an end. I believe you have told the truth in one respect, Miss Trafford, in that someone else will soon come looking for you. Unfortunately, I cannot allow any of you to be found.' He paused. 'At least, not alive.'

Nia audibly gasped. 'The game is up, Mr. Kenton. Your deception has been exposed. If

I were you, I would forget about us and concentrate upon making good your escape. After all, putting your own welfare first is an area in which you excel.'

'I have not the slightest intention of abandoning my rather profitable scheme. I had thought one more commission would be sufficient for my needs, but further consideration has convinced me that I need at least two before I shall be in a position to support Lady Fairstock in the style to which she is accustomed.'

'But you cannot — '

'Oh, but I can.' His chuckle was disconcertingly confident. 'If you imagine I will permit this little setback to alter my plans, then you are the one who's deluded. Only the four of you know my identity. If I am not at the unveiling of the duke's portrait, which obviously cannot now be unveiled anyway because it has been destroyed, then I can't be identified.'

'You are insane!' Annie screamed.

'Very possibly, but I am alive and intend to remain that way. You four, on the other hand . . . '

'I hesitate to spoil your party,' Nia replied, her sweetly sarcastic tone belying her disgust at Kenton's behaviour, to say nothing of her increasingly fear, 'but I caught Annie before she could do any harm to the painting.'

'What?' Kenton glared at Annie. 'Is this true?'

'I wouldn't help you if you were the last man in England,' Annie spat in response.

'Which does not answer my question.' Kenton took several deep breaths and the madness Nia had espied in his expression was replaced by disconcerting calm. 'Not that it really matters. If the unveiling goes ahead, I shall not be there.'

'You will be identified by your absence,' Nia pointed out. 'We have known for a while that the forgeries could only have been painted by one of three people, including you . . . ' She allowed her words to trail off without stating the obvious.

'Your family will have greater concerns in a short time than a mere art exhibition. It would be the height of bad manners to go ahead with it while they are in mourning.'

His smile was pure evil as he produced more rope and bound Annie hand and foot. Dear God, Nia had made the situation worse by goading him! A squealing noise caused her head to swivel in the boys' direction. They were fighting against their bonds, their faces puce with rage, and Leo was trying to say something around his gag. Nia's heart went out to them when it occurred to her that *they* were trying to protect her. She sent them a reassuring smile.

'Don't worry, boys. Your papa and Lord Vincent will be here directly.'

Kenton shrugged as he turned his attention to binding Nia, seemingly unconcerned about her threat. He must know that if Sean and Lord Vincent were close by, they would never have allowed Nia to confront him alone.

'Such a shame you could not be made to see reason,' he murmured, his hands lingering insolently upon her ankles. 'Such spirit; so independently minded; such strength of character and will. We should have made a formidable pairing, after I had brought you to heel, of course.'

She sent him a derisive look. 'I am not a dog.'

'That you are not, my dear. That you are not.' He sighed. 'However, much as I'm enjoying this little exchange, now is neither the time nor the place to continue with it. Please have the goodness to wait here. I shall be but a moment. My carriage is close by and I shall take you all somewhere more private where we shall be at leisure to continue our delightful discussion.'

'Such a shame the only way you can force a lady to discuss anything with you is by binding her hand and foot.'

Kenton chuckled. 'If that is what you really think?' He nodded towards Annie. 'Ask her if you doubt my word.'

'And yet she is now trussed up as well.' Nia raised an indolent brow. 'It did not take her long to see your true colours.'

Kenton executed a dismissive shrug. 'She was simply a means to an end.'

Annie hissed at him but if Kenton noticed, he gave no sign. Instead, he doffed his hat at them both and left the barn.

Nia struggled against her bonds as she watched him go; feeling furious, helpless and afraid. She tried to appear resolute for the sake of the boys but when the ropes chaffed against her wrists and ankles, remaining tightly in place, she was forced to accept that they were all at Kenton's complete mercy.

She tried to work out how long she had been there, and how long it would have taken Sean to ride to the Park, conduct a search for his sons and return home to hear news of proceedings from Sophia. Her spirits plummeted when she realised she had most likely not kept Kenton talking for long enough. She had failed her beloved nephews when they were most in need of her protection.

Unless salvation arrived within the next few minutes — a remote possibility at best — they were all going to die.

★ ★ ★

Kenton cursed his bad fortune as he strode off to collect his carriage, assuaging his wounded dignity by telling himself he could not have foreseen this development, could not have made allowances for it, and so his meticulous planning was not at fault. If Annie had played her part right and done as she was told, if the boys had not managed to dislodge their blindfolds, it would not be necessary to kill any of them. Kenton was not a violent man by nature, but circumstances had forced him to become one. He had not been born into poverty and did not intend to live the rest of his life as a pauper, suffering for the sake of his art. He was too talented, too intelligent, too accustomed to the good things in life to make such an almighty sacrifice while he waited for the world to wake up and offer him the acclaim he so richly deserved.

Why society had not already fallen at his feet to pay homage to his artistic skill was a puzzle to which he had devoted many hours of contemplation. He was as good as Trafford — better even — but those fools who had seen his work exhibited alongside Trafford's were so busy fawning over Trafford himself that they barely spared Kenton's superior efforts a glance.

That situation could not be permitted to continue. Humiliation still washed through Kenton whenever he recalled the disaster that ought to have been his moment of triumph. That was when he finally ran out of patience and decided to take matters into his own hands. God helped those who helped themselves was the mantra by which he lived his life, and thanks to his courage, his determination and willingness to act decisively, his star was finally in the ascendency.

He had been shocked when Nia Trafford declined his proposal of marriage — truly shocked — at first not believing she was serious. All of his plans had hinged upon her accepting him, and not for one moment had he considered she would prefer to remain single rather than marry a man with his looks, talent and charm. He had gone to considerable trouble to cultivate her friendship and thought she genuinely admired him. He was universally popular with the ladies, though he did say so himself, and could pick and choose which particular ones enjoyed the privilege of keeping him warm at night.

Matrimony was a last resort, albeit a necessary one, if he was to achieve his ambitions. The prospect of being united to Miss Trafford was appealing in many respects, and not only because of the connection to her grandfather.

There was just something about her that stirred Kenton's baser instincts: her innate femininity perhaps, or the detached air that made him want to exert himself in order to secure her regard. Kenton was not in the habit of putting himself out for any female and it still irked that Nia Trafford appeared immune to the very great honour he had accorded her.

It had all worked out for the best, of course, just as things almost always did. He had met Arabella Fairstock, purely by chance, soon after he left Trafford's household at Sean Trafford's insistence. That was another cause for complaint. He might have pursued Nia a little aggressively, but he refused to accept she was serious in her rejection of his suit, and he didn't have time for her games. He was a man in a hurry to make his mark and needed Nia to help him do it.

Kenton stopped walking, blew air through his lips and felt his anger reigniting, as it always did when he thought about his ignominious ejection from Trafford's house-hold. He had left with his head held high, pretending he was leaving through choice, unprepared to let them see just how humiliated he felt by the little tramp's rejection. A plan to exact revenge had already been incubating in his brain, and he needed to ensure the family thought he bore them no ill-will in order to bring it about. But inside, he continued to seethe. It was not as if he had actually tarnished Trafford's precious sister's reputation. Damn it all, he hadn't laid so much as an inappropriate finger upon her.

Calm again, Kenton continued his walk and returned his thoughts to Arabella Fairstock. As soon as they were introduced he immediately recognised in her a kindred spirit. She was just as ruthlessly determined as he was, but her husband had proved to be far less well off than he had led her to suppose when she agreed to marry him. The fool appeared to think it was a love match and that his lack of money wouldn't signify. As though a lady of Arabella's sensitivity and beauty would marry a man twenty years her senior because she loved him!

Kenton was happy to be of service to her. With the inconvenience of a possessive husband swiftly eradicated, Arabella and Kenton reached an agreement. They would marry as soon as they decently could, Kenton would provide Arabella with all the luxuries in life a woman in her situation was entitled to expect, and in return she would ensure his acceptance into the top echelons of society.

All that was left for Kenton to do was to accrue the blunt he had assured Arabella he already possessed. This time she was taking no chances and although they made ideal bed-fellows in every possible respect, she would not agree to become his wife until she had tangible proof of his wealth. Kenton was well on the way to accruing that wealth. Wealth that would ensure his genius finally received the acclaim it so richly deserved. A couple more forgeries and he would be set. And no one — not those troublesome twins, certainly not Annie, not even Nia Trafford, would stand in the path of his ambition.

He thought of Arabella's husband, and how he had pleaded for his life like the snivelling coward he had been. Gentlemen do not plead, Kenton had wanted to tell him as he broke his miserable neck and then arranged things so it appeared like an accidental death. Having committed murder once, he found himself less reluctant to do so again, multiple times. Even so, a small part of him regretted the loss of Nia Trafford.

He strode along, wishing he could have found a closer place to hide his carriage, wondering if there would be time for a little revenge against Miss High-and-Mighty before he sent her on to the next life. He hardened at the prospect, just as he always had whenever he contemplated becoming inti-mately acquainted with the chit. What he did not feel was regret at what he must do. She had brought this on herself. No one rejected Tobias Kenton without facing the consequences.

Yes indeed, he thought, as he finally reached his carriage and turned it back onto the track. He had a destination in mind where he could dispose of the meddlesome four and where their remains would not be discovered until he was long gone — if ever. The location was so remote that he would also be at leisure to take his pleasure with Miss Trafford first. He idly wondered if she would follow Sir Edwards' example and beg for her life, to say nothing of her virtue.

19

The moment Kenton left the barn, Nia sprang into action. Finally she had reason to be grateful for the man's arrogance. He was so sure of himself that he had not thought to search Nia for concealed weapons. Fortune had smiled upon her when she picked up Annie's discarded dagger and absently slipped it into the pocket of her skirt. Somehow it had not fallen out during her mad dash through the trees, and Kenton had not found it, as she was sure he would, when he bound her hands. Her scathing words to him, designed to distract, had had the desired effect.

'Oh, miss, what are we going to do?' Annie wailed.

'Shush, Annie, and allow me to think.'

The last thing Nia required was Annie wailing, distressing the boys more than they already were. Besides, she had a plan forming, thanks to the convenience of the dagger. Her hands were tied behind her back but it was the work of a moment for her to slide them beneath her bottom and raised legs and bring them up in front of her.

As well as failing to detect the dagger,

Kenton had also made the mistake of binding the boys together with a strong rope around their torsos, their arms pinned to their sides, their hands free to dangle helplessly below their bonds. He thought himself so intellectually superior to just about everyone, and that arrogance just might prove to be his downfall.

'Leo, Art,' she said, sending the boys a reassuring smile. 'I am going to shuffle across to you and get close enough so you can reach into my pocket. Do you understand?'

They both nodded vigorously.

'Now listen carefully,' she said, as she started her awkward wiggle across the hard earth floor. 'There is a dagger in my pocket. I want you to grasp it with your free hands and carefully cut through the rope binding my hands. Do you think you can do that?'

More nods.

'Good boys. We shall soon make Mr. Kenton see that he is not quite as clever as he thinks he is. Then he will be very sorry indeed for what he has done.'

It seemed strange not to be greeted with the loud, simultaneous shouts of agreement or the squabbling Nia had grown to expect when engaging in conversation with the twins. Even though they still seemed terrified, only gagging them could prevent a torrent of false bravado spilling from their lips. But at least now they had a task to concentrate upon, which would help to divert them. Even though Nia hoped soon to have them all free from their bonds; even though they possessed a dagger; she was not foolish enough to imagine they were safe. Something told her Annie's loyalty was still questionable and, even with the twins' help, she could not match Kenton's superior strength.

'Do not on any account, attempt to cut the rope binding the two of you together.' They looked disappointed. 'You might cut yourselves by mistake.' Nia had now reached their position and Leo's hand delved into her pocket. It came out again clutching the dagger. 'Quickly now, Leo,' she said, when it appeared that a wordless argument was taking place between the boys to ascertain who would get to do the cutting. 'We do not have much time.'

The tip of Leo's tongue protruded between his lips as he commenced sawing at the thick rope binding Nia's hands. The dagger was sharp, which ensured quick progress, but one slip of the hand and it could well be Nia's wrist that was cut instead of the rope. She closed her eyes, trying to banish such defeatist thoughts.

'Aw, miss, what is to become of us all?' Annie wailed.

'Stop that, Annie. It isn't helpful.'

Nia's sharp words reduced Annie to snuffling and crying.

'You are doing really well, Leo. Just a little more. I can feel the rope loosening.'

The dagger nicked her wrist, sending a sharp pain spiralling through her. She cried out and felt warm blood spilling over her hands. Leo's eyes were wide with guilt, and fear, and he stopped sawing.

'It's all right, Leo. It's a tiny cut. Keep going. I am almost free.'

A moment or so later, the rope binding her hands fell away.

'Well done, Leo!'

Nia delved into her pocket for a handkerchief and tied it tightly around her cut wrist. She felt light-headed, disorientated, but could not allow her own situation to distract her. The lives of everyone in this barn were in her hands. She reached forward and awkwardly untied the boys' gags, bracing herself for a barrage of words.

'Are you all right, Aunt Nia?' Leo asked, tears trailing down his cheeks.

'Leo didn't mean to hurt you.'

'I know that.'

'Can we stab that nasty man with the dagger?' Leo asked.

'It's my turn,' Art protested.

Nia managed a brief smile. So far, the boys

didn't seem much the worse for wear. She sliced through the rope binding them together, watching as they flexed their arms to restore feeling into them. She was reassured to see all their limbs appeared to be in working order. She released her own ankles from the rope that bound them too tightly, and sighed with relief when the blood began to flow freely again.

'What about me?' Annie wailed when no one took any notice of her.

It was actually a good question. Nia couldn't decide whether to trust Annie and release her or not. In spite of her anger at Kenton's relationship with another woman, Nia had noticed the way her eyes followed his every movement with total adoration writ large across her face. Would she try to regain favour with her erstwhile lover by warning him about the dagger? Before she could decide, the sound of a conveyance approaching drove all thoughts other than protection of her nephews out of her head.

'Quick, boys. Sit back where you were.' Nia loosely fastened their gags back in place, and wrapped the rope around their waists so they appeared to still be bound. 'Wait for my word and do as I say. Do you understand?'

Eyes once again round with apprehension, both boys nodded. Nia just had time to arrange her skirts to cover her now untied feet and place her hands behind her, as though they were still bound together, when Kenton appeared in the doorway.

'Ah, there you all are. Just as I left you.'

'Where else would we be?' Nia asked scornfully.

'Where indeed?' Kenton took a moment to consider their situation. 'Right you are, lads. You two first, I think.'

Damnation, that was what Nia had been worried about. She had hoped he would conduct her to the carriage first, giving her the opportunity to launch an attack with her dagger and disable Kenton for long enough that they could all make a dash for safety. Kenton stepped towards the boys, presumably intending to pull them to their feet and drag them to the carriage. She could not allow him to do that. The moment he approached them he would see their rope was not properly tied. Precious seconds slipped by as she tried to decide how best to divert him.

'Dive!' she yelled at the boys.

'She has a dagger!' Annie shouted simultaneously.

In the pandemonium that ensued, Kenton moved with the speed and agility of a large cat. He lunged at Leo, sending both boys tumbling to the floor, where they remained without moving. At the same time he turned to face Nia, who had leapt to her feet and held the dagger out in front of her. She was right handed, and it was her right wrist that was cut and continued to bleed copiously. Her hand wavered and Kenton actually laughed as he reached forward to take the dagger from her.

'I always knew you were a wildcat beneath that prim exterior,' he said. 'You really should have accepted my offer. Now come along, my dear, give that knife to me before someone gets hurt.'

Feeling nauseous and more light-headed by the moment, Kenton's arrogant assumption that she would simply bow to his authority, strengthened Nia's diminishing . . . well, strength. She thought of the boys, of what would happen to all of them if she failed to get the better of Kenton, and refused to meekly give in. She found further resolve in thoughts of Lord Vincent, the man she now accepted that she loved with single-minded, albeit one-sided, passion. She definitely wanted to experience more of those kisses of his for as long as he was prepared to administer them — another reason why it was absolutely necessary for her to remain alive.

With a disarmingly sweet smile of compliance that clearly confused Kenton, who was probably expecting anger and defiance, she pretended to hand the dagger to him. At the vital moment, she drew her hand away and then thrust it forward again, aiming the pointed end of the knife directly at his heart.

'Definitely a wild cat,' Kenton said, laughing aloud as he grabbed her cut wrist and squeezed it until spots appeared before her eyes and the dagger clattered to the floor.

It was too much. Nia had failed and she had nothing left to fight back with. His strong arm circled her waist as she crumpled to the floor beside the boys.

★ ★ ★

Vincent plunged along the narrow path, noticing freshly broken branches and trampled twigs underfoot in what used to be an orchard. The trees were in full bloom, littering the ground with fragrant pink blossom. Blossom that had recently been disturbed by several pairs of feet, if Vince was any judge. In his haste to rescue Nia and the twins he had not had the foresight to bring a weapon with him; a grave error. Resigned to improvisation, he picked up a stout branch and tested it against his open palm. It was strong and could knock a man senseless. It would serve, he fervently hoped, because he would be facing just one man and a maidservant.

He thought of Nia, of the twins, but tried not to lose his focus by being drawn into images of how afraid they must be. Why the devil had Nia not waited for him or her brother to arrive before charging off on an ill-conceived rescue mission? It was a rhetorical question that Vince already knew the answer to. Fears for the twins' safety had caused her to act without thought for her own welfare. Brave, foolish child! If he lost her, if the forger harmed one hair on their collective heads, he would beat the man to death with his bare hands. He might well do that anyway in retaliation for the trouble he had caused for Nia and her grandfather.

He strode on, not bothering to move stealthily, but alert and ready for any danger that presented itself. He prayed he was not too late. The forger would be desperate to cover his tracks, and would not care about collateral damage. Nia had a good twenty minutes head start on him. If she had blundered into a dangerous situation the consequences could well be catastrophic. This villain was as cunning as he was desperate and Vince would not make the mistake of underestimating him.

Vince did have one or two advantages of his own. He knew the lie of the land. The small track he was approaching was a turning off the Winchester road just wide enough to accommodate a man on a horse, or a small carriage. Even if the forger had already taken Nia and the twins elsewhere, he didn't have much of an advantage. With superior horses Vince and his brothers would soon overtake him. Besides, he could not have got away because Zach would have sent someone to block off the end of the track by now.

He reached the end of the path and glanced across the width of the track that bisected it. Of course, there was an old barn here, long disused. He ought to have remembered that. He and his brothers had often played in it as boys.

As he arrived he saw a small closed carriage pull up outside. The driver jumped down and entered the barn. He was alone. Presumably Annie was inside, keeping watch over Nia and the twins. Did the arrival of the carriage imply that the forger was about to leave with or without his captives? It was impossible to know, and there was no time to consider all the possibilities. If he planned to leave without Nia and the twins, there was every reason to suppose he would kill them first and make a clean getaway. Vince suspected there was little he would not do to protect his identity.

He stepped out from the trees, grim-faced and determined. Still clutching his club, he slipped silently into the barn a very short time after the forger left his carriage. His heart lurched when he observed the twins huddled together on the floor, looking dazed and frightened, but thankfully alive. Their eyes widened when they saw Vince, but he held a warning finger to his lips. They were gagged, but even so, it was important that they remained passively where they were. They were quick on the uptake and made no further attempt to attract Vince's attention.

The forger was preoccupied with Nia and had not yet noticed his approach. The serving girl's eyes widened and she seemed on the verge of shouting a warning. It seemed strange that she was tied up when she was the forger's accomplice, but Vince didn't have time to worry about the mind-set of a deranged criminal. He sent her a warning glower and she wisely closed her mouth without speaking, looking sullen and afraid.

Satisfied that Annie would probably change sides on a whim, depending upon who appeared to be in the ascendency, Vince turned his attention to Nia. She was also crumpled on the floor, blood pouring from a wounded wrist. Anger surged through Vince at the sight of the forger standing over her with a dagger raised. Nia was holding his gaze defiantly, refusing to cower or beg.

The forger must have sensed Vince's movements in the periphery of his vision. He turned his head just fractionally, shock registering in his expression when he saw Vince.

'Try fighting a man instead of picking on women and children,' Vince invited in a tone tight with controlled anger.

The forger swung around, thrusting the knife towards Vince. Having anticipated such a move, Vince knocked it from his hand with a vicious swipe of his improvised club. He heard bone shatter, and the forger cried out in agony. Vince glanced at the twins, at Nia's pale face and the blood-soaked handkerchief wrapped around her wrist. He wanted to kill the blaggard for what he had put them through, but even through the blinding mist of his anger, he knew better than to attack a man who could not defend himself.

But the forger didn't seem willing to give up so easily. He made a desperate attempt to reach for the fallen knife with his left hand. Vince was delighted by his stupidity, since it gave him *carte blanche* to retaliate, now that his foe was attempting to arm himself. He brought his club down again for a second time, this time on the back of the man's head, with considerable force, probably shattering his skull in the process. He fell to the ground with a sickening thud and didn't move.

20

'Lord Vincent . . . '

'Is Aunt Nia all right?'

The twins pulled off their gags and ran to crouch beside Vince, not seeming to care about the forger lying prostrate on the floor, blood pouring from the back of his head.

'I didn't mean to cut her wrist,' Leo said, tears pouring down his face. 'Will she die?'

'She won't die,' Vince assured them, helping Nia to sit. Her eyes blinked open and she looked at him as though she didn't know him. 'It's over,' he said softly, somehow resisting the urge to reassure her with kisses. 'You are safe.'

'The boys?'

'We're here, Aunt Nia,' Leo said.

'Kenton is dead,' Art said with great satisfaction. 'Lord Vincent killed him.'

Annie wailed. Everyone ignored her.

'Unfortunately I didn't hit him hard enough,' Vince replied when Kenton, since that was obviously who the forger was, stirred and groaned.

Vince examined the slit on Nia's wrist as the boys took it in turns to explain how she had come by it. The bleeding had slowed, but the cut was deep. He extracted his own hand-kerchief and tied it tightly around the wound, suspecting that it would need stitching.

'We shall all have to return to the house separately,' Vince said. 'That carriage isn't big enough to take everyone at once. Can you walk back, boys, and reassure your papa that you are safe and well?'

'Yes,' Leo replied. 'We can do that. But what about Aunt Nia?'

'And Annie?'

'She deceived us.'

'She was working for *him* all the time.'

'I helped you,' Annie wailed.

'And then you warned Kenton that Aunt Nia had a dagger.'

'You almost got her killed.'

Annie wailed even louder. 'I love him, and he loves me, deep down. We were to have such a fine life together.'

Vince shared a helpless glance with Nia. Between the boys' chatter and Annie's pathetic noise, it was impossible to think straight. For-tuitously, Sean Trafford and Amos burst through the door at that moment.

'Papa!'

The boys threw themselves at him and Trafford crouched down in order to embrace them both at once. 'Thank the Lord you are safe.'

'It was not our fault, Papa.'

'Kenton held our heads under the pond and we nearly died.'

'We would have fought him, but he was too strong.'

'Shush, I'm thankful you are safe. You can tell me all about it later.' He turned to Vince. 'How is Nia?'

'She has a wounded wrist that will need stitching.'

Trafford persuaded his sons to walk back to Stoneleigh Manor with him. They appeared to be recovering from the ordeal with remarkable speed, vying with one another in a verbal contest to decide which of them would have overpowered Kenton, given the opportunity. Amos unceremoniously lifted Annie over his shoulder and threw her onto the floor of Kenton's carriage, still bound hand and foot, still wailing that none of this was her fault.

'Take Miss Trafford home, Vince, and send Trafford back with the carriage for this bounder,' Amos said, glancing with total disregard for his obvious distress at Kenton. 'I will stand guard over him until then. With great good fortune, he will try something foolish.'

Vince nodded as he swept Nia into his arms and carried her from the barn. Briefly alone with her, he covered her pale lips with his own, revelling in their sweetness and thanking God for her relatively safe deliverance.

'Don't you ever frighten me like that again,' he said as he carried her to the carriage and gently deposited her on the seat before driving the conveyance the short distance back to Stoneleigh Manor.

A welcoming committee awaited them on the terrace. Sophia gasped when she saw the state of Nia, as did Hannah. When Nia herself assured them she was not mortally wounded and that Sean and the boys would be back at any moment, some of the tension drained from the atmosphere.

'What about her?' Hannah asked, pointing an accusatory finger as the sobbing Annie.

'Lock her in somewhere secure,' Vince replied, heading for the stairs with Nia in his arms. 'We will deal with her later. Come with me, Miss Ash, if you please, and direct me to Miss Trafford's chamber.'

⋆　⋆　⋆

A voice repeatedly called her name. Nia willed it to go away and leave her in peace. She was sleeping for the first time in what felt like days and had no wish to interrupt a vivid dream that centred upon Lord Vincent and his rather skilful fingers teasing at her body.

The voice persisted, which was perhaps just as well. There was a very good reason why she should not be thinking about Lord Vincent. Unfortunately, she couldn't recall what it was. Her head throbbed and thinking exhausted her. So too, did the sound of the persistent voice. It would be easier, she supposed, to open her eyes and be done with it.

Sophia's lovely face loomed above her when she forced her eyelids to lift.

'How do you feel?' she asked.

'Like I have been trampled by a horse.'

She lifted her right arm, and immediately lowered it again. Her wrist was heavily bandaged, which brought all the memories of Kenton's demented behaviour flooding back.

'You have been seen by a doctor,' Sophia explained. 'The duke was here and arranged everything, as only dukes can. Your wrist has been stitched but you will have a scar.'

'The boys?'

'Are full of their adventure. Their only concern was for Ruff. He bit Kenton, apparently, and Kenton responded by kicking the poor little chap quite viciously. Anyway, all is well since Ruff found his way home and has nothing wrong with him other than bruised ribs, according to Lord Amos, anyway.'

'That's a relief.'

'And before you ask, your grandfather is

working contentedly on the duke's portrait. He has recovered from Annie's barbaric assault and doesn't seem to remember much about it.'

'Thank goodness for that.' Nia stretched and wiggled into a more comfortable position. 'How long have I been asleep?'

'All night.'

'All night!' Nia attempted to sit up too fast and immediately flopped down onto her pillows again, her head spinning. 'You should have woken me sooner.'

'The doctor gave you something to make you sleep. Besides, Lord Vince would have scolded me if I had tried to rouse you before now.'

A small part of Nia rejoiced at his concern. The sensible part chided her for her stupidity. 'My actions are no concern of his,' she said, her voice sounding prim and unconvincing.

Sophia smiled. 'You can tell him that, if you like. Speaking personally, I do not dare.'

Nia eased herself into a sitting position, lured by a tempting aroma. 'I brought you some breakfast, which is why I woke you.'

'Thank you.' Nia gratefully accepted a cup of tea and nibbled at a slice of buttered toast. 'What has happened to Kenton?'

'The duke had the local constable take him in charge. He will stand trial and most likely be deported, if he is fortunate enough to escape the hangman's noose. Abducting children is not a crime that will be looked upon with leniency.'

'He was in league with Lady Fairstock.'

'Yes, so we understand.'

'He implied that he killed her husband so they could be together.' Nia wrinkled her nose. 'It would not surprise me if he did, but I don't suppose he will actually admit it and there is not the smallest possibility of proving it after all this time.'

'There is more than enough to charge him with. He will not escape justice.'

'And Annie?'

'She is still locked in the cellar. We wanted to consult with you before we decided what to do about her.'

'She was quite taken in by Kenton, you know. She actually believed he was in love with her and would give her the life of a lady to which she aspired.' Nia cautiously shook her head. 'Foolish child! She cannot stay with us. She assaulted Grandpapa and allowed the twins to be abducted without trying to prevent it, or at least warning us. *And* she was going to destroy the duke's portrait. Then she helped me, only to change sides again.' Nia spread her hands. 'But still, she is not the first woman to be deceived by a handsome rogue, and I don't believe she's inherently bad.'

'I tend to agree with you. Her father is a parson, you know, in a small village in Devon. Beth tells me she ran away from home because he was too strict and she wanted excitement. I think the worst punishment would be to send her back to her father.'

Nia took a moment to consider the matter. 'Yes, it very likely would be.'

'I will make sure Sean arranges it.' Sophia took Nia's empty cup from her. 'Now then, the boys are anxious to see you. Are you up to it if I send them in?'

'No, I shall get up. I have no excuse to laze about in bed.'

'Oh, Nia, are you sure?'

'Perfectly. Now will you help me or must I dress myself?'

'Very well, if you insist.' Sophia pulled the covers back. 'Oh, by the way, I have some good news. My sketches have been found. When Kenton regained his senses, Lord Vincent questioned him about them.'

'Whereas I had forgotten all about them.'

'You had more pressing priorities.'

'Where had Kenton hidden them?'

'As it transpires, he didn't have them. The wretched man talked his head off before the constable took him in charge, hoping to save his miserable skin. But he denied all knowledge of the sketches, claiming he was not in the habit of stealing other artists' work — '

'Merely forging it,' Nia said disdainfully.

'Quite. He seemed to think there was an important difference. Anyway, we have Lord Vincent to thank for their recovery. He saw Annie and Kenton together in Compton a while back and saw Annie pass something to Kenton. He assumed it was the sketches but both Kenton and Annie denied it vehemently. They both said the papers were sketches drawn up by Annie of the layout of this house and the grounds.'

'Because Kenton thought he might need to break in, or at least gain access to the grounds, which of course, he did.'

Sophia nodded. 'Lord Vincent believed them, especially since Kenton admitted to painting the forgeries. Being under lock and key, he could not benefit from the sale of the sketches, so why not give them up, if he had them?'

'Yes, I can see Lord Vincent's reasoning.'

'He deduced that if Kenton and Annie both knew nothing of the disappearance of the sketches then someone living beneath this roof must be responsible for their theft.' Sophia laughed. 'You should have seen him, Nia. He was like a dark, avenging angel. He stormed into Drake's room, ignored its occupant's protests, and turned it upside down until he found the sketches hidden at the back of his wardrobe.'

Nia, in the process of stepping into the petticoats Sophia held out for her, paused and widened her eyes. 'Mr. Drake stole the sketches?'

'Yes, he was put out when you rejected him — '

'So was Kenton, apparently, my refusal being the catalyst for his subsequent activities.' She sighed. 'What is so special about me that it drives men to criminal activities?'

Sophia shook her head. 'You still do not know?' Even after Lord Vincent — '

'There is nothing to know.'

'Have it your way.' Sophia flashed a smug smile. 'Anyway, Drake stole them as an act of revenge. He anticipated being evicted from this household when we return to Ireland and wanted something to live on. Suffice it to say, he too is now under the constable's care.' Sophia grinned. 'At least he still has free accommodation.'

'How very clever of Lord Vincent,' Nia mused. 'But I wish I had arrived at the truth myself. I do so hate being beholden to him.'

Sophia chuckled. 'Do you indeed?'

* ★ *

Vince visited Stoneleigh Manor that afternoon, more in hope than expectation of
seeing Nia. After her ordeal, she was likely to
remain in bed, recovering her strength, for
several more days yet. He was both surprised
and delighted to see her sitting alone in the
sunshine on the terrace, staring into space.
The boys bounded up to him, seeming none
of the worse for their ordeal, Ruff dancing
around their feet. He handed Forrester over
to them, took a few minutes to answer their
barrage of questions, and then presented
himself to Nia.

'How do you feel?' he asked.

'Much better, I thank you. Without you . . .
well, without your timely intervention I do
not care to think how matters might have
resolved themselves. I am very much obliged
to you, Lord Vincent.'

'It was a pleasure to be of some small
service to you.'

'Small!'

'How is your grandfather?'

'None the worse for his ordeal, thankfully.'
She smiled at him. 'We are returning Annie to
her very strict clergyman of a father whom
she was at pains to escape from. We think that
will be punishment enough for her.'

'Why am I not surprised at your soft-heartedness?'

'She is a very silly girl, but I believe she has learned her lesson.'

'Let us hope so.' He paused. 'Zach hopes to arrange a private viewing of his portrait in two weeks' time. I know it's no longer strictly necessary, since we know the identity of the forger, but he is determined to do it.'

'He has not seen it yet. It might be unflattering.'

Vince laughed. 'He is not so conceited that he would let that concern him. You have declared it to be amongst your grandfather's best work, so too has Sophia. That is enough for Zach.'

'Then I am sure it can be ready in time. Then we can concentrate upon arranging the exhibition in London and return to Ireland in the interim. But this time we shall be living without the usual entourage my grandfather manages to attract. I only have Miss Tilling to be rid of and we will be ourselves again.'

'Just so long as your grandfather doesn't adopt any other good causes.'

Nia shuddered. 'We shall ensure it doesn't happen. Grandpapa means well, but we now have definite proof of just how ungrateful people can be.'

'Quite so.'

'I never did like Mr. Kenton. He definitely had an inflated opinion of his own self-worth. I just didn't realise that by adopting him, Grandpapa had only made matters ten times worse.'

'Your grandfather had faith in him, reinforcing Kenton's self-belief. And by having the good sense to reject his proposal, to his warped way of thinking, you gave him justification to feel resentful.'

'Odious man!' She shuddered. 'He was convinced I would accept him with open arms. However, enough of him. I have yet to thank you for recovering Sophia's sketches and exposing Mr. Drake's treachery.'

'When one understood his reason for feeling aggrieved, he was the obvious suspect.'

'Not to me.'

'That is because you underestimate the effect you have on the opposite sex.'

Nia laughed, already shaking her head in denial. 'You mistake the matter.'

'I am obviously not the first man to think so.' His smile was deliberately provocative. 'You inspire men to great love, and equally great iniquities, without having to lift a finger. That must be a very heavy burden to bear.'

'No, Lord Vincent, this has nothing to do with me.'

'It has everything to do with you,' he replied softly.

She shook her head, clearly not convinced. 'It is ladies like Sophia who inspire men's artistic souls, not I. Kenton and Drake both wished to exploit me for their own personal gain. I am not such a numbskull that I cannot recognise false flattery when I hear it.'

Vince was filled with admiration for the modest, headstrong and determined female who had so effortlessly captured his heart. Part of him wanted to shake that modesty out of her, turn her in front of a mirror and make her see herself as others did.

As he did.

Now was not the time to tell her how he felt, but there never would be a right time. He reached for her hand and held it between both of his own, drawing patterns on her palm with the pad of one thumb.

'I have no reason to offer you false praise.'

'I don't know what to say. I . . . ' Her pale cheeks were suffused with a pink glow. Her lips parted as though she knew precisely what to say, but no words came out.

'I admire your dedication to your grandfather, your determination to do the right thing by him and all of your family, regardless of the personal sacrifices involved.'

'I cannot take any credit for that,' she

replied, looking embarrassed. 'Grandpapa is an impossible person not to love. I am fortunate to have him in my life.'

'I dare say he would say the same thing about you, and he would be in the right of it.' He wagged a finger at her. 'Now stop interrupting when I am attempting to pay you compliments.'

'I beg your pardon, Lord Vincent,' she said with an engaging smile. 'Pray continue.'

'Very well. Now, where was I? Ah yes, I adore your staunch defence of Sophia, your efforts to keep the twins from running completely wild, and so many other things about your character.' He paused to offer her an intensely passionate smile. 'But most of all, I love your modesty, your sharp mind, the natural beauty and vitality you don't seem to be aware of.' He shook his head. 'The list is endless, you know.'

'Lord Vincent . . . Vince, I don't quite know what to say to all of that.'

'There is only one thing you need to say,' he responded in a stirringly passionate tone. 'Say you will do me the very great honour of becoming my wife.'

Nia's mouth fell open. 'Your wife!'

21

Nia trembled with a combination of dizzying shock and momentary joy. She was acutely aware of the honour of his proposal, even though it would be impossible to accept it.

'Thank you.' She shook her head, dazed and deeply disappointed. 'If circumstances were different I would accept you with pleasure. But alas, we are not all masters of our own destinies.'

Still holding her hand, Vince pulled her onto her feet and into his arms. Nia definitely should not go quite so willingly into them. All the time he was simply holding her hand, she could find the strength of will to disappoint them both — just about. But if his arms closed around her or, worse, if he brought his lips into play, then it would be a very different matter.

'I know you have decided against matrimony, but then you did not expect to ever fall in love. Situations change.'

She moistened her lips and attempted a haughty toss of her head. 'What makes you suppose I am in love with you?'

He chuckled. 'Then deny it. Convince me,

if you possibly can, that I have got it wrong and that you do not return my feelings.'

She immediately lowered her gaze. 'Even if what you say is true, I cannot leave my grandfather.'

'Your grandfather has Sophia, your brother and the boys. Besides, once the exhibition is over, he will have the money to live wherever he likes. This place could be renovated. I will pay for it if your grandfather cannot.'

She looked up at him and gasped. 'You would do that. For me.'

'I would do that for my wife, and much more besides, with gladness in my heart. Your grandfather could divide his time between here and Ireland. Or, if he decided to live permanently in Ireland, we could visit as often as you wish. We could even purchase a house of our own, close to his. My duties for Zach do not require my continual presence at the Park.'

He linked his hands behind her waist and pulled her fractionally closer. She really should not allow him to. Passion overcame clarity of thought whenever he crowded her with his masculinity. Worse, her hands appeared to have taken up a position on the back of his coat quite without her giving them leave to do so. She could feel sculpted muscles rippling beneath her touch through the layers of his clothing. Dear God, this simply would not do! She instructed both her hands and her body to distance themselves from him.

Absolutely nothing moved and she remained captive in the circle of his strong arms. Rather too willingly.

'Painting Zach's portrait appears to have reignited your grandfather's ambition,' Vince said in a velvety drawl that sent shudders running through her entire body. 'It would be criminal if he did not do more portraiture. I am sure we can find sympathetic subjects who would understand his fragile state of mind. People will overlook much, put eccentricities down to artistic temperament, to acquire an original masterpiece.'

'Are you suggesting that painting landscapes contributed to Grandpapa's deterioration? Lord above, please do not say it is so. It was my idea that he take a different direction.' He had shocked her limbs into activity with his words and she was able to remove one hand and clap it over her mouth. 'I was trying to help.'

'You did help, my love. You did what you thought best for the grandfather you adore.'

'And sent him into a spiral of depression?'

'Not at all. You gave him the breathing space he didn't realise he required. Now it's time to think about what you want for yourself.' His hands gently caressed her back as he pulled her closer again, closing the distance she had briefly managed to put between them. 'Anything is possible, if one has the will and the means. Don't throw away your own happiness for the sake of an ideal.'

'You don't know what you are saying!' She found the strength to wrench herself out of his arms. 'I don't know what has brought this declaration on — '

'Do you not?'

His knowing smile told Nia what she already suspected. He could see she had fallen in love with him — to a man of his experience the signs must be obvious — and was not permitting her to keep her secret. He must be accustomed to women falling for him. Frankie had told her once that all four brothers spent their time dodging young ladies determined to tempt them into matrimony. Nia was *not* trying to do any such thing. So why did he feel the need to declare himself? She shook her head. It made no sense at all.

'Putting aside for one moment my disinclination to marry, I can think of a dozen different reasons why we would not suit.'

'Name them.'

'Oh, for goodness sake, you do not intend to make this easy for me, do you?'

'If I thought you were serious in your refusal, if I thought you did not care about me, then I would accept your decision. Although, if those circumstances existed, I probably would not have declared myself.' His smile was infuriatingly confident. 'As it is, you will have to do better than citing nebulous reasons. I can be very determined, you know, when there is something I want. And I have never wanted anything more passionately, with more single-minded determination, than I want you for my wife, lovely Nia. I think I have known it almost since first setting eyes on you.'

Nia couldn't remain insensible to a compliment, so obviously genuine, spoken with so much desire writ large on his face. She ought to turn him down and have done with the matter. If she could convince him that she genuinely did not wish to marry him, then he would do the gentlemanly thing and walk away.

The only problem was, that with a few tender words and a scorching expression, he had made her doubt the future she had always envisaged for herself. She was not unaware of the honour he had bestowed upon her — how could she be — but did he really mean it? Had he spoken in haste, following the extraordinary events of the past day? She couldn't think straight while he hovered over her. She needed quiet and solitude in which to think the matter through.

'You must excuse me, Vince,' she said softly. 'This has all come as a huge shock. Give me time to consider, if you please.'

His smile was victorious; as though she had already agreed, which she most emphatically had not.

'By all means. Take all the time you need. I shall call tomorrow afternoon and expect your answer.'

'Tomorrow! That hardly gives me any time at all.'

'You know your own heart, sweet Nia,' he replied softly, briefly resting his knuckles against her cheek. 'Even if you are not ready to admit what it tells you. Yet.' He raised her hand to his lips and chastely kissed the back of it. 'Until tomorrow,' he said, turning on his heel and leaving her standing on the crumbling terrace.

★   ★   ★

Nia watched him with the twins as they produced Forrester and plagued him with their usual barrage of questions. He hunkered down and answered them, seemingly in no hurry to escape. Was she out of her senses, even hesitating to accept such a handsome, compassionate gentleman? A man whom she loved with single-minded passion, and who could offer her and her family every advantage in life.

A man who was so sure of himself that he seemed to think one day was sufficient time for her to reach a decision that would affect the rest of her life.

This timely reminder of his forceful personality helped to put the matter into perspective. With a disgruntled harrumph, she resumed her seat as she watched him ride off down the weed-strewn driveway, waving over his shoulder to the twins as he went.

'You look as though you still have the weight of the world on your shoulders.'

Nia had not heard Sophia approach, but smiled at her and patted the seat beside her. 'How is Grandpapa?'

'Sleeping.'

'Ah, that's good. This portrait must have exhausted him.'

'More to the point, my dear, how are you?'

'Oh, I am perfectly fine.'

'Was that Lord Vincent I saw with you just now?'

Nia treated Sophia a droll look. 'You know very well that it was. You ought to have joined us.'

Sophia chuckled. 'I think my presence would have been unwelcome and unnecessary.'

Sophia said nothing more, leaving Nia to fill the silence. She felt a sudden urge to confide in the one woman whom she could rely upon for sound advice. The woman who was more of a mother to her than her own had ever been.

'He asked me to marry him,' she said offhandedly.

'Ah, I imagined he might.'

Nia was unsure what reaction she had expected, but it had definitely not been calm acceptance of such a monumental and highly surprising development. 'You suspected he might propose and did not warn me?' Nia glowered at Sophia. 'You are supposed to be my friend.'

Sophia raised an ironic brow. 'Would you have believed me if I had said anything?'

'No, I suppose not, but you might at least attempt to conceal your amusement. I am a tangle of uncertainty and you find it amusing.' Nia scowled. 'That is not at all helpful.'

'Ah, I knew it would be too much to expect you to follow your inclination, and your instincts, to say nothing of your heart.' Sophia sighed. 'Foolish child!'

'He doesn't really love me,' Nia said, sounding less than sure of herself.

'Believe me, my dear, Sheridan men do not say what they don't mean. If they did, all four of them would have become leg-shackled long since.'

'Hmm, but what if he decides he has made a mistake? What if I do?'

Sophia lifted her shoulders. 'I very much doubt if that situation will arise. But life is all about risks. You ought to have learned at least that much by now.'

'Anyway, it is quite impossible. I have Grandpapa's welfare to consider.'

'Excuse me, my dear, but that is not precisely true. I have never liked to mention this before, what with me being a courtesan and all, but Patrick is more my concern than yours. After all, it is me who shares his bed.'

'Sophia!'

'I am his wife in every respect, except in the eyes of the law. If it would make you feel better, I will marry him and make it completely legal. He has asked me often enough — '

'He has?' It was Nia's turn to exercise her brows. 'You never said.'

'The subject did not arise.'

'But you love him. Why would you refuse?' When Sophia remained silent, the truth dawned on Nia. 'You refused for my sake. You thought it would reflect poorly on my . . . on my what precisely?'

'I thought a situation might arise when you decided against remaining single. I was not about to hamper your prospects of making a good marriage by tarnishing your family's name.'

'Oh, Sophia!' Nia threw herself into the older lady's arms. 'You should not have made those sorts of sacrifices on my behalf. If anyone who cares for me disapproves of you, then they are not worthy of my regard.'

Sophia flashed a wicked smile. 'Lord Vincent doesn't disapprove of me. In fact, I think he rather likes me.'

Nia shook her head, endlessly amused by Sophia's irreverent attitude. 'I really was sincere in my intention never to marry.'

'Because you had not met a man who stirred your passions.'

'And now I have?'

'You don't need me to answer that question for you.'

'He has given me until tomorrow to offer him a response.' Nia puffed indignantly. 'One day to make such a huge decision.'

'A decision which, unless I mistake the matter, you have already made, which implies he was very generous in his allocation of time. The poor man must be in a plethora of anxiety.'

'The suave Lord Vincent in a fit of anxiety.' Nia giggled. 'That I would very much like to observe for myself.'

★ ★ ★

Nia was again on the terrace when Vince called the following day. The boys didn't run to greet him and so he was obliged to stable Forrester himself. He raised a hand in greeting as he strode onto the terrace, nervous yet optimistic as he tried to read Nia's face for early signs of her decision.

'Where is my reception committee?' he asked by way of greeting.

'Sean has taken them tadpoling. He thought it important that they return to the pond and not be afraid of it. Not that they showed much fear, but then this is normally the time set aside for their lessons, so I suppose that might have had some bearing on their enthusiasm.'

'Very likely.' He proffered his arm. 'Come and walk with me.'

'Matrimony seems to be in the air,' she remarked as they strolled down a track beneath the unpruned apple trees.

'Is someone other than you and I planning a union?'

'We have no such plans.'

'Not yet, no.'

'I was referring to Sophia. She is thinking of accepting my grandfather's proposal.'

'How very sensible of her.'

Nia looked at him in evident surprise. 'You don't mind?'

'Why should I mind if he makes an honest woman out of her?'

'Yes, but if I were to accept your proposal, which is far from certain by the way, then you would be related by marriage to a courtesan.'

'She would not be a courtesan, she would be your grandfather's devoted wife.' He stopped walking and pulled her into his arms. 'But, enough of Sophia. That is not my immediate concern. Stop keeping me waiting, Nia, and tell me if you will devote your life to being my wife.'

'Well,' she replied with a playful smile that gave him hope. 'That rather depends.'

'Upon what?'

'Would I have to ask you for permission for all my activities?'

'Good God, no!' He laughed. 'I can just imagine Crista's reaction if Amos enforced such draconian measures in their marriage.' He caressed her with his eyes. 'You are a free spirit, Nia, which is one of your many endearing features. I would never attempt to tame that spirit; on that you have my solemn word.'

He watched a kaleidoscope of emotions flit across her countenance as she considered his assurance. There was so much more he could do to persuade her, but he resisted the urge. She must admit that she loved him and wished to spend the rest of her life with him without any further coercion on his part.

After what seemed like an hour, but could only have been a minute or two, a radiant smile illuminated her features. She stood on her toes and placed a delicate kiss on his lips.

'I do love you, Vince, more than you could possibly know, and if you really want me for your wife, then I accept your proposal with gladness in my heart.'

Vince whooped as he bent his head to seal their agreement with a searing kiss.